The
Book of Sarah

For Kieth

with thanks

and good wishes

Beth

The Book of Sarah

BETTY WILSON

COTEAU BOOKS

This novel is a work of fiction. Names, characters, places, and incidents
either are the product of the author's imagination or are used fictitiously.
Any resemblance to actual persons, living or dead, is coincidental.

Edited by Geoffrey Ursell.

Cover painting, "Mama's Memories: The Day," by Laureen Marchand.
Cover design by Horst Hamm.
Book design by Karen Thomas.
Printed and bound in Canada.

The publisher gratefully acknowledges the financial assistance of the
Saskatchewan Arts Board, the Canada Council for the Arts, the
Department of Canadian Heritage, and the City of Regina Arts
Commission, for its publishing program.

Coteau Books celebrates the 50th Anniversary of the Saskatchewan
Arts Board with this publication.

Canadian Cataloguing in Publication Data

Wilson, Betty, 1923-
The book of Sarah
ISBN 1-55050-136-4

1. Title.

PS8595.I58 B66 1998   C813'.54   C98-920123-6
PR9199.3.W4964 B66 1998

COTEAU BOOKS
401-2206 Dewdney Ave.
Regina, Saskatchewan
Canada   S4R 1H3

AVAILABLE IN THE US FROM
General Distribution Services
85 River Rock Drive, Suite 202
Buffalo, New York, USA
14207

For
Dod and Davey

THE BOOK OF SARAH

PART ONE: YOUTH

1. THE ALDRIDGE QUARTER

J UST BEFORE SARAH'S FIFTH BIRTHDAY, Father sold a load of wheat at the elevator in Rattlesnake Park and came home with a gasoline lamp and a radio.

"Was that bit of money burning a hole in your pocket, James MacKenzie?" Mother gasped. "I thought we'd agreed to save every penny against the down payment on this place."

"Ah, hell, Beth, we deserve a little pleasure too."

"Pleasures can wait. Barton's not going to wait forever for us to make up our minds."

"Gotta stay with the times. Hell, woman, it's 1931. Most people already got gas lamps and pretty soon everybody's gonna have a radio."

"If we're ever going to get anywhere farming, we'll never do it as renters. We need land of our own."

"We'll get land of our own. Don't you worry about that," he said, rooting happily in cardboard boxes full of excelsior and treasures.

At first the radio seemed like magic to Sarah – strange voices coming out of a little wooden box hooked up to a bunch of mysterious and dangerous looking batteries which Father had gingerly placed in a wooden box under the radio proper. She thought the music was kind of nice too, but Mother, whose family were classical musicians back in England, kept asking Father to find something *worth* listening to. Between stations, the radio squalled and howled like a tortured cat, and the programs on one station sounded very much like the programs on any other.

Just before dark, Father filled the gas lamp, set it on the kitchen table, and pumped air into it. Then he tied two little silken sacks he called mantles onto the burners. When he had finished puzzling over the instructions, he set the mantles alight. As blue smoke curled away from them and they burned to white ash, Mother grabbed Sarah and retreated to the door. "Are you sure you know what you're doing with that thing, James?"

"Ee-e-yep. Nothin' to it," he said, fixing the fluted green glass shade into place. When Sarah saw the beaded fringe hanging from its edge, she cried, "Oh, look, Mother. Isn't that pretty?" She tried to wriggle free to go for a closer inspection. Mother's grasp tightened.

Father, with the lordly air of a master alchemist, struck two kitchen matches on the thigh of his overalls, opened the lamp's valve a couple of turns, and held the matches up to the generator. The lamp lit with a roar. Father sprang back. Blue and orange flames licked the ceiling; the thread running through the beaded fringe caught fire. Beads hopped and popped in every direction.

"*Do* something, James!" Mother screeched, dragging Sarah outside.

2

Shading his face with one hand Father sidled up and turned the valve off. Gradually the flames died. The lamp sputtered and flared a few times then settled down to a steady hiss and a bright white light. Father cautiously opened the valve a quarter-turn. "There you go, Beth," he said shakily. "Throws a real nice light, don't it?"

"Lucky the fool thing didn't burn the house down."

"Takes a little getting used to is all. And it'll be great for you to work on your tapestry."

"I won't sit anywhere near it."

What Sarah liked best about the lamp had been the fringe, but that had been burned off; within a week she hated the radio. She had always been able to talk or make as much noise as she wanted; now it was "Keep still, Kiddie. We're trying to hear."

Hear what? Just a bunch of tinny voices blathering about stuff she couldn't understand and people singing the same dumb old songs over and over again. She learned to hate "The Daring Young Man on the Flying Trapeze" and "Molly and Me and Baby Makes Three"; she wanted to do terrible things to their stupid "blue heaven." Father even shushed her for sawing doors and windows in a grocery box with the bread knife to make a house for old Kit's family of new kittens. The only thing she could do, without being shushed, was to draw. Then Mother scolded her because, when she went to write her weekly letter to Grandma, Sarah had used up all the letter pad.

But worst of all, Father had made a new friend, the bachelor, Willie Stainthorpe, who lived on a quarter section three miles west of the Barton place. When Willie heard the radio, he thought it was wonderful;

Father invited him to come and listen any time he liked. "Real gentleman, that, and a well-educated fella too," he told Mother.

"So are most remittance men."

"Well, Beth, he's a –"

"Bum," she finished for him. "Should be ashamed of himself, squatting on that homestead waiting for his stipend. Then it's off to Medicine Hat for a three-week toot."

"Can't be much of a stipend. The poor bugger lives on oatmeal and spuds, and he can't afford a radio or a decent chair."

"From the tales I hear from people who see him on his 'toots,' he could afford a dozen radios and a dozen chairs. And I don't want him squatting on ours."

But the damage was done; Willie appeared most nights to shush Sarah and twiddle the radio dials until he had found something he wanted to hear. Then he hunched forward, his ear six inches from the speaker, from time to time slapping his thigh and emitting a loud "Har! Har! Har!"

After two weeks of his visits, Mother protested, "Our home is not our own anymore, James. I don't like that man taking over the radio and shushing Sarah. And furthermore," she set her tapestry aside and turned stern eyes on him, "what's this Aldridge quarter you and he keep talking about?"

"Quarter section right next to Willie's. Municipality's letting it go for taxes. Figure it might be worth looking into. Willie says it's a good deal."

"*Willie* says? What farming does Willie do? He hasn't even planted a crop these past two years."

"Well, he *is* an educated man."

"In what? Romance Literature?"

"Ah, Beth –"

"I know his type. A great authority on everything but work. And mark my words, the time you need him he won't *be* there."

"You're awful hard on the poor bugger."

"You're not considering that Aldridge quarter, surely?"

"Well, I – Gosh, I dunno, Beth. It might be a good –"

"I don't understand you. I thought we'd agreed to meet Barton's price for this place?"

"Too damn much money."

"For decent land and buildings? And don't for one minute think I'm going to live next door to Willie Stainthorpe. You'd have him in the house *all* the time."

Father didn't argue, but he didn't do anything to discourage Willie's visits either. Several times, when Mother was not about, Sarah heard them talking about the Aldridge quarter. "Wonderful opportunity for a chap with a bit of initiative, James. Real bargain. Where would one find a fenced quarter section with forty acres broken for seven hundred dollars? True, the buildings could do with a bit of repair, but they are quite adequate and as for a well – all a chap need do is dig deep enough and he'd be bound to strike water. That place has real possibilities."

On the third of March, Sarah's birthday, a warm day for that time of year in Alberta, Father took her to town with him. For her birthday present, he bought her a box of Cracker Jack and left her to eat it in the wagon while he went into the municipal office. Sarah felt very grown up and very rich. She betted that not many five-year-olds could be trusted to wait by themselves in their fathers' wagons and she betted that not many fathers bought their kids boxes of Cracker Jack either. But she was disappointed with the prize, a miniscule replica of a barn lantern with a red globe that broke when she touched it; the tin whistle that came in some packages was what she wanted.

Father was a long time in the municipal office. For a while, Sarah watched a flock of horned larks, the first of the spring's migrants, moving steadily northward, hunting for seeds on patches of bare ground. Then three boys passed with schoolbags over their shoulders. They were arguing in strident voices, each trying to outshout the other. Sarah sat very still in case they should notice her. Kids scared her. She seldom saw any, excepting for cousins, and she didn't like them much. She was relieved when Father appeared, humming to himself as he untied Dick and Danny.

When he turned the horses towards home, Sarah said, "Don't forget we still gotta go to Thomas's store to buy Mother that butter press."

"That's gonna have to wait, Kiddie. I'm broke."

"But when you bought me the Cracker Jack you had lots of money."

He looked startled. "Now, listen, Kiddie, don't you say anything to your Ma about me being in the municipal office. All right?"

"I won't."

"Promise?"

"Cross my heart and spit to die."

As they rattled on homeward, Father started to sing:

Old Dan Tucker's a fine old man,
Washed his face in a frying pan,
Combed his hair on a wagon wheel,
And died of a toothache in his heel.

Sarah knew the chorus. She hollered it out with him.

Look out the way for old Dan Tucker,
He's too late to get his supper,
Supper's over and dinner's cooking,
And old Dan Tucker just stand there a-looking.

ON SUNDAY, AS USUAL, Uncle Johnny and Aunt Jane, along with their thirteen-year-old son, Billy, came for supper. Billy, who was repeating Grade Six, always brought his guitar and sat beside his mother on the couch, struggling to master a few basic chords. After he and his family had gone, Mother always said, "One of these days, I shall take that instrument and tune it. Otherwise, there will come a time when I will surely break it over his head." Father didn't like Mother picking on his family, but even he couldn't think of much to say in Billy's defense.

But Uncle Johnny more than made up for Billy. Mother and he were both from "the old country," England and Scotland respectively. After Father got the radio, Uncle Johnny told Mother that he'd heard that they broadcast church bells from the old country at five o'clock on Sunday afternoons. Mother was thrilled. She asked Father to turn the radio on and Uncle Johnny told Billy to "Leave off that racket for a minute."

Father and Aunt Jane barely tolerated each other. Father still held it against Aunt Jane that she had been *their* father's favourite, but they banded together in mutual disdain when the bells rang and Mother and Uncle Johnny wept. Sarah sided with Father and Aunt Jane; she thought the bells were awful too. "Why would anybody bawl over that jangle?" she whispered to Billy. He squeezed an acne pustule on his chin and shrugged.

But there was a worse jangle when the radio was turned off – the Aldridge quarter.

"Are ye forgetting the Aldridges nigh starved on that place, Jamie?" asked Uncle Johnny. "And God alone knows the wells they dug and never got a drop of water fit for drinking." His fierce blue eyes blazed with intensity.

Father took his glasses off, yanked a piece of shirt tail through the side slit in his overalls, polished the glasses and asserted in a low stubborn mutter, "Oh, I think a fella could make a go of her, Johnny."

"Ye're daft, man." And, with an abrupt change of tactics, "What's Barton asking for this place?"

"Six thousand. And he can go to hell."

"For decent buildings and a quarter *worth* farming?" Frustration always made Uncle Johnny holler.

"And I'm supposed to go into debt for the next twenty years when the municipality is letting the Aldridge place go for seven hundred and I can buy her free and clear?"

"It's well ye know there's not a decent building left on that place and Bert Thompson's been using the house as a granary this past four years. Forget the Aldridge quarter, man."

8

Sarah, sitting in the middle of the wrangle, wanted to side with Father, but she knew Mother sided with Uncle Johnny. She tried to take her mind off them by staring at the little oil painting that Mother's friend, Miss Hindman, the art mistress at the English boarding school, had given Mother when she gave up her own position as matron there and emigrated to Canada. The picture was of a nude young woman wading through drifts of apple blossoms; her face was slightly averted and her body glowed with radiant health. Mother often looked at the picture, straightening it lovingly and sighing that she believed Miss Hindman had become quite a well known artist, although they had lost touch with each other.

Sarah wondered why it was that Aunt Jane always saw to it that Billy and she sat with their backs to the picture when they came to visit. Sarah thought the picture was beautiful. She often tried to imagine herself into it – tried to imagine herself as that young woman. Once she had asked Mother what it would feel like to wade through apple blossoms. Mother got a dreamy look in her eyes, "Like wading through bits of silk, Pet, and the smell is wonderful." Now, when Sarah tried extra hard to imagine herself into the picture, she could almost shut Uncle Johnny and Father out, she could almost feel the silky apple blossoms between her toes.

After supper, when Uncle Johnny and Aunt Jane had gone and Father was gathering up the milk pails to go and do chores, Mother said, "You should try to get the chores done while it's still light enough to see what you're doing, James. I don't like the way that young bull looks at you. I don't think he's safe."

"You been listening to them old hens in town again. What do they know?"

"They know the town children teased that animal. I don't know why you let the creature run with the town herd all winter anyway."

"Never got around to fetching him home and it saved our pasture a little."

"When are you going to see about cutting him?"

"Don't figure I'm gonna. He's a pretty nice looking little animal. Should throw some decent calves."

"You're going to keep a bull that's been teased?"

"Well, for chrisake, I ain't teasing him!"

He sounded so put upon and beleaguered that Sarah felt sorry for him. She thought Billy – her name for the bull – was a pretty nice looking little animal too. He was Bessie's calf from two springs ago. She remembered Father carrying her down to the barn to see Billy when he was first born. He had been too dumb to drink from a pail. Cousin Billy was pretty dumb, too. "Why don't we call the calf 'Billy,' Father?" she'd said.

"Well, for evermore!" Mother bristled. "If you're insisting on keeping that beast, you'd better build a good solid corral for him and get a ring into his nose right away."

"He ain't hurting a soul and it's not something that can't wait till after we move."

"Move?" She dropped a pile of plates into the dishpan with a clatter and swung around to face him. "You're surely not considering that Aldridge quarter?"

Father sounded pretty desperate. "Beth, you don't always have to listen to Johnny Graham. If he was so goddamned smart, he wouldn't be walking around with the arse out of his pants, now would he?"

"He may have the arse out of his pants, as you so delicately put it, but he obviously knows a hawk from a handsaw when it comes to land."

That did it. Father always blew sky high whenever she started in with her "highfalutin' language." When he'd more or less run down, Mother said, "All *right*, then. We'll just see what Cecil has to say."

Mother's brother, Cecil, who had taken up good farm land south of the CPR tracks, was well on his way to becoming a successful farmer. Mother was not above pointing that out to Father, even though it made him mad.

When the fireworks died down, Mother was grimly silent. Father took to humming under his breath and studying her out of the corner of his eye when he was sure she wasn't looking.

Father's friend, Pete O'Donnel, showed up, and the two of them went to town to the beer parlor, something Father almost never did, excepting when he and Mother were mad at each other. Father came home a little tight, hauled a packet of Cracker Jack out of his coat pocket, and gave it to Sarah.

She took it out to the verandah. As she began to demolish it, the cattle wandered into the barnyard. When Sarah had licked the last sticky kernel from her fingers, she spotted the prize, the little tin whistle with a tiny wheel which rotated rapidly when you blew into the tube. Cousin Lloyd had had that whistle once. When he blew hard enough, it would screech so loud that it had made her ears feel funny. She wondered what the cattle would do when they heard the whistle. She shut her eyes and blew with all her might.

Wow! Her ears *did* feel funny; it must have made Billy's ears feel funny too. He left the herd and trotted along the fence that separated the house from the barnyard. He didn't look like a calf any more. There was a big bulge on the hump of his shoulders and a wild expression in his eyes. Long strings of saliva dripped from his muzzle, his tail curved high over his back, and he moaned in a low, dangerous rumble.

Sarah was delighted. She blasted the whistle again. Billy roared, got down on one knee, and pawed dirt over his back.

Oh, boy, this was fun! Sarah dragged in her breath and blew again. Billy's roar broke on a high, wild note. He stalked off a dozen paces, turned and rushed the fence. It was a stout one. It shrieked, but it held. Last week Father had put a poke around Billy's neck. The combination of poke and fence threw him back. He half fell, regained his feet, then stalked along the fence, rumbling deep in his throat and staring at Sarah with bloodshot eyes.

She was scared. She slunk into the house. It occurred to her that what she had been doing was teasing Billy. She didn't think she'd better tell Father or Mother. Mother was baking bread. There was a good fire burning in the stove. Sarah lifted a stove lid and dropped the whistle on the hot coals.

WHEN UNCLE CECIL and Aunt Frances dropped in on Saturday afternoon, to Sarah's relief, they didn't have the three kids with them. Somehow or other, whenever Cecil Junior and his sister, Gwendolyn, appeared, Sarah got into trouble.

Aunt Frances said, "Cecil and I have been discussing it and we think Lloyd is quite capable of looking after his younger brother and his little sister for an hour or two. My goodness, he's going on fourteen. When I was that age, I had already started working in the mill."

Mother agreed with her politely, and after she had poured the tea, she brought up Father's notion of making a deal for the Aldridge quarter.

"The Aldridge quarter?" Uncle Cecil threw back his head and brayed. "Jamie, lad, don't even think of it. That place won't grow enough prairie wool to feed the jackrabbits. This is the place for you, laddie, right where you are."

"Oh, I dunno, Cecil. I think a fella could make a go of the Aldridge quarter."

After Uncle Cecil and Aunt Frances left, Father said, "Beth, there's something.... We'd just as well have this out right now." He sent Sarah out to feed the chickens. She never knew what happened, but, for the next two weeks, every time she looked at Mother, Mother was weeping.

Several times she made dark references about going back to England. That scared Sarah. Would Mother take her back to England too? Would England be anything like Miss Hindman's picture? And what about Father, what would happen to him?

From time to time, Father said, in a voice that tended to crack on him, "I'm the man of the family, Beth. It's up to *me* to make decisions about what's best for us."

"Best? *Best?* Can nobody tell you anything? You heard what Johnny and Cecil said about that place. And did it never occur to you that I had a right to be consulted?"

"Oh, sure! Johnny and Cecil are smarter than me any day, ain't they? Well, for your information, Willie Stainthorpe thinks a fella could make a go of the Aldridge quarter and Willie Stainthorpe's an Oxford-educated man."

"You'd listen to that drunken fool when Johnny and my brother told you – ?"

"Well, Jesus, the deal's made now." Father sounded desperate. "How was I to know you'd be so dead set against it? Jesus, it's *our* place. Paid for. Can't you get *that* through your head? On the first of April, we're moving, so you better start packing. And for chrisake, turn off the water works. I figure a fella could make a go of her."

Mother made no move to pack anything. Any day it was warm enough, Father escaped to calcimine the walls of the house over on the Aldridge quarter. Mother and Father never spoke to each other. Sarah hated it. And on top of everything else, a vicious spring blizzard blew up one evening just as the smelly little guy who sometimes came to buy horsehair, hides, or any other bit of junk he could peddle, drove his crowbait team into the yard.

Father would never think of turning anybody away in such a storm. In the western ranch tradition where he had been raised, any stranger and his horse were welcomed for the night. He stabled the peddler's team and invited him into the house.

Mother disliked foreigners; she hated garlic, and

the peddler reeked of it. The peddler, dark and speaking nothing but the most rudimentary English, looked no happier to be in her house than she was to have him there. He refused supper, except for a slice of bread and a cup of tea.

Father dumped a whole bucket of coal into the heater and forgot to close the draughts. The overheated room brought out the strong smell of the peddler's garlic diet. As soon as Mother had finished dishes, she stalked off to bed, after telling Father that he could jolly well wash the guest bedding himself the next day.

That the peddler understood. Huffily, he told them that he would get his own blankets out of his rig and sleep on the floor beside the heater. When he ducked out into the wild night, Father said, "Beth, for chrisake, do you have to be...?"

"What are you going to wish on us next, James MacKenzie? First it was Willie Stainthorpe, then that goddamned farm, and now this stinking peddler...."

Sarah, whom neither Mother nor Father had thought to send to bed, shrank as though somebody had burned her with a branding iron. Mother never, never swore.

When the peddler came back into the house, he spread his blankets on the floor, sat down on them, and drew them around him as though protecting himself from the contamination of his surroundings. All Father got from his attempts at conversation were grunts and wry shrugs. Several times, as the little man's eyes roamed the room, they came to rest on Miss Hindman's picture. Finally, he said, "How much?"

"Oh, hell, I dunno. It was a gift to the wife."

"Vat you take?"

Father's tone was jocular. "What're you offering?"

The peddler rose and examined the picture closely with narrowed eyes. Colour rose in his sallow face. He turned back with a deprecating shrug, not meeting Father's eyes. "Tree hundred, might be."

"Dollars?"

The voice faded to a reluctant whisper. "Tree fifty. Might be."

Father gawked at him. Money was very tight since he had paid cash for the Aldridge quarter. "Well, it ain't mine to sell, but – but I – I don't think you'd better mention it to the wife."

It was he who mentioned it to Mother the next morning as soon as the peddler had gone.

"How dare you, James MacKenzie? The one thing that I truly value of the little I could bring with me. If I sell Miss Hindman's picture, it will be for a return passage to England and for no other reason. Assuming, of course, that it is worth anything. What would that fool of a peddler know?"

"Wouldn't hurt to check it out."

"You had better *not*."

For a week they passed each other like strangers.

FATHER HAD BEEN LETTING the calves run with their mothers that spring, but as the day of the move approached, the money situation became desperate. One evening, as he and Sarah watched the cattle trail into the yard for water, he said that he had decided that he was going to wean the calves, milk the cows, separate the milk, and send the cream to the dairy in Medicine Hat for a little ready cash. The calves would just have to get by on skim milk.

"Does Mother know?"

"Nope," he said as he closed the gate, "she'll just damn well have to get used to the idea."

Sarah stood outside the corral, watching as Father, with the whole herd of cattle, including Billy, in the corral, started grabbing calves away from their mothers, dragging them by one leg across the corral and firing them into the barn. The calves bawled, the cows bawled, and soon the cattle were in a milling turmoil.

Billy, at first, milled along with the cows, but as they became more and more upset, he started to roar in a low, dangerous rumble. Once he stopped, faced Father, and gathered himself. Sarah's upper arms went heavy with dread, but Father ran at Billy, shouting threats, arms flailing. Billy shied off into the cow herd. Father grabbed a calf and dragged it toward the barn. The calf bawled as though it was being ripped apart. The mother followed, snuffling at it.

While the cows stared at the scene, Billy shouldered through them. Sarah screamed a warning a moment before the bull rushed Father and knocked him end over end. Before Father could gain his feet, Billy went at him again. At Billy's second rush, Father managed to grab the poke he had fitted around Billy's neck to keep him from crawling fences.

Father was a powerful man. Billy dragged him all over the corral, but he couldn't back off to get another run at him.

Sarah stood, rooted, too horrified to move. Out of the corner of her eye, a moment before she came to herself and ran screaming to the house, she saw Willie Stainthorpe peek out from behind the granary, take in the scene, and duck back out of sight again. That she'd seen him at all barely registered. "Mother ! Mother !" she screamed as she crashed through the kitchen door.

Mother jumped up from the sewing machine. "What?"

"Billy's – Billy's got Father down."

Mother froze, staring at her.

"Mother!"

A shudder passed over Mother. She looked left and then right as though she was searching for something before she rushed out of the house, snatched the axe from the chopping block, and made for the corral. As she opened the gate she turned on Sarah. "Stay out of the corral! Stay away!"

Billy moaned and roared, pawing at Father's blood-ied and almost naked body, tossing it back and forth while Father clung to the poke with both hands. The rest of the cattle, always the meekest and humblest of beasts, milled about in a frenzy of excitement. Bessie, tossing her head in a goring motion, made a half-hearted rush at Mother. Mother turned on her, swip-ing with the axe. Bessie thought better of her venture, rushed back to her sisters, and gored the meekest of them instead.

"Hit this bastard, Beth!" Father croaked. "For god's sake, hit him!"

Mother sidled up to the bull and gave him a tap on the head with the blunt end of the axe.

Billy emitted a sound somewhere between a screech and a roar and rammed Father's body against the feed yard fence. Father didn't exactly scream, it was more a cry of absolute despair.

This time Mother opened Billy's head with the blade of the axe. Billy shuddered and staggered away. Blood gushed from the wound. Mother held Father with one hand, clutched the axe with the other, and tore towards the fence. "Over the fence, James. Over!"

As long as she lived, Sarah carried a mental picture of Father grasping the top wires of that fence in both hands and somehow somersaulting over it like an acrobat turning on a bar, Mother right after him, just as Billy, spurting blood, came thundering behind them. Often Sarah wondered if she had made the picture up. It seemed highly improbable that a man who had suffered such terrible injuries as Father's could have somersaulted over anything, but she knew she remembered the three of them creeping around to the back of the barn and waiting for dark, while in the corral the cattle milled and moaned like wild beasts. When a hard early-spring frost made waiting intolerable, the family sneaked far out through the stubble field where the cattle could not see them and circled back to the house.

Mother was practically carrying Father. He was in terrible shape, his every breath a sobbing moan. The cattle were still bellowing and roaring when she phoned Uncle Cecil.

Long after Sarah was supposed to be asleep, she heard uncles and aunts and neighbours – trucks and cars coming and going. Then a strange voice, cultured and clipped. "Is there someone you could hire to take over for you here, Mrs. MacKenzie? Your husband has sustained serious internal injuries, besides broken ribs and a dislocated shoulder. He won't be capable of work for many weeks."

"Hire, is it?" Uncle Johnny bristled. "There'll be no need of the lassie hiring some stranger, doctor. Cecil and me can manage chores between us. Tomorrow we'll butcher that beast, and when it's time we'll seed the Aldridge place down for Jamie too."

Barton was a decent guy; he let the MacKenzies stay on his land until Father recovered – as much as he was ever going to recover. He was never able to ride a horse again and he never could raise his right arm properly either.

When the family arrived on the Aldridge quarter one June morning, driving the cattle and horses before them and with all their possessions piled on two wagons, it was scarcely a triumphal procession, but Sarah noticed a wild rose growing at the south side of the house beside a big blow hole that the wind had scooped.

When she went into the house and looked around, she realized that it was pretty awful in comparison to the Barton's, even though Father had done a nice job of calcimining the walls. For some time, she had been wondering how a person would draw a horse and rider with a dog following a long way behind. With this much space on a blank wall, it would be easy. She had a stub of pencil in her pocket.

When Mother caught her, she scolded her and told her to get outside. Sarah slunk off to explore the other buildings while Father and Mother set up the stove and unloaded the wagon. Buster and Molly, the two young cats they had saved from old Kit's last year's litter, trailed along with Sarah.

As she was coming out of the barn, she saw Willie Stainthorpe skulking along the road allowance.

Last Sunday, when Uncle Johnny and Aunt Jane came to visit, Uncle Johhny said that Willie had been on a terrible "toot" in Medicine Hat early that spring. Among other things, he'd broken the plate glass mirror in the bar at the Arlington Hotel and they'd tossed him in the hoosegow for thirty days for being drunk and disorderly.

Willie didn't speak to Sarah, but when he started to shuffle a little faster, she knew he'd seen her. Something sneaky and ashamed in his gait made her remember the last time she'd seen *him*.

She stuck her tongue out at his retreating back. I'm telling on you, Willie Stainthorpe. So there, too.

When she got back to the house, Mother had hung Miss Hindman's picture on the wall, scrubbed the floor, and put down a piece of matting beside the table. Buster and Molly sniffed the air. Sarah could smell them too. Mice. She remembered Uncle Johnny saying that Bert Thompson had used the house as a granary. That night, lying in the dark after the lamp was out, she could hear the cats pounce and the sound of mouse bones crunching.

2. VENIE THE WIENIE

"THREE MILES IS A HELL OF A LONG WAY for a six-year-old to hike in the winter," Father said. "Blizzards blow up on these bald-headed prairies. If we gotta start Sarah to school, we're gonna get her a gentle pony."

"You know perfectly well I think she's too little to ride a pony." Mother was peppery. "Why couldn't she start school next spring when the weather is better?"

"Now, Beth, just 'cause you're scared of horses –"

"Ordinary people never ride horses in England. Only the gentry and –"

"Well, ordinary people ride horses in Alberta, and when we start her to school, we're gonna get her a pony, that's all there is to it."

"A pony!" Sarah scrambled onto his lap and hugged him so tight she almost choked him. "Boy, oh boy, am I glad we live in Alberta."

"Hey, Kid, let up," Father said, prying her arms loose and settling her on his lap. "Now, listen, don't you go worrying about this school stuff. Your Ma's gonna send away for stuff from the Correspondence

School Branch. Her and me can learn you good as any damned schoolteacher."

"What kind, Father?"

He blinked at her. "What kind of what?"

"Pony. To ride to school. You *know*."

A grin pulled at the corner of his mouth. "Well, now, let's see. Gotta have a coupla ears, I guess. Needs a tail too, don't it? I was thinking of getting one with three legs, but I guess we'll have to make it –"

"Fath-er!" she giggled, somewhere between exasperation and delight as she scrambled out of his lap and scampered outside.

While he had been teasing her, she'd heard the work-horses coming into the yard; she had invented a wonderful new game of "store" to play with them. She let herself into the feed yard, climbed the stack, picked stalks out of the oat bundles, leaned over the high board fence, and enticed the horses to come and "buy." She usually discussed their "accounts" with them in the same super-refined and affected manner that Mrs. Thomas, the general store owner's wife used when she discussed Father's overdue accounts with him, but today she couldn't keep her mind on the game. Pictures kept hopping into her head of the pony Father was going to get for her when she started school. Black? No, bay. No! White. White, with a long tail that blows in the wind. That's what it's gonna be, white.

When the correspondence school lessons came, Mother and Father set about "learning her as good as any damn schoolteacher." Within a month, Father was making her struggle to read the Childrens' Page from the *Winnipeg Free Press*, a tough task for a Grade

Three student. She sweated from word to word, trying to "sound 'em out," understanding nothing, and hating every minute of it. Arithmetic was worse. "Quickly now, Sarah," Mother insisted, "what is six plus eight plus three? And don't count on your fingers." Then came the day when Mother announced there was no reason that Sarah should not get a head start on the multiplication tables.

The only thing Sarah liked about this school business was Father's map game. He had taken a big sheet of brown paper and drawn squares on it. He told her that every square was like somebody's farm. "This is our place, see?" he pointed out. "And here's our house right in this corner, and here's the Belly River four squares to the north of our place, and here's the islands where the Belly meets the Bow," he said, drawing them in as he talked. "We went to this island for the Church picnic, remember?"

Sarah could instantly see it. "And over there's the other island where we picked saskatoons last summer."

"Yep. You got it. Now, if this is our place right here, where would Willie Stainthorpe's quarter be?"

That wasn't hard. Willie's quarter was one square down towards the river and kitty-corner from their place.

"Right, that's northwest, you understand? And where'd the old Barton place be where we used to live?"

She counted three squares over. "Here."

"Yep, that's east."

"But where's Thomas's store?"

"Well, we gotta draw in the CPR tracks, don't we?"

He traced a line carefully across the squared paper, mouthing and squinting at it; then he drew in a bunch of tiny squares beside the railway tracks and said, "Now, these here are the houses and the grain elevators in Rattlesnake Park and about here'd be Thomas's store."

"But you forgot the highway, and there's the school across the railway tracks, right?"

He blinked at her. "Well, all right, Miss Smartie, where's Aunt Jane and Uncle Johnny's place, then?"

"One square east of Rattlesnake Park. Right – there."

"And that great big old poplar?"

"On the east side of the road, one square north of town. And Uncle Cecil's and Aunt Frances's place would be –" she counted very earnestly, "right – there. Three squares south of the railway track and two squares – east."

"Holy doodle, Kid. I can't figure out how come you can't learn to read."

Neither can I, she thought miserably. If only it was easy, like the map game. But she didn't say it; Father was liable to get the bright idea of trying to turn that awful Grade One primer into something like a map. Every day she ached for lunch time and the glorious freedom of the afternoon; for time to stare at clouds, to revel in sunshine and the mighty arch of the prairie sky, to sometimes hear the shivery thrill of a coyote's howl or to watch one of the old bachelor neighbours rattling by in their buggies. And there were chickens and kittens and lambs, the sage hen that wandered through the yard, and the mystery of how anyone squeezed milk out of a cow's teats. Best of all, there was her game of store. She held the horses in thrall for hours while she admired their rippling muscles and their tails, blowing in the wind. She would love to comb those tails if only she could find the courage. When she got that pony of her own, she was certainly going to comb its tail.

Then it occurred to her that she had been gypped, that all human beings had been gypped. They had no tails. She discussed the matter with Mother.

Mother laughed. "You make a fuss when I braid your hair. You don't need a tail to braid too."

"If I had a tail, I wouldn't let anybody braid it. Not ever. And when I get my own pony, nobody's going to braid its tail neither."

"When *you* get a pony?"

"When I start school. Father said."

"Oh, Pet, I don't know if we can afford that."

"But Father promised!"

"Well, Baby, we'll just have to see how things go. I don't know how –"

Don't know how? Don't know *how?* Well, Father *promised* and I hate Mother. Hate her, hate her, hate her!

She stomped outside.

Father had dug post holes to cross-fence the yard. She hopped down into one. When she scrunched down small, she was completely hidden. *Good. I'm gonna stay here for ever and ever, and Mother will never find me no matter how hard she looks, and Mother will cry and cry and it will serve her right.*

When she got tired of hating Mother, she tried to lever herself out of the hole. Hopeless. She tried kicking steps, but the earth crumpled and trickled into the bottom. The more she struggled, the more it trickled. Sweat mixed with dirt and tears.

The horses came tearing into the yard. Along with Father's workhorses were five half-wild four-year-olds he was breaking for other farmers. They swirled around Sarah's head, kicked up dust, and nipped and kicked at each other. A colt, bigger than a grain elevator, came within nothing of stepping on top of her. She screamed until Mother came tearing out of the house wielding the broom.

Father and Mother had words. Something to the effect that he was always running off and leaving jobs half done.

"Horses don't step into holes. That kid couldn'ta been safer in the Church."

He looked somewhat taken aback when Mother reminded him that he had said that badgers were a menace to cowboys since horses stepped into *their* holes. He turned on Sarah. "You're too little to be out in that yard when them horses are around. Stay out of there. You hear?"

"But it was just because I couldn't run when they –" Sarah howled. "I love the horses, Father. I only want to –"

He cleared his throat, avoided Mother's eyes, and roared, "Well, then you just watch yourself, Miss."

In ten minutes Sarah was back at her "store" game. The horses were so beautiful; their tails were so beautiful. It was just not fair that people didn't have tails.

Then she remembered the hide of the steer Father had butchered last fall. It had been a nice red steer and it had a nice brown tail. Nice for a cow, that is. It struck her that if she could not grow a tail, she could at least pretend to have one. If she could get the tail off the hide.... She sneaked a butcher knife out of the house and tried to saw the tail off; the hide was too tough. The axe was obviously the answer. Two whacks, and the prize was hers. She took it to the barn and curried it, then held it up to the appropriate place on her behind and paraded up and down the yard, craning over her shoulder to study the effect. Not bad. Holding it in place scarcely cramped her style as she doled oat stalks out to the horses, and it did make her feel so much more like a horse.

She became quite blasé about the horses. When she was sure neither Mother nor Father could see her, she walked out among them. The gentle old plough-horses bent their great heads to her and blew softly against her face and hands, but she was determined to make friends with the half-wild colts. After all, she was soon going to have to make friends with a pony of her own. She inched up to a big grey, holding out a hand and talking to him. He shied away and snorted. Old Baldy, Father's favourite breaking horse, dived at the colt and nipped him. Sarah was caught in a swirl of dust and heels.

When she came to, the world came and went in dizzy black waves and the horses were nowhere in sight. She could scarcely get her breath and her stomach hurt something awful. She picked herself up and retrieved her tail. Trailing it in one hand, she wobbled to the house and told Mother that she had a stomach ache.

"Something you ate, Pet? Well, never mind. Just go and have a little lie down."

With Mother out of the way, Sarah pulled up her

shirt. A huge bruise in the shape of a hoof print covered her belly. She yanked her shirt down and curled up small. I'm never gonna tell Mother. If she saw my belly, I'd never get a horse of my own.

March, and spring work loomed. Father hauled his "harness horse" into the house, straddled it, awl and black waxed thread in hand, and cursed as he broke needle after needle, while he struggled to mend the traces and britching on his horses' work harness.

"No time to fool around playing teacher any more," he declared. "After your birthday, Miss, you're gonna go to school."

School. Sarah had shied away from thinking about it. Now, a butterfly began to flutter in her belly. She hardly knew any kids, except for the cousins who came to visit with their parents sometimes. Aunt Jane's Billy was no problem. He simply sat beside his mother, breathing through his mouth or whanging on his guitar, but Uncle Cecil's Gwendolyn, who was a year older than Sarah, was forever tattling on Sarah to get her in trouble. And as for Cecil Junior – one moonlit night last fall, when he had been twelve, he had dragged Sarah's Red Flyer wagon across the pasture just for the fun of it. Sarah and Gwendolyn went along too. To be out in the moonlight with the kids seemed like a wonderful adventure to Sarah, but when they returned to the house, they discovered that one of the wagon's wheels was missing. Cecil Junior warned Sarah not to blab, but Father discovered the loss the next day. Sarah was dragged onto the carpet to explain herself. Red Flyer wagons didn't grow on trees. It didn't occur to her to tattle on Cecil Junior. The three-wheeled wagon sat, like a rebuke, on the verandah all winter. Just a few days ago, Father had found the wheel, all rusty and faded from the snow. Sarah got scolded all over again. If the kids at school were anything like her cousins, she didn't expect to like them much, but there was one great compensation. "So, you're going to get my pony right away, eh, Father?"

He looked startled. "Oh, gosh, Kid, I dunno about right away."

"Sarah, don't bother your Father."

"But he *promised!*"

"Well, maybe sometime when you're older. If you do well in school. Now, it's past your bedtime."

Sarah was too shocked to argue. She crept off to bed and cried herself to sleep. Even when the colt kicked her in the belly, she hadn't felt so bad.

For the first day of school, Mother made a great show of decking her out in "a proper little English schoolgirl's uniform," a hand-me-down from cousin Rosemary in England. Sarah hated it.

She hated trudging to school with Mother too. Three miles – past the big old poplar, beyond the village, across the highway and the CPR tracks. Mother lectured her about looking both ways before she crossed the highway, and warned her to never, never, never crawl under a train standing in the station.

The thought of crawling under a train made Sarah's guts knot, but she figured she'd stand a fair chance of seeing a car coming on the highway; bald prairie stretched for miles in either direction. It wasn't cars and trains that worried her, it was that two-storey red brick building looming ahead, with its slitted windows and the thousands and thousands of kids of all ages, yelling and pummelling each other in the cinder-strewn yard.

As they approached the school, Sarah crowded close to Mother and took her hand. Kids, who had been yelling and tearing around the yard, stopped to stare at them. Sarah spotted Marjorie Strider. Mother and Mrs. Strider both belonged to the Church. When Mother was in town, sometimes she would stop at Mrs. Strider's house for a little chat and a cup of tea. Sarah, naturally, had to tag along. Marjorie always tried to entice her into "playing house." Sarah didn't like playing house; she detested toy tea sets and dolls, even the ones that piddled and squalled "Mama" when you turned them over. Marjorie was eyeing her now and whispering behind her hand to another kid.

Cousin Gwendolyn came around the side of the school with another little girl. Gwendolyn's pale blonde hair was in beautiful ringlets and she was wearing a smart little tartan skirt and one of Aunt Frances's famous home-knit sweaters. Sarah could have died. Here she was, dressed in a middy and knee socks, with her braids tied with big red bows. Gwendolyn stared at her for a second, then ducked back out of sight around the corner of the school.

Mother, quite unaware, swept through the double doors, up the worn steps, across a bare hall with oiled floors, and tapped on a closed door.

A young woman, whom Sarah knew must be the teacher, opened the door, and stood, frowning slightly, while Mother explained who she was, who Sarah was, and what was wanted.

The teacher sighed and backed out of the doorway. "Well, come on in. Sarah MacKenzie, you say her name is?" She went to her desk, sat down, and pulled a longish, soft-covered book out of a top drawer, opened it, dipped her pen into an inkwell, and scratched Sarah's name in the book.

She looked at Mother over her glasses. "Birthday?"

"Just seven. Her birthday was on March the third."

"Why was she not sent to school last fall?"

Mother went through the whole rigmarole.

The teacher sighed even more deeply. "You understand, I have thirty students in Grades One to Six in this room? I have no time to give individual attention to any one child."

"Father and Mother learned me some reading and some numbers, Teacher. And I had lots of practice sitting still," Sarah offered hopefully.

"My name is Miss McCrostie. You do not address me as 'Teacher,' and your parents didn't learn you, they taught you." She turned to Mother. "Mr. Wasdon and I will have to find time to assess her progress. Unless it is significant, I should not be surprised if it should prove necessary for her to repeat the first grade."

Sarah didn't understand what that meant, except that it was bad. Mother looked crushed.

The bell rang; the riot outside quenched like a fire with a barrel of water dumped over it. The only sound was the scuffle of boots as thousands of kids filed into this room or climbed the stairs to the room above, which Sarah knew must be the lair of the principal, Johnny Wasdon. Father said Wasdon "had been brung into the school to whip kids like that young bugger of a Billy and that slimy little bastard of a Lloyd into shape."

The teacher looked quizzically at Mother, who was

still standing beside the desk. "You can leave her now, Mrs. MacKenzie. She'll be all right."

Mother drew Sarah to her and kissed her. "Now, be a good girl, Pet, and come straight home after school."

A titter passed though the room. "Pet! Get a load of that," one of the boys breathed. "And get a load of them pigtails and that outfit," another jeered before wilting under Miss McCrostie's gimlet eye.

With a pang of terror, Sarah realized that Mother had gone and she was alone staring into sixty eyes, among them Cousin Gwendolyn's and Marjorie Strider's.

"Come, Sarah, you'll be sitting with Kenny Krebs. That's the only seat available." She followed the teacher to the back of the room and slipped reluctantly into a scarred double desk beside a big boy who breathed through his mouth. He regarded her with mean grey eyes, scowled, and wiped his nose on his shirt sleeve.

The only thing Sarah understood of the confusing first ten minutes was "The Lord's Prayer." Mother had drilled that into her. "O Canada" she'd never heard. It sounded as dreary as the chanting Mother and the other ladies did in the Church. When the class was seated, Miss McCrostie said, "Get your library books out, class. I don't want to hear one peep out of a soul. Now, Sarah MacKenzie, up to the front here, if you please."

The teacher handed her the Grade One primer. "Are you familiar with this book?"

"Yeah. Well, it's kicking around the house. I look at the pictures sometimes, but Father says it's just garbage, so...."

A suppressed giggle ran through the room.

"Really?" The teacher did not look amused. She opened the book at random and thrust it into Sarah's hands. "Read. From the top, if you please."

Sarah could scarcely see the letters let alone read; everything Father had taught her flew out of her head. Finally the teacher took the book from her. "Very well, then. Can you count for me?"

Sarah got to thirty, then stopped with a shrug.

"Well, go on."

"What's the sense? It just goes thirty, forty, fifty, and like that."

Another titter passed through the room. The teacher eyed her with a tight-lipped expression, took a pad from her desk, wrote on it briefly, and handed it to her. "Take this upstairs to Mr. Wasdon."

Johnny Wasdon! Sarah's scalp prickled. All the way up the stairs she tried to picture the feed yard at home with the chickens singing in the sunshine and scratching in the dust. From the hall at the top of the stairs, she saw two closed doors, one to the left, the other to the right. Not one sound came from behind either door. Which was Wasdon's room? Nothing for it but to open the doors and look. She chose the door on the left, opened it, and stuck her head into the room. Good! The right one. There was Cousin Billy, who was repeating Grade Eight. He had a sullen look and he was too big for his desk. At the very back of the room, she spotted Cecil Junior and his older brother, Lloyd. She waved and grinned. None of them waved back.

Then she noticed Wasdon sitting behind the desk at the back of the room. He was wearing an expression that reminded her of old Baldy when he was about to punish a colt. She walked down the aisle, rounded the desk, and held the note out to him with a trembling hand. "Miss McCrostie said to give you this."

Wasdon rose, but he did not take the note from her. "Do you not know to knock on a door before you open it, Miss?"

"Well, yes, I – but –" How could she explain? Maybe if she twirled one of the buttons on the front of his jacket between her fingers for a second or two she would have time to figure out how to tell him –

Wasdon batted her hand away. "Keep your hands to yourself, Miss MacKenzie. You're not 'Father's little Kiddie' here."

Sarah could not have been more shocked. She flinched when he took the note from her.

"All right, let's see what you know, then," he said after he had read it. "What's eight plus seven?"

Blood roared in her ears. She began to count on her fingers.

"We don't count on our fingers here."

"But I know seven *times* eight is fifty-six. Sir." She didn't tell him that it was one of only six or seven combinations in the multiplication tables that she did know for sure.

Wasdon stared at her. "Well, I don't know what to do with you, Miss MacKenzie. Miss McCrostie and I will have to discuss it after school. Return to your class now."

She didn't remember much of the rest of that day or much of anything else for the next three weeks. Miss McCrostie didn't bother with her. All day she drew pictures of horses and dreamed of the comforting details of home, old Kit's litter of new kittens, Cherry's heifer calf, and the way the noonday sun slanted across the kitchen table. The only way Mother could get her to go to school at all was to walk with her halfway. That was nice, since the cats came too, but when Sarah had to go on alone, she always bawled.

After a visit to the school, Father came home wearing a grim expression. "Now, listen, Kiddie, you just gotta try to read. That teacher says your numbers ain't too bad, but if you can't read, you're gonna have to start Grade One all over again next fall." He picked up the primer from the top of the sewing machine. "Now, you *know* how to sound 'em out. Let's —"

Mother snatched the primer from his hands. "The two of us have done quite enough damage, James. If she has to start over, then she has to start over, that's all there is to it."

It was seldom Mother backed him down, but when she did, he stayed backed.

So there it was. Sarah hated school; she couldn't read, it didn't look like she was ever going to learn, and she didn't even have a pony. But at least she had the weekends when she could play "store" and after school, once past the range of prying eyes, she could pick three sprays of pasture sage. Bunched together, they made quite a good substitute tail, and there were three miles of prairie where she didn't see a soul, except for the odd gopher and maybe a hawk or two riding on the wind. Every night Father asked her what she had learned. She hated the question; she could never remember learning anything.

Finally, well out of range of Mother's hearing, Father said, "Tell you what, Kid, the time you can pick up that primer and read me a page, all by yourself, I'm gonna see if I can't make a deal for a pony I've got my eye on. Thing's as gentle as a pet dog and I figure she'd make you a dandy school pony."

Aunt Jane had an old Manitoba reader. In it was a picture of Arabs watering their horses at an oasis. One of the horses was a gorgeous white mare. Every time the MacKenzies visited Aunt Jane, Sarah stared at that picture. It sprang to mind now. For a horse like that white mare, she was darn well going to learn to read.

The next day, instead of drawing horses or gawking around at what other kids were doing, she hauled out the Grade One primer. On one page was a picture of a bird with a red breast. Beyond was a little grey church that looked something like the church where she and her mother went every Sunday. She forced her eyes away from the picture and stared at the print, trying to remember what Father had taught her. Suddenly the word "robin" jumped at her. Then "bell," then "church."

The robin is sing – singing in the r – ain wh – while the church bell rings, ding, dong, ding.

She grabbed the primer in both hands and scampered to the teacher, who had a class of Grade Fives at the board, drilling fractions into them. "Miss McCrostie, I can read! See? It says 'The robin is singing in the rain while the church bell rings, ding, dong, ding.'"

"Well, yes, Sarah, that's right. But you really must learn to control...."

"But I can read, can't I? I can read?"

"Well, you've read that. Now, take your seat, and perhaps when I'm finished with this class you can read me the whole story."

Sarah didn't give a rip that the whole school was laughing at her. She ran most of the way home. Before she could blurt out her news as she burst through the door, Mother said, "James, do you really think she's ready? She's so tiny."

"Pshaw! Started when I was four. Head on down to the barn, Kiddie. Surprise there for you." Then, hollering after her, "Hey! Hang on a minute. Go tearing up to that little mare and you're liable to get the guts kicked...." Sarah didn't hear the rest.

She ploughed to a stop in the doorway of the barn and stared at a moth-eaten, pot-bellied rack of bones that stopped grinding straw long enough to turn and glance at her. A ten-pound rock landed in the bottom of her belly; she had seen this creature following old Bill Mitchell's dray around town. It had a disgusting habit of half-sitting against the trough of the town's artesian well and rubbing its backside, pendulous upper lip waving, while it wore what little hair there was off its ratty stump of a tail.

Father's hand was on her shoulder. "Well, Kiddie, whadda you think?"

"All – all right," she managed.

"Now, listen, Kid, I know I said I'd get you a pony when you learned to read but – well, hell, I just wanted –"

"But I *did* learn," she cried. "Tonight I was going to show you."

He looked like he was going to bawl. "One of these

days, when I'm in the chips, Kid, I'm gonna get you an honest-to-god horse. But right now –" He stared at the rack of bones for a long minute. "Got a nice white blaze on her forehead, anyhow, ain't she?" he ventured. "You could call her Venus, after the evening star."

"Yeah. Venus. I guess."

"Oh, she's a little skinny right now. Kinda lousy, too. Winter-poor, yuh know? But just wait till green grass when she fattens up and slicks off. Wanna go for a ride?"

"A ride?"

"That's what we got her for, ain't it?"

He bridled the creature, led it out into the corral, and heaved Sarah aboard. She grasped a hank of mane in each hand and clung like a burr to a sheep's pelt while Father led the pony around the corral.

"How's that?"

"G-great."

Father handed her the reins. She felt empty and helpless, staring down a mile of neck ending in a pair of floppy ears.

"What do I do now?"

"Kick her in the ribs and make her go."

Sarah tried very tentatively. Nothing happened.

"Kick her like you mean it, for chrisake, and let up on the reins a little."

"What if she runs away?"

Father was grinning. "Gotta walk before she can run, Kiddie."

That time the rack of bones moved. A little.

"That's it. Keep her going. You're doing fine."

Round and round the corral Sarah went, feeling very strange and very powerful. The other farm kids who brought horses to school came from big families who drove buggies or democrats, like Uncle Cecil's kids. Not one of them had a horse of their very own, even a moth-eaten one.

"How'd you like to ride down in the pasture there and fetch the cows? A couple are about due to calf, and I gotta keep an eye on 'em."

"Alone?" she squeaked.

"Sure, alone. Nobody goes along holding a cowboy's hand, do they?" He opened the gate and stood back while Sarah urged her charger through. She had a small problem getting Venus headed in the right direction, then the mare walked along, very sedately. For a few yards.

April was at work. The odd shoot of green grass was beckoning. Venus gave a tug on the reins asking for freedom, lowered her head, and started to graze. Sarah did her best to haul the mare's head up. Useless. She kicked her in the ribs. Useless. She pleaded. Useless. "Father, she won't go," she screamed.

Father was leaning on the fence, laughing. "Guess you got yourself a problem there, ain't you, Kiddie?"

Tears gushed from Sarah's eyes. She redoubled her efforts. She might have been a gadfly for all the attention the mare paid. Finally it occurred to her that she could use the ends of the reins as a whip. Venus started sharply. Sarah had to grab a hank of mane to keep from falling off. And all the time Father was laughing his head off. But she was riding. She was. Venus was moving, obedient to the rein.

Filled with a tremendous sense of pride and accomplishment, Sarah gathered the cows and headed them toward the corral. It was not until she was almost home that she realized her rear end was sore.

"Well, how was your first ride, Kiddie?"

"Just –" Unexpectedly the mare shook herself and Sarah too. "Wu-wu-wu-wu-wonderful."

"Bum not sore?"

How could he have known? "Maybe, a little," she admitted.

When he swooped her to the ground she caught sight of the black wool stockings covering her legs. Wherever they'd touched Venus, they were matted with dead-looking blackish hair and something else besides – dozens of yellowish, maggoty-looking things stuck in the wool. She screeched and ripped the stockings off.

Father was cackling again. "Don't get your arse in an uproar, Kid. Them's only horse lice. They won't bite you."

"But they're biting Venus! They must be."

"Well, yeah. Happens after a real hard winter when a horse ain't been fed too good, but they'll disappear come spring."

"I'll curry 'em out. Every one. I will."

Father laughed again. "You got your work cut out for yuh, Kiddie."

"But what about her tail? What can I do to – ?"

"Pinworms. They won't be so bad once she gets a good bellyful of green grass."

"And her tail will grow out nice and long and shiny, won't it?"

"Oh, hell, Kid, I wouldn't count on that. She's wore it right down to nubbins, and I figure she's just a nat-ural rat-tail anyhow."

What a blow. What a disappointment. Sarah could

have wept. But perhaps Father was wrong. Anyhow, she took Venus into the barn, climbed up the side of the stall so she could reach, and began currying. Hair came out in ugly matted clumps polluted with horse lice. Venus ignored the operation and went on placidly chomping straw.

When Mother called her in for supper, Sarah overheard Father saying, "I never exactly said it was *hers*."

"I should hope not. Not when you say he wants the plough and five dollars to boot."

"If he ain't satisfied, he can go take a running jump at hisself. A deal's a deal."

"You should have settled this matter before...." She broke off when she noticed Sarah.

Sarah wondered what they were talking about, but she didn't wonder long; she was bubbling over with the need to tell them about her plans for her Venie, her treasure, her joy. Well, she was going to *make* her her treasure and her joy, and maybe Father was wrong about her tail.

After a week of decent feeding and Sarah's brush and curry comb, Venus began to look a little better, but her tail remained disgracefully ratty. Still, Sarah continued to hope. Every night after school she rushed home to ride around the farm and bring the cows in so that Father could check the ones that were calving in the night.

"I can ride to school tomorrow, can't I?" she badgered on Sunday night.

"Oh, Pet, I don't think you're ready."

"That hunk of crowbait ain't likely to get the kid in trouble, Beth," Father cut in. "It'd take a quirt and a pair of spurs to get a trot outta her, let alone –"

43

"But Sarah can't even mount unless she leads the thing up to a fence. If she had a saddle –"

"Not on your life. A kid can fall and get tangled in a stirrup. Sarah's gonna learn to ride Injun style."

So, on Monday morning, ears filled with stern warnings to be sure to look both ways before she crossed the highway and the railroad tracks, Sarah set off for school mounted on Venie. The school bag slung over her shoulder contained two sandwiches wrapped in the *Free Press and Prairie Farmer* and two handfuls of rye for Venie that she had filched from the feed bin. She could hardly wait for the gasps of envy from kids that didn't own horses of their own.

Well, it wasn't quite like that.

Cecil Junior overheard Sarah fondly calling Venus "Venie."

"Venie? You mean wienie!" he hooted. Marjorie Strider picked it up, "Venie the wienie!" Then Kenny Krebs. Soon they were all chanting, "Venie the wienie!"

At first, Sarah was mortified, then she was furious. Wasn't it bad enough having a lousy horse with a hopelessly ratty tail without having people call her a a wiener? "You stop that. You just stop it!"

They danced around her, just out of reach. "Venie the wienie. Venie the wienie."

When the bell rang, Marjorie forgot the game and bent down to pull up one sagging stocking. Sarah grabbed a handful of her ringlets and gave a good hard yank.

"Ow! Ow! Ow! I'm telling, Sarah MacKenzie, and you're gonna get the *strap*." She raced towards the school; when she was close enough for everybody to hear, she started bawling as though somebody was sticking hot pokers in her eyes.

Sarah considered mounting Venus and fleeing, but Johnny Wasdon threw open an upstairs window and bellowed, "Sarah MacKenzie! In my office. On the double!"

Her world tipped. For a moment, everything went hard and cold and grey. The office! It could only mean one thing. She had heard big tough boys howl in anguish when Wasdon applied the strap to their shrinking palms.

She never remembered climbing the stairs, never remembered opening the office door, but she would never forget the strap, a length of two-inch-wide grey machinery belting lying on a dusty old desk.

Wasdon picked it up with one hand and slapped it into the palm of the other. "You see this, Miss MacKenzie? We have discovered that boys and girls who get the strap don't start fights in the schoolyard."

But I didn't start a fight. I didn't. They called her wienie.

But she never said it.

He brought the belt down with a reverberating crack on the desk. "Be warned, Miss MacKenzie, I stand for no fighting in this schoolyard. You understand?" He glared at her. "Well?"

"Yes, sir," she quavered.

"Very well, then. Go to your class."

Sarah sat numbly through classes. Again and again, the crack of that belt exploded along her nerves. At recess, she told Miss McCrostie that she wasn't feeling well, that she wanted to stay at her desk. How could she go outside and face the taunts of the kids calling Venus a wienie when she didn't dare say one word to defend her?

When school was out, Marjorie Strider took up the "Venie the wienie" chant again.

Sarah untied Venus, bridled her, and climbed up the side of the stall so she could mount. Once up, she backed Venus out of the stall and rode out of the barn. From this vantage point, Marjorie Strider looked little and mean and her stockings were wrinkled at the ankles.

"Go home and tell your mother to make you some new garters, Marjorie Strider."

"Go home and tell *your* mother to pick the horse lice out of your socks."

The unkindest cut of all – Sarah hadn't had time to pick lice out of her stockings before the trouble started that morning. She raked her dignity together, urged Venus into a shambling trot, and headed for home.

How could a day that should have been so wonderful turn out so awful? And there was nothing for it but to face days just as bad, tomorrow and all the days and days and days after that. Venie would always be a wienie, and, deep down, Sarah knew that she would never have a decent tail.

But the awful day wasn't over. When she got home Father and old Bill Mitchell were sitting side by side on a wagon tongue, both looking sour. Father took off his cap and punched his fist into the crown. He only did that at moments of great crisis. "Nothing doing, Bill. A straight swap. A deal's a deal."

"I never said a straight swap. I said the sulky plough and maybe another five bucks. And we never shook on it."

Father looked grim, then he glanced sharply at
Sarah. "You better stable that cayuse, Kiddie, and give
her a good feed. Might be the last she gets for a while
if Bill's gonna take her back tonight."

"Take her – ? What – ?"

"Now, don't get your shirt tail in a knot. We can
make a deal with Albert Peterson for a better looking
pony than that crowbait, and Albert's *looking* for a
sulky plough."

"You mean I can't have Venus?"

Father's eyes flinched away, his brow washboarding
up into his hair line, but the stubborn set of his jaw
did not relax one bit.

Sarah knew she was going to blubber and she didn't
want Father and old Bill Mitchell to see her. She rode
Venus down to the barn and gave her an extra good
feed, then leaned against her shoulder and wept.

It was Mother who found her. "Oh, Sarah, Pet, I'm
so sorry, but you see, we haven't got five dollars.
There hasn't been that much money in the house
since Christmas time. Baby, I know how disappointed
you must be, but your father says that pony of Albert
Peterson's is...."

Sarah didn't hear the rest. She was watching old
Bill Mitchell, looking somewhat shamedfaced, leading Venus away.

She couldn't eat supper, but she was made to sit at
the table.

"Do try to eat something, Pet."

"I hate pickled beets."

"You could try a little scrambled...."

"Smells yucky."

"Well, just this once, it wouldn't hurt for you to

47

have your doughnut before...."

"I don't want a doughnut."

"Ah, Beth, for chrisake, let up on her." Father turned to Sarah. "Now, listen Kiddie, I'm going over and talk to Albert Peterson first thing in the morning."

"Why? I'm not riding some lousy horse with a ratty tail. And I wish you and Mother would quit calling me 'Kiddie' and 'Pet' and dumb stuff like that. Everybody laughs at me. Even Mr. Wasdon said –"

"Said what?"

"Said I wouldn't be 'Daddy's little Kiddie' in school."

Father's face went white. "Well, that son of a –"

Mother threw her hands up. "We should have started her with the other Grade Ones last fall, James. Then we could have afforded to get a decent pony for her too."

"The hell you say? After all the bawling and squalling you done about getting her any kind of a pony?"

Sarah could bear no more. She started a "Wah! Wah! Wah!" chant, clapping both hands against her ears and squeezing her eyes tight to shut them out.

Father drew her onto his lap and gently pulled her hands away. "She ain't lousy, Kid. I know that for a fact. When I go to look at her tomorrow, how'd you like to come with me? Missing one day's school ain't gonna make that much difference."

In spite of herself, dream pictures of the Peterson pony kept popping into Sarah's head while she was drifting towards sleep. She squelched them ruthlessly. Well, anyhow, it can't look any worse than that wienie. Never know, it might even have a decent tail. And I'm going to named it Skeezix after that kid in the funny papers. Marjorie Strider and Cecil can't make fun of that. And I'm never going to love it, neither. She drew herself into a tight little ball and crossed her fingers. Never.

3. COYOTE TRAP

SARAH WAS PELTING ALONG ON SKEEZIX, skimming a crest of dizzy elation. Ahead of her stretched two glorious months of summer, in her school bag was a report card saying that she'd passed into Grade Two, and between her knees was her very own pony, not exactly a white Arab, but not bad either. And she did have a nice tail.

When she topped the hill between the village and the farm, she spotted Uncle Cecil's truck in her parents' yard. He *had* come for her! It was to be her first visit away from home, a whole week to spend with her cousins.

Last week, when Gwendolyn had invited her, Sarah had been puzzled. Ever since she'd started school, Gwendolyn had avoided her; now she had suddenly become friendly. She knew Gwendolyn well enough to wonder why. Still, when she saw the truck and her three cousins waving to her, she was thrilled. She kicked Skeezix into a gallop and skedaddled for home. She was so excited she forgot to turn the pony loose in the pasture. Father said he'd see to it after the truck had gone.

Sarah assured Mother that she would not be home-sick and, after a flurry of exhortations, kisses, hugs, and good-byes, she climbed into the truck box with the kids. As Mother handed her a little suitcase containing enough clothes to do her for the week, Cousin Gwendolyn, quite the young lady, even at eight, said, "Don't worry about Sarah, Auntie Beth. We'll take good care of her."

Why did I ever think that Gwendolyn didn't like me? Sarah wondered.

That night was delicious, lying in bed in the dark talking to Gwendolyn, giggling until their ribs ached. Uncle Cecil called to them to go to sleep, but there was a smile in his voice. They knew he didn't really care.

The next morning each of the children was issued a tomato can with some kerosene in the bottom and sent out to the potato patch to pick bugs.

Lloyd bossed the job in a quiet, reassuring voice, mature and exciting. Several times Sarah caught him watching her with a veiled, speculative expression. The look flattered her, puzzled her, and stirred a vague apprehension.

The potato patch was enormous and the work nasty, but Sarah was too excited by the company to mind. It was Cecil Junior who began to whine.

"Quit complaining or you're not getting any you-know-what in the loft this afternoon." Lloyd's voice was mild and unstressed.

"You can't stop me."

Lloyd crouched between the rows; the tips of his white, even teeth showed in a smile. "You can't lick me, little brother, and I don't think you're gonna tattle."

"I'm not your 'little brother,' Shit Face," Cecil snarled, gathering a handful of half-grown orange and black bugs, and flinging them savagely into the can. "Next week I'm gonna be thirteen."

The bugs smelled of partially digested potato leaves and besides had a peculiar sickening odour all their own. They exuded a sticky, orange-colored gum that befouled Sarah's hands. As the morning grew hot the world swam with the odour of potato bugs and kerosene. The sun punished her bare head. When she looked over the tops of the potato plants, a violet aura hung above them. She was thinking she couldn't bear another minute when Gwendolyn announced, "Sarah and me are quitting."

"Gwendolyn!" But all the authority had gone from Lloyd's voice.

"C'mon, Sarah." Gwendolyn's silver-blonde ringlets bounced in the sun as she bounded over the somber rows of green leaves with their white and purple flowers. Avoiding Lloyd's eyes, Sarah screwed up her courage and scampered after Gwendolyn as she said, "If he wants us in the hayloft this afternoon, he can darn well pick our share of the bugs, eh, Sarah?"

"What're we gonna do in the hayloft?"

It was a moment before Gwendolyn answered. "Play with the horses, dummy."

The only horses Uncle Cecil still kept were the team that the kids drove to school, a couple of broken-winded, spavined relics that had once been racehorses. "How do you get Margie Belle and Tinker up into the hayloft?" Sarah asked.

Gwendolyn's laugh was a tinsel glitter of sound ending in a small catch of breath.

Sarah's face felt hot. Here was something she didn't understand. Something exciting and a little sinister. For the briefest moment she tried to picture Skeezix at home in the pasture and wished she was there too, combing her tail.

Gwendolyn darted from granary to hedge to machinery to fence, always keeping something between Sarah and herself and the house as they made their way to the horse trough. When they had washed the stench and gum of potato bugs from their hands, Gwendolyn said, "Let's go see the coyote."

"Coyote?"

"In the granary there. Lloyd and Cecil trapped it."

They sneaked across to a small building of weather-greyed wood and peered between the slatted boards covering the door. For a moment, Sarah could see nothing, but there was a musky animal smell coming from the granary and the sound of some creature rushing about inside. Before her eyes adjusted to anything else, she saw the flame of terror in its frost-jade eyes. Soon she could see the whole animal, a beautiful little creature, its luxurious fur now matted with straw and filth. It limped back and forth against the back wall, keeping as far away from them as possible. One of its hind legs was broken. The leg, befouled, and attached now only by a bit of skin, flapped uselessly with the coyote's pacing.

"Isn't he hurting?"

Gwendolyn shrugged. "So? He's only a coyote. Lloyd'll probably kill him this afternoon. The hide's no good at this time of year, but Lloyd and Cecil make quite a bit of money trapping in the winter. Weasels and jackrabbits, too. See that trap hanging there?

That's a coyote trap. The spring's so strong Lloyd has to step on it when he sets it."

Sarah stared at the jagged steel jaws of the trap. She tried to imagine what the coyote had felt when those jaws had snapped. She would have liked to turn the coyote loose, but she didn't know how.

Gwendolyn wrinkled her nose. "Whew! He stinks. Let's go sit in the toolshed. It's cool in there."

Soon Gwendolyn was telling Sarah that Tilly Wannamaker had a baby and it was born with the snout of a pig, honest to God it was, only it had died and they'd buried it out beside the root cellar and, if Sarah didn't believe her, she would take her down to Tilly Wannamaker's place real early in the morning before the sun came up and she could see the grave for herself, so there.

"But why did Tilly Wannamaker's baby have a pig's snout?"

"'Cause Wannamaker's old boar, Sampson, caught Tilly out in the yard and fucked her one time."

Sarah slapped her hand over her mouth in guilty delight. Fucked! The bad word Mother says you're never supposed to say. But I bet Gwendolyn knows what it means. "How did Sampson fuck Tilly?"

"How?" Gwendolyn examined her with a sidelong glance. "Gosh, Sarah, don't you know *anything?*"

Sarah picked up a twig and began drawing a pig in the sand. She pressed her lips together to stop them quivering. Her eyes felt uncomfortable and hot. She wanted to get away from Gwendolyn. She wished she could see Mother and the two orphan lambs that hung about the house. "Guess I'll go see Aunt Frances."

"You will not."

Sarah couldn't stop her lips from quivering. She looked across the prairie towards home, away beyond the CPR tracks, away beyond the far hill. Could she walk that far? How long would it take?

"It's nice in the hayloft, Sarah, honest. And we've got quilts and everything."

But what do horses have to do with quilts? She looked the question without daring to ask it.

"Don't you believe me?"

"I don't...don't know what you're talking about."

"Sare! Sure you do."

Just then the triangle clanged, calling them to dinner. Sarah was so relieved that she dashed toward the house.

"Sarah, you dummy!" Gwendolyn's screech stopped her in her tracks. "Lloyd says we've all got to go in together."

They retraced their dodge-and-hide path, one eye on the windows of the house. When they were back in the potato patch, Cecil thrust a canful of dying bugs under Sarah's nose. "Yum-yum! Here's your dinner, Sarah."

She recoiled. Cecil advanced on her. She stumbled over a clod of earth and sat down hard. Cecil grabbed her by the back of the neck and forced her face towards the mouth of the can. "C'mon, Sare. Eat up."

Lloyd grabbed the can. "Cecil, quit that." Cecil fled. Lloyd chased him between the potato rows and caught him a hard boot in the backside.

Sarah couldn't fight back tears. Gwendolyn crouched beside her. "Don't be a bawl-baby, Sarah. C'mon. Let's watch Lloyd burn the bugs." She pulled

Sarah to her feet and they approached Lloyd, who took a bunch of matches from his overall pocket, crouched on a patch of bare earth, ripped the label from the tomato can, and using that for a wick, set can and contents alight. The fire flared, caught the kerosene and played over the mass of squirming orange bugs that writhed and popped until there was nothing left but a charred, smoking heap.

"That's it," Lloyd said. "Let's go to dinner." He put one arm around Gwendolyn's shoulder and the two of them sauntered towards the house.

Sarah trailed behind. Cecil ranged up beside her. "You blab about me teasing you and you're gonna get it," he muttered before he sprinted ahead to join the others.

Sarah trudged behind. I will not be a bawl-baby. I will not be a bawl-baby, she repeated to herself.

When they were all seated at the table, Auntie Frances said, "Sarah, are you feeling all right?"

She nodded vigorously.

"Tara Tenzie wouldn't be homesick, would she?" Uncle Cecil teased.

Her flesh crawled when he called her Tara Tenzie. When she was learning to talk, she hadn't been able to say 'Sarah MacKenzie.' Uncle Cecil never let her forget it.

"No, I'm not," she denied.

"Eat your dinner then."

She forced herself to swallow gravy and potatoes. She wished she was hungry, wished she could go on eating for the rest of the afternoon, then she wouldn't have to play that game, whatever it was, in the loft.

"Fine meal, Frances. Fine meal," Uncle Cecil pronounced, shoving his chair away from the table and patting his flat, muscular belly. "Now, I think we all deserve a little rest."

Gwendolyn climbed onto his lap and locked her arms around his neck. "Sarah and me want to nap in the house, Daddy."

He tousled her silvery ringlets. "Nothing doing, Pet. Mummy and I want to snooze, not listen to you two chatter." He patted her backside, gently broke her hold and set her on her feet. "All right, away you go, all of you. Shoo!"

Lloyd was holding out his hand. "C'mon, Sarah."

Her heart pounded and her apprehension deepened, but she didn't know what to do except allow him to lead her along. While Cecil raced for the barn, Gwendolyn dawdled behind. "C'mon, Gwenny," Lloyd coaxed, "I'll take it easy, I promise."

The inside of the barn was dark, musty. Strips of blue light found cracks between the boards and lay like parallel shimmering wands on the floor.

"Up in the loft with you," Lloyd commanded, standing back while Gwendolyn and Cecil climbed the ladder. There was nothing for Sarah to do but follow. To her relief, the hayloft door was wide open; the sun blazed on the loft floor in a brilliant white square. Just as Gwendolyn had said, a pile of quilts lay in one corner. The loft, which still held the scent of hay, was swept clean. What was there to be afraid of?

"You wanna be first, Sare?" Lloyd said, caressing her bare arm.

She stepped away from him. "First what?"

Lloyd looked at Gwendolyn. "Didn't you tell her?"

"She's such a dummy she didn't understand."

Anger and something like fear crossed Lloyd's face, then he forced a laugh. "Gwendolyn and I will show you, Sare. Then, after a while, you and me can try it. It's nice. You'll see."

To Sarah's amazement, he whipped out of his overalls, stripped the dress over Gwendolyn's head and shoved her down onto the quilts. Sarah knew fellows had wormy-looking things that dangled between their legs. Once she had seen Father's when she walked in on him when he was bathing, but Lloyd's was not like a worm. It was thick and it stood up and jerked. There was a funny-looking purplish lump on the end of it. Suddenly he was over Gwendolyn, on his knees between her spread legs. The stiff thing with the lump on the end of it disappeared inside Gwendolyn. He rammed it into her again and again.

Amazingly, Gwendolyn scarcely seemed to notice; she stared off into distance and hummed a tuneless little song. Sarah had the weird feeling that Gwendolyn wasn't really there. Then Lloyd started ramming the thing in real hard.

"Ow, ow, ow! Lloyd, you said –"

Lloyd groaned, his face twisted as though in pain, and he collapsed on top of her.

Sarah was trembling, faintly sick. She had seen animals do something like what Gwendolyn and Lloyd were doing, but it seemed to her that the animals were angry with each other when they did it. She expected Gwendolyn to bawl, to threaten to tell. Instead, she tangled her fingers in Lloyd's hair and jerked hard enough to make him wince.

He raised his head from her shoulder, cuffed her, and grinned at Sarah. "See, Sare? It's fun. Now, you try it with Cecil and after a while, you and me –"

"Yeah!" Cecil grabbed at the hem of Sarah's dress and tried to lift it over her head. She tore away from him. He grabbed at her again. When she ducked away that time, it was into Lloyd's arms.

He clapped one hand over her mouth. "Sh-hh, Sarah! Sarah! Just shut up, will you? Look, you don't have to if you don't –"

She twisted free and made for the ladder.

"Cecil, stop her!"

Cecil flung her to the loft floor, straddled her, held her down and slapped one dirty hand over her mouth. "Shut up, you dummy! Just shut up. Do you want Daddy out here?"

"Cecil, don't you hit her. Don't!" Lloyd sounded desperate. He shoved Cecil away and lifted Sarah to her feet. "Sarah, honest, you don't have to do it if you don't want to. Listen, wipe your nose on my shirt here, okay? We won't hurt you, Sare. Honest we won't. There's nothing to be afraid of."

"Bawl-baby! Just listen to her." Gwendolyn, scornful.

"Sare, you're not going to tell, are you?" Lloyd pleaded.

"You do and we *will* make you eat potato bugs," Cecil threatened.

"Tell? No!" She shuddered. Not if they saw my bare belly on the barbed-wire fence.

When she finally quit sobbing, Gwendolyn took her to the horse trough and helped her wash her face.

The three of them followed her around all afternoon, hatred in their eyes, never leaving her alone with Uncle or Auntie.

At suppertime Aunt Frances said, "Are you not

feeling well, Sarah? You've hardly eaten anything all day and you're very pale."

Three pairs of eyes bored into her, dared her.

"My stomach hurts," she whispered. "I want to go home."

Uncle Cecil groaned. "Typical only child! Lord, spare me. Well, all right, Tara Tenzie, get your stuff and I'll drive you as soon as I finish my tea."

The kids tagged along, of course. But Sarah was never in their house again, except for those times when she had to go with Mother and Father. She was never invited; if she had been, she wouldn't have gone.

Several times, over the years, Mother said, "I simply don't understand *why* you can't get along with your cousins, Sarah. They are quite the best brought-up children in Rattlesnake Park. Nothing shows like quality and breeding."

4. BUFFALO CHIPS AND BLANKETS

OTHER FORGETS THE PANCAKE SHE IS about to flip, turns around and gasps, "Wash blankets at the *river?* James MacKenzie, I never heard of anything so ridiculous."

"Well, they gotta be washed before winter. And down at the river there's lots of water. Wood for heating it and everything."

"*If* you could find wood dry enough to burn. Besides, the river water is so hard that soap curdles in it like –"

"Gets stuff clean, though, and after we spread the blankets to dry, we can pick chokecherries. Be a nice little outing for Sarah before she's gotta go back to school."

"Outing, indeed," Mother snorts, batting at greasy smoke. "You heard the radio. Snow flurries in Edmonton this morning. A regular arctic outbreak."

"Ach! Edmonton's three hundred and fifty miles north." He wrinkles his nose. "You gonna flip that flapjack or let it smoke us out of here?"

"Oh, bother!" She scrapes the ruined pancake into

the slop bucket and adds more batter to the griddle. "You know perfectly well that when Edmonton gets a storm on Tuesday we get a storm on Wednesday."

While her back is turned, Father sneaks a fistful of kitchen matches out of the box and pockets them before lighting his pipe. "Today ain't Tuesday though; it's Saturday."

She gives him the kind of look that withers attempts at humour.

"It's not gonna storm, Mother," Sarah bursts out, "It's real warm outside. And why can't we just do something for fun? Other people do. Other people go to the river just for the fun of it. Other kids get to swim."

"We're going," Father says with the air of the lord of the manor. "You go run the team in, Kid. I'll round up the blankets and soap and stuff, and your mom can fix us a lunch to take along."

"James MacKenzie —" she begins.

"Oh, fer chrisake, Beth, don't go ruining the day," he overrides her. "We deserve a little change, just like everybody else."

When Father talks like that, Mother caves in, not necessarily with grace, but she caves.

Riding Skeezix, Sarah gallops off to find Father's driving team. Jake and Baldy are a pair of tough little cayuses. Their mother, Daisy, was a wild horse captured in the mountains. In Daisy's blood ran the pure fire of Arab ancestors that escaped conquistadors centuries ago; the same fire runs through Jake and Baldy's now. The two are never to be trusted. For the mere the hell of it, they whistle alarms that turn sensible spans of workhorses into quivering idiots. If there is a runaway, Jake or Baldy are always involved and, in spite of the poorest feed and the hardest work, they manage to prance after a hard day in the fields. They also manage to be devilishly hard to catch. Before Sarah runs them into the barn, she and Skeezix are both lathered.

Proud of her accomplishment and feeling very grown up and daring (after all, she *is* eleven-and-a-half), Sarah ties the team up and sets about harnessing them. She has never harnessed a horse, but she has watched Father dozens of times. She is trying to figure out how to attach the britching, the straps that pass around the horses' rumps to hold the wagon from running up on the team's heels when they are heading downhill, when Father enters the barn. "God, Kid, what're you doing fooling around with Jake and Baldy? You're liable to get the guts kicked outta –"

"No, I'm not," she says saucily. "Give me a hand with this britching, will you?"

"We don't need no damned britching."

"We do so. You know Mother hates it when you don't put it on and the team have to outrun the wagon on the river hill."

"Ah, don't hurt nothing. Safe as a church. Your Ma just needs something to squawk about is all."

"Well, outrunning that hill scares me too. If you don't put the britching on the team, I'm not riding in the wagon; I'm riding Skeezix."

"You're doing no such a bloody thing."

"Why?"

"Well – well, you're just not. That's all."

"Do you always have to be the boss? I'm not a baby any more."

"Now, look here, Kid –"

"What are you scared of? That I might get out of your sight for ten minutes so you can't tell me what to do?"

"Now, look *here*, Kid –"

"If I can't ride Skeezix, *I'm* not going."

"You either ride with your ma and me or *none* of us are going."

When she realizes that she has backed herself into a corner, she is furious, but she still glares at him defiantly.

"C'mon, Kid, it's a great day," he wheedles. "Let's not waste it. Tomorrow there might be a foot of snow and nobody'll be going to the river."

"Yeah, right," she is relieved to admit, "but just in case it storms before we get back tonight, I'd better go put the coats in the wagon."

"That's using your head."

But when she goes into the house to get the coats Mother says, "There's nothing but a little slack coal left in the bin and hardly enough kindling to start a fire. If it storms before we get home tonight, we'll be in a nice mess. You'd better take your little red wagon and go and gather buffalo chips, Sarah."

Gathering "buffalo chips" is the job that Sarah detests above all others. What she is really gathering is pancakes of dried cow dung. (Cow pies, Father calls them.) Sun baked and dried, they are almost odourless and they throw off considerable heat when they are burned, but Sarah looks upon gathering cow pies as the greatest disgrace of their poverty, and it makes it no less shameful that Father tells her that buffalo chips, the real article, was what the Blackfoot burned in their campfires when they roamed these plains fifty years ago. She sets off on the task, yanking the toy wagon behind her and cursing under her breath.

The morning started with the penetrating somnolent heat of a late August day with a washed-out pale sky; a day when no one can believe that they ever had to wear coats and overshoes and mittens, or that they will ever have to do so again, a day when the dusty prairies dream under the heat and the only energetic creatures are clattering grasshoppers. But by the time they are four miles from home the fierce heat is leeched from the sun; the blue of the sky has changed to a darker hue and ragged clouds scud out of the north-west.

Mother says, "If we had any sense, we'd turn around right now and go home."

The coats! A shiver passes over Sarah. She is struggling to work up the courage to admit that she has forgotten them when, inadvertently, Father lets her off the hook.

"Ah, hell, another mile and we'll be at the river. We'll have water heated and them blankets washed and spread to dry before you know it."

To Sarah's surprise, Mother hasn't complained once about Father not putting the britching on the harness, but at the top of the river hill she says, "All right, James, you can let me out right here. I'll walk. I'm not riding while that crazy team tries to outrun the wagon on the river hill."

"Beth – !"

"You heard me."

"Oh, Jesus!"

"Supposing one of them stumbled?"

"They never have."

"Or a wheel came off?"

"Oh, for chrisake – !"

"And swearing doesn't help. Now, let me off."

"Supposing some neighbor sees us? This is gonna look like hell."

"It looks like hell, you trying to act like some tough old cowboy at your age too."

"I ain't!"

"You could fool me." She climbs out of the wagon. "Come along, Sarah."

Sarah is about to hop out of the wagon too, when she glances at Father. His face is quivering with indignation and hurt. "Guess – guess I'll ride with Father," she mutters.

"Very well then, but if the two of you get into trouble, don't expect any sympathy from me." She turns and starts resolutely down the hill.

"Dang woman," Father says. "Never seen anything as stubborn in all my –" He thrusts the lines into Sarah's hands. "Here, hang onto this team till I get my pipe to steaming."

He taps the dottle out of his pipe and refills it, his baleful gaze on Mother's retreating figure. "Old cowboy, huh? We're gonna show her a thing or two, Kid. We're just dang well gonna show her." He draws his brows together, fishes a match out of his pocket, and huffs and snorts as he lights the pipe. When he has a little cherry-red furnace burning three inches from the end of his nose, he rises, grabs the lines from Sarah, whaps them down on Jake and Baldy's backs, and yells, "Yaaaa-ho-o!"

Within three strides, the team is running flat out,

ears back, bellies to earth, tails and manes streaming. The wagon jounces and bounces and clatters behind. Father hangs onto the lines, feet braced against the footboard, an expression compounded of terror and fiendish glee on his face as they tear past Mother, who has stopped to stare at them, the fingers of one lady-like hand pressed against her lips.

The wagon hits a hummock. To save herself from pitching out, Sarah grabs at Father anywhere she can get a handhold. The fingers of one hand claw into his braces, the other crunches the fistful of matches in his overall pocket. The matches explode with a puff of smoke.

"Jesus!" Father yells. "Jesus!" Sarah bats at his thigh with one hand and hangs onto his braces with the other. He reefs on the lines with all his might. "Whoa, you bastards! Whoa, you sonsabitches! Whoa, goddammit! Whoa!"

The horses come to a plunging halt, eyes rolling, slavering, dripping sweat and breathing in great wheezing heaves. While Father bats at his smoking thigh, Sarah pries the lid off the lardpail of milk that Mother brought for tea and sloshes it over his leg. A puff of acrid smoke peels off on the chilling air.

"Father, are you burned?"

"Burned? Nah! Singed a little is all."

"You're sure?"

"'Course I'm sure."

She is trembling, partly from fright, partly from pure elation. When she glances at him, there is a gleam in his eye too, and a grin tugging at one corner of his mouth. She smacks him on the shoulder with the heel of her hand. "You're awful!"

"That's what your Ma keeps telling me." They lean against each other and giggle.

"So, what're we gonna do now?"

"Head down to the bottom of the hill there and wait for her. She sure as hell ain't gonna be too pleased with us if we leave her to wade across that ford alone."

"You mean, we're fording across to the small island?"

"Yep. There's a good patch of chokecherries there." He shifts the stem of his pipe from one corner of his mouth to the other, fishes all the matches out of his pocket, and stares at them. The ends of all but three are charred brown stumps.

"Well, at least you've got enough left to light the campfire," Sarah chirps.

He gives her a sour look, knocks the dottle out of his pipe, shoves it into his pocket and squints back up the trail. "I wish that woman would get a move on. Them storm clouds are moving in pretty fast."

The afternoon is a disaster. The ford is deeper than Father figured. Water coming over the floor boards ruins the lunch. They have trouble finding dry wood. Twice Father scrabbles together dead grass and dry leaves for kindling but he can't get the wood to catch. He is down to the last of his three matches when Sarah, who has been ranging the island, comes upon a dry poplar branch, grey with age. Father slivers it up with his jackknife, makes a tiny tipi of the slivers, nurses it into flame, and finally gets a sulky fire lit under the tub of wash water.

Mother keeps eyeing the sky and predicting that the storm will hit before supper time.

The wash water turns to grey scum when soap is added. Mother says that they will be lucky if the blankets are not completely ruined.

Father says, "Bullshit," and takes the first clean blanket into the river to rinse. He is backing into the river, trailing the blanket behind him, when he steps off into deep water and disappears. He surfaces, sputtering and choking, while the blanket sails serenely downstream.

"Get the blanket, James!" Mother screams. "Get the –"

He strikes out in a floundering dog paddle, grabs the edge of the blanket, clamps it between his teeth and wallows to shore, dragging the blanket behind him through the mud.

Mother bursts into tears.

Muttering and cursing, Father drags the blanket back into the river, sloshes mud off of it, and staggers out of the water with it in his arms. "Give me a hand to wring the water out of her," he puffs.

"One does not wring woolens. We shall have to spread it to dry, wet as it is."

"If we wrung some of the water out of it, it'd –"

"I refuse to ruin the only blankets we own."

By the time all the blankets are spread to dry on clumps of buckbrush, the sun has disappeared and the air is chilly. The family hunches, waiting around the campfire.

"If we even had some tea..." Mother mourns.

Sarah moves closer to the fire, praying that they will get home before the storm hits. Father, dressed only in long johns, since *his* clothes are also drying on the buckbrush, rises to adjust one of the blankets that is sagging to the ground and exclaims, "Christ! Look at what's coming!"

From the northwest a great wall of purple clouds rushes down upon them. A blizzard of dust, choked with tumbleweeds, flees before it. Great splotches of ice-water rain slap against their skin, so shocking that, at first, they seem impossible to bear.

"Where's them coats, Kid?" Father gasps.

"I forgot to bring them."

He stares at her, flinching away from the rain. "Christ all Friday! Well, don't bawl about it. It ain't the worst thing you coulda done. You and your Ma heave them blankets into the wagon fast as you can, and I'll hitch up the team."

The full force of sleet, rain, and driving wind blasts them when they are out of the shelter of the island's trees crossing the river ford.

"Oh, mercy!" Mother moans.

"Christ all Friday!" Father gasps.

Jake reaches over and bites Baldy and Baldy bites him back. Father curses them and they both caper. Sarah rolls herself into a ball to try to conserve body heat and clamps her jaws to keep her teeth from chattering.

"I cannot bear this, James," Mother cries. "I am perishing with cold."

"So am I," Sarah whimpers.

Once across the ford, Father pulls the team to a stop. "All right, get out. Beth, you hang onto Jake's hame and Sarah, you hang onto Baldy's. We'll all warm up when we start running ."

"You know I'm terrified of horses," Mother cries.

"Well, then, trot along behind."

Sarah grabs Baldy's hame, one of two steel contraptions that pass around his collar, and swings along, half carried by the horse's strength. Soon she begins to warm up. It is an adventure now, almost fun. Father trots gamely along, clinging to the lines, but Mother falls farther and farther behind. Finally she stops and calls after them, "I cannot do this. I cannot run any further."

Father stops the team, hops up into the wagon, swings the team around beside her, and offers her his hand. "C'mon, wifey. We'll get you home and thaw you out."

Once in the wagon, he shelters her with his body from the wind and driving rain which is now peppered with snowflakes, and lays the lines on the horses' backsides. The old wagon bumbles and clatters along at an only slightly more sedate pace than the runaway he had staged for her benefit that morning. Sarah, clinging to Baldy's hame, has the sensation of running without effort, almost flying, the horse half carrying her. She is thoroughly enjoying herself, except for the slight anxiety that she might step on a rattlesnake, too sluggish from the cold to get out of their way.

But when Father stops the team in the farmyard, Mother climbs out of the wagon like a creaky old arthritic, blue and shivering violently. Father looks at her askance, his face red and apprehensive. "Figure you could unharness the team and turn 'em loose while I get the fire started for your ma, Kid?" he asks. "And there's some old horse blankets in the granary. Fetch 'em in when you come."

Sarah strips the harness off the team and turns them loose. They tear across the pasture, bucking and kicking as they disappear into swirling snow which is collecting in every little hollow on the ground.

When Sarah staggers into the house with a load of horse blankets, Father has a "buffalo chip" fire burning in the kitchen stove. Mother and he, dressed in every bit of winter clothes that they own, crowd as close as they can to the fire, but Mother is still shivering. "This'll thaw you out, Beth," Father says, as he wraps Mother in a horse blanket that stinks of chicken shit and mice.

"Oh, but my poor feet. I don't think I shall ever feel them again."

Sarah puts the pot containing the remnants of last night's stew on the stove to heat and sits down beside her mother.

Father lights his pipe, then pulls his blanket tight around his shoulders. "Well, sir," he says, heaving his feet up to rest beside Mother's and Sarah's on the open oven door, "she ain't such a bad world, after all."

5. WORMY APPLES

I T IS A HOT SEPTEMBER NIGHT; THE AIR IS filled with the odour of bush fires in the far-off Rockies and an eerie purple dusk creeps across the prairies. Sarah is sitting in the doorway of the old farmhouse admiring the calluses she has built up from going barefoot all summer to save shoe leather. When she hears the jingle of trace chains, she looks up and sees a Bennett buggy approaching. This contraption, which had once been Uncle Johnny's Model A Ford, stops at the fence. Aunt Jane and two other women dismount. After a moment, Sarah realizes that they are Father's other two sisters, Aunt Jessie and Aunt Mary. Sarah hasn't seen them for a long time. Practically nobody drives cars any more, and even though the sisters live in Taber, a little more than thirty miles away, they would think three times before they spent the money for bus fare, simply to come visiting.

Something must have happened, Sarah realizes, as they troop past her into the house. All three are dressed in their Sunday best. Aunt Jane has even put in her false teeth, something she does only when she is going to Women's Institute or to Church. Once seated in the living room, Aunt Jane turns to Father. "Us MacKenzies are family, Jamie. We stick together. You gotta remember that."

"What're you blabbering about?"

She bursts into tears, digging a balled-up hankie into the corners of her eyes. "It's Donald –"

Aunt Mary starts bawling too, while Aunt Jessie wails, "I can't believe what's happened to our brother."

"Hurt, is he?" Father demands, alarm flaring in his face.

They shake their heads.

"Not *dead*, surely?"

"No."

"You mean he's married that whore of a Nancy he's been shacked up with since Lottie took off on him!"

"James!" Mama snaps. "Not in front of Sar –"

"Any kid going on twelve knows what a –"

"Never mind." She turns on the aunts. "Pull yourself together, Jane. Now, what has happened to Donald?"

"He's in jail."

"Jail?" Mother slaps one hand over her mouth, her eyes wide with horror.

Sarah shrivels against the door frame. Wait till the kids at school hear about this.

"What'd the damn fool do this time?" Father groans.

Aunt Mary, the flighty one, bursts through tears into a shriek of laughter. "Walked off with two kids' bikes."

"He *what?*"

"You know Proudfoot, the big-shot lawyer in Taber? Bought his kids a coupla fancy bikes. They rode around town all day, snooting all the other kids, and when suppertime came they dropped the bikes on the sidewalk in front of Proudfoot's house as if new bikes were nothing to them and –"

"For chrisake, get to the point."

"After the beer parlour closed, Donald and Nancy came rolling home, a little tight, picked up the bikes and wheeled 'em –"

"That jackass of a Donald!"

"He wasn't gonna *steal* 'em," Aunt Mary intercedes. "He was just gonna let his kids ride around on 'em till Nancy and him had slept it off the next morning, then he was gonna take the bikes back, but –"

"But Proudfoot got old Cappy Falls out looking for the bikes," Father divines.

"Drove that town truck up one street and down another until he –"

"Why didn't the old fart just take the bikes offa the kids and dump 'em back at Proudfoot's place?"

"He maybe would have, but Donald got feisty."

"Took a punch at –"

"And Proudfoot said to make an example of him. Said he wasn't living in any town where –"

"So Donald got a week in the Taber lock-up!" Father whoops and slaps his knee. "Serves the bugger right."

"A *year* in the Lethbridge jail!" the sisters chorus.

"A year in the – ?" He gapes at them. "A *year*, you said? For snitching two kids' goddamn bikes and taking a pop at old Cappy Falls? I'll get a real lawyer after that silly – I'll appeal the –"

"And what do you plan to use for money?" Mother is as crisp as lettuce.

The aunts start bawling again.

"But the children?" Mother asks. "Lottie's surely taken them?"

"Won't."

"Won't? But they're *her* children."

"That new man of hers don't like kids."

"That is outrageous."

"You mean them kids are with that whore of a Nancy?" Father bristles.

"Donald says it's all right with him."

"And she's gonna feed 'em offa what she rakes in peddling ass?" Father's face is scarlet and he is shouting. "There's no bloody way. Us MacKenzies are respectable people. We look after our own."

Aunt Jane beams approval. "We knew you'd see it that way, Jamie."

Mother turns to him. "And how do *you* propose to look after Donald's children? We can scarcely look after the one we've got."

He blinks at her, mouth opening and closing like a landed pike's.

"Me being a widow now, there's no way I can take them kids." Aunt Jane starts to bawl again, as she does every time she remembers that last winter, Uncle Johnny died of pneumonia. "My Billy's a real responsible boy, and I feel real blessed that he's going to take over the farm," she says, "but you can't expect a young fella of twenty to take on a couple of cousins."

"And I've got the old folks to look after. What between them and working at that telephone exchange –" Mary reminds the company.

"And what with five kids of my own –" Jessie spreads her hands.

Five kids? Sarah thinks. Last time I heard, there were three, and I can't even remember their names.

Father rakes his fingers through his thin hair, turns to the left and blinks, then turns to the right and blinks. Then he looks at Mother and spreads *his* hands.

"*Us* take those boys? What are you thinking of?"

"Well, they could sleep on these two old winnipeg couches here in the living room."

"And what about blankets? We've scarcely enough to cover ourselves."

"Donald must have blankets," Mary says. "I don't see how that Nancy character could stop you from taking them when you go to get the kids."

"Go to get those children?" Mother cries. "James, this is madness! We'll be begging the municipality for relief when I've used up the bit of the flour I've got left, and you want to take Donald's – ?"

"It ain't as though the rest of us wouldn't take them if we could," Aunt Mary interrupts.

"The municipality's bound to give you relief for 'em if you need it," Aunt Jessie says.

But Aunt Jane knows where to zero in. "It's the Christian thing to do, Beth," she says, eyeing the palm leaf cross the priest gave Mother the Sunday before Easter, which has been drying all summer on top of the Thomas Trading Company's calendar.

"Look at it this way, Beth," Father says, after the aunts have gone, "it'll be kind of like having a coupla brothers for Sarah."

"Brothers for Sarah! Are you out of your mind?

They are horrible children. Jane says the little one wets the bed. And the other one.... Well, he's –" Her face crimsons. "Well, he's *at* himself all the time."

Sarah doesn't understand what "at himself" means; she doesn't care. She is so tickled she hugs herself. I don't care what Mother says. I think it's gonna be great, having a couple of little brothers.

But far into the night she hears Father and Mother's voices rising and falling. Once she hears Mother say something about an orphanage and Father shouting, "That ain't the way us MacKenzies do things, Beth. We look after our own."

The following morning, looking wan and miserable, he stands humbly by while Mother raids the coffee can. Bus fare to Taber for Sarah and him from the money Mother had squirrelled away, pennies at a time, to buy ingredients for a Christmas cake. Mother says it is an awful extravagance, Father taking Sarah with him, but he says he'll need help to pack the kids' stuff.

Two hours later he is stopping strangers on the streets of Taber, asking if anyone knows where Nancy Cannon lives. Some guys giggle; some stare at him as though they'd like to pop him one. One points to Sarah and says, "Farming her out to Nancy? A little young, ain't she?"

Father's face turns purple. "Look, I just asked you if you knew where a guy'd find Nancy Cannon."

"North edge of town. Camped in an old cook wagon somebody used to use on a threshing outfit. Yah can't miss it."

When Father and she are out of earshot, Sarah asks, "What did that guy mean, 'farm me out to Nancy'?"

"Never you mind. Goddamnit, I dunno if this was such a good idea, fetching you along."

"Well, I just asked."

"Well, don't."

They don't speak again until they spot the cook wagon, a dilapidated little shack on wheels parked on a vacant lot by the side of an irrigation ditch. Two dirty kids of about nine and six, wet from playing in the ditch, stand up and stare at them. Each has a partly-eaten apple in his hand.

"Poor little devils," Father mutters. He turns away, takes a hankie out of his hip pocket and honks his nose. "Well, we're gonna do the best we can for 'em, and that's all there is to it."

Sarah goes all mushy inside with good intentions. While Father heads for the cook shack, she races across to where the kids are standing. "I'm Sarah," she burbles, "and you must be Willie and Ned?"

The older kid looks her up and down, spits a bite of apple core in her direction and says, "So, who the fuck is Sarah?"

"Watch your tongue, Mister. You can't talk like that when you come to live at our place."

"Live at your place? Who says? You're nuts."

The littlest kid crowds against his older brother, his face pinched and frightened. "She can't make us go with her, can she, Willie?"

"Nah! She can't make us do nothin'." He cocks what remained of the apple and throws it at Sarah. "Bugger off, you. Beat it."

The apple leaves a wet splatter on her dress. She is furious. "Throw something at me again, Mister, and I'll teach you some manners."

"You and whose fucking army?"

Outraged, all romantic notions about little brothers knocked out of her head, she retreats to Father who is standing on the top step of the cook wagon talking through the screen door.

"Listen, Nancy," he is saying, "you got no right to them kids, no matter what Donald says. I'm taking 'em. You better get that through your head. Now, if you'll let us in, we'll start gathering clothes and stuff for 'em."

"You're not taking the kids."

"Figure we are, Nancy, and there's no arguments." He grabs the handle of the screen door and yanks. The hook that had been holding it on the inside goes flying. He steps into the shack with Sarah on his heels.

Nancy, dyed red hair in curling rags, and rouge spots standing out on her cheeks like a paint job on a cheap doll, backs towards the bed and screeches, "Willie, Ned, get in here!"

The kids burst through the door and line themselves up beside her. "You're not letting them take us, are you, Nancy?" Ned pleads.

"Over my dead body, sugar."

"Let her keep them, Father," Sarah blurts. "*Let* her! Mother's right. They're awful kids."

"Fine way for a MacKenzie to talk! No goddamned whore looks after a kid of –"

"Whore?" Nancy springs at him. Her nails leave bloody scratches on his cheek; his glasses go flying. He grabs her wrists and holds her at arm's length. "That's enough. Cut it out right now, unless you want me to get the cops."

She starts to bawl, throwing her head from side to side. "You can't take the kids."

Father gives her a shove that sends her sprawling across the bed. "Now, listen here, you got a choice," he says, blinking at her myopically. "You either let me take them kids, or I'll see they get sent to an orphanage. What's it gonna be?"

"Not an orphanage, Nancy," Willie wails. "They beat you there and make you work and feed you just bread and water if you're bad. I read all about it. I'd sooner go with the old bastard."

"No!" Ned cries.

Nancy scrambles to a sitting position and takes Ned's face between both hands. "Sugar, looks like you are gonna *have* to go with him. But it's only for a year. When your dad gets out, we're gonna get hitched, and then –"

"Quit fillin' the kid's head with shit," Father snorts.

"It ain't shit." She casts him a venomous look, fishes five dollars out of the garter roll above her knee and hands it to Willie. "That's for stamps and writing paper and stuff, sugar. If the bugger don't treat you right, you let us know. Your dad'll fix him good when he gets out." With a defiant toss of her head, she slides one arm around each kid. "C'mon, let's go wait outside. He can bloody well find your stuff himself if he wants it so bad."

Sarah can hear them bawling. She feels like bawling herself, but for different reasons. After she has found Father's glasses, he bends them back into shape with trembling hands and hooks them over his ears. Reluctantly, Sarah helps him go through all the boxes and cupboards in the shack; they don't find enough clothes to fill one gunny sack.

Why did we bring three sacks? Sarah puzzles, but the expression on Father's face forbids silly questions.

It is dark when the four of them get off the bus in Rattlesnake Park. Sarah's belly is rumbling. She hasn't eaten since breakfast; neither has Father. She wonders if the kids are hungry too, but they, at least, have had an apple apiece. As they tromp along, Indian file through the dark, following the ruts of the wagon trail on the long trek home, she hears them sniffling. She tries to put herself in their place. They must be scared, she thinks. I sure would be if I was heading out through the dark with a couple of strangers and I didn't even know where I was going. "You'll see the light in our window from the top of the next hill," she offers. "Mother's probably got supper ready for us too."

Willie mutters something under his breath. The only word she can make out for sure is "fuck." Father grabs him by the shoulder. "You clean up your tongue, young fella. We don't stand for dirty talk around our place."

Willie wrenches away. "Keep your hands offa me. You're not the boss of me."

"I'm the boss of you until your dad gets out, and don't you forget it." But he doesn't sound like he's the boss of anybody. When they enter the house, he falls into his rocker like a weary old man. "God, what a day!"

"And you're hungry, I suppose," Mother surmises. "Well, there's porridge ready on the back of the stove and I managed to get a little milk out of the cows."

"Mush? Ugh!" Willie sounds as though he is about to throw up.

"Young man, before this winter is over we'll all be

happy for a bowl of 'mush,'" she tells him. "Now, wash your hands and sit down at the table."

Willie shrugs insolently, but does as he is bidden.

Sarah, Father, and the kids have started eating when Mother says, "I had just as well make down the winnipeg couches for them now. Where are their blankets, James?"

His eyes grow enormous behind his glasses, his jaw sags, and he drops his spoon into his bowl. "Jesus Christ! We forgot the blankets!"

Sarah stares at him, horrified. *That's* why we took all those gunny sacks.

After a long silence, Father says, "We'll have to ask the rest of the family to share. They're bound to have a couple of extra –"

"The rest of the family! They were telling me the children piled all the coats in the house on their beds to keep from freezing last winter. The only thing I can think, is to make up one winnipeg couch and have the kids sleep together to share what blankets we've got."

"I'm not sleeping with Ned," Willie cries. "He pees the bed."

Mother looks a little sick.

"Well, we can't expect him to, can we, Beth?" Father says. "We're just gonna have to divide up what blankets we got and pile coats on our beds too."

Mother looks at him for a long minute, her lips pressed tightly together. "James MacKenzie, you had better pray that this won't be a hard winter."

He shoves away from the table without finishing his mush.

Mother, who has started going through the kids'

clothes, looks up at him. "Where are their winter clothes?"

"All we could find is just what's in the sack."

"No overshoes. No coats – and winter coming on."

"Jessie's bound to have some hand-me-downs from her kids."

"For me to mend and make over."

"Beth, for chrisake, we'll have to do the best we can."

"I may be a good manager, but I can't manage on nothing. There's a municipal meeting tomorrow night. You can go and humble yourself. They might give us a few dollars for relief."

"Oh, Jesus, Beth, I was figuring we wouldn't have to ask until maybe November."

But the following night Sarah watches him walk away, heading for the meeting, a small man wearing much-patched overalls and a shirt that Mother had cobbled together out of two bleached flour sacks. A few hundred feet from the house, he stops, turns his back to the wind, and lights his pipe. When he returns at ten o'clock, Mother looks up from patching overalls. "Well?"

"Seven bucks a month for you and me and Sarah. Nothing for the kids."

"Nothing for the – ?"

"Well, Donald wasn't living in this municipality, so –"

"Seven dollars! Not half of what we were making from the cream cheques when the cows were milking last summer."

He fishes his pipe out of his pocket and puts it in his mouth.

"You'll be giving that thing up when you've finished the tobacco you have left, won't you?" Her tone is as dry as chalk.

His face twitches and he returns the pipe to his pocket.

The next day the complaints begin. "Why do us guys have to sleep in the living room?" and "Did you *forget* to put any sugar in these cookies?" And, as time goes on, "Don't you ever buy any apples or oranges or *any* of that good stuff?" and "Do we have to eat salt pork and spuds *every* night and mush *every* morning?" Or, "Isn't there even a ball for us guys to play with?" And, most bitterly, "Why *can't* we go visiting the neighbours?" and "Why can't we invite other kids here?"

Then Willie figures out a delicate little game of nerves. He buys a writing pad, stamps and envelopes with the five dollars Nancy gave him. Several times a week he composes letters to either his father or to Nancy, sly little smiles playing around his mouth and his eyes roaming from Sarah to Mother and Father and back again. While he writes, Father sits, the stem of his cold pipe clenched between his teeth and one hand drumming an irritating little tattoo on the arm of his old rocker, while Mother strains her eyes darning socks or mending overalls, glancing at Willie from time to time, an anxious frown between her brows. When Willie has finished his letters, he seals the envelopes, tucks them under his pillow, and mails them before he goes to school.

NOVEMBER COLD CREEPS through the skimpy patchwork quilt and pile of old coats that cover Sarah's bed. She pokes her head out of the tangle to peer at the window. Frost ferns half an inch thick. Outside, wind whines and whimpers around the corners of the old house. Northwester. First honest-to-god blizzard of the winter. And I've got to help Father get Crip and Cherry to town for that buyer today.

She covers her head against the cold and scrunches back down. I know we gotta sell Cherry. Father needs overshoes and Cherry's just a useless dry cow now. But I feel awful. When I was a little kid, she put up with me pestering while I learned to milk. And poor old Crip – his foot froze off when he was born last winter – Father says he'll never make it through till spring, so....But he was always so happy to see me last summer when I carried skim milk out to him after we'd finished separating.

She is cramped from holding still, but if she moves she will break the cocoon of warm air that surrounds her. When misery finally forces her to turn, icy draughts invade her nest. Isn't Father ever going to get up and start the kitchen range? She draws herself into a tight little ball. She is about to get up and start the fire herself when she hears Willie pad into the kitchen, pee in the slop pail and scuttle back to bed.

But not Mr. Ned. He's not getting up in the cold. Why would he, when Mother will melt snow to wash his sheets every day?

When her misery becomes worse than her dread of the cold, she scrambles out of bed, yanks on shoes and a coat, clamps her jaws to keep her teeth from chattering, and rushes to the stove. A few faint red coals among the grey ash wink at her when she lifts the lid. She lays kindling on the coals and opens all the draughts. Shaking like a person with a fever, she repeatedly checks her handiwork. A few wisps of smoke – no flame.

Father's voice comes from the bedroom, muffled with sleep, "You shake her down, Sarah?"

She goes at it vigorously.

"Hey! Take it easy. Shake them coals clean through the grate, and you'll have to start her from scratch."

With a whimper of apprehension, she lifts the stove lid and peers inside. Tender tongues of flame now play with the kindling. "She's going, Father, she's going!"

"Good. You'd just as well put the kettle on then."

"I can't," she crows, more delighted than appalled. "The dipper's frozen solid in the water bucket."

"Hell! Gonna be one sweet day to move stock."

"How're we gonna move Crip, anyhow? He can't walk."

"You're gonna have to help me get him in the bob-sled and we'll tie him down."

Why me? Why not Willie? He eats here too, but he doesn't have to do anything excepting haul in a little kindling, and Mr. Ned doesn't have to do anything at all, she grouses, as she dumps half a bucket of coal onto her fire and rushes back to bed.

When the fire begins to roar and the stove pipes are pinging, she scrabbles her clothes together, takes them into the kitchen, dresses in front of the stove, then goes to the window and melts a peephole with her breath. Outside, snow-wraiths flee before a north-west wind; ice crystals dance in the light of a lemon-pale sun which struggles above the horizon only to disappears among scudding clouds.

An hour later, when the house is beginning to thaw out and be almost bearable, Sarah is headed for the barn, old Skeezix's bridle in hand, and face averted from the wind. When Mother calls her back, she finds Father in the kitchen wrapping his feet in gunny sacking. He looks both sheepish and mad. A pair of ancient cowhide overmitts, which, up to now, he has been wearing without woolen liners, lie on the table in front of him. He glances at Sarah, then turns his back on her.

"Sarah, dear," Mother apologizes, "your father can't drive a team on a day like this without liners in his mitts. Could you possibly – ?"

During the first cold snap of the winter, Ronnie Beans, the meanest kid in school, had asked Sarah how she liked having a jailbird for an uncle.

"About as much as you like being a bastard," she'd shot back.

After school, when she went to dress to go home, she found her overmitts with "FUCK SARAH" written on them with indelible ink. She would sooner have died than let anybody see those mitts. When she got home, she hid them under her mattress and told Mother somebody had stolen them. Mother helped her unravel an old pair of socks and use the wool to knit mitts to wear over top of her liners. The two pairs together were tolerably warm, but a single pair was little better than no mitts at all.

Fighting tears, she peels off her top mitts, shoves them at Father, goes into her bedroom, drags the FUCK SARAHs from under her mattress and flings them down on the table in front of him.

He winces. "Damn it, Kid – ! Look, I'd trade you these overmitts, but that pair of yours are too small for me."

Tears of rage and humiliation splash onto her

cheeks while Willie watches with a grin of smug satisfaction that she wants to slap off his face.

As Father heads for the barn, she calls after him, "I hate us tying Crip down when it's so cold. Couldn't I take the quilt off my bed to cover him?"

"Your quilt? Supposing somebody stole it or Crip peed on it? We've hardly got enough to cover ourselves as it is."

In a red-edged rage, Sarah screams, "Is that Crip's fault?"

There is a savage satisfaction in seeing Father's eyes swimming in tears while she helps him lift and boost Crip into the bobsled. As Father ties the calf down, the beast looks about him with an expression of pained bewilderment which reminds Sarah of Ned when he realized that he could not stay with Nancy. She cannot bear to look at the calf, nor at Cherry either, trailing along so patient and trusting behind Skeezix.

The cattle buyer is a pot-bellied guy with a purple face and a large cigar which he chews but never lights. In the CPR stock yards, he looks at Cherry with arched brows, then walks around the bobsled staring at Crip. "What do you expect me to do with that piece of shit?" he says, gesturing with his thumb.

"Should be worth a buck or so," Father says tentatively.

The man snorts. "Five bucks for the two of them."

"Five bucks for – ?"

"Take it or leave it. That's the deal."

"YOU SHOULDN'T HAVE TAKEN IT, Father. You shouldn't have," Sarah rages, as the two of them are tying their horses up behind the Thomas Trading Company store.

"What would you have done? Turned around and taken them home again, when we've hardly got feed enough for the stock we've got? You think that's kind? And I *gotta* buy a pair of overshoes if I'm gonna get out and haul straw and stuff all winter."

"And what about overmitts for me?"

She knows that he has turned his back so that she cannot see his face. Choking on shame, she leaves him and races ahead to the store.

THE THOMAS TRADING COMPANY, which seldom has as many as three customers in its premises at one time, is overflowing today. Mostly men, crowded around the pot-bellied stove talking in high, excited voices. Something about boxcars of food that has been sent from the Maritimes for the drought-ravaged prairies.

Father corners the widow Crosby, a Maritimer herself. "You know anything about this grub they're talking about?"

"There is dried cod, great rounds of cheese, and apples for everybody. As you can see, people are already lining up their rigs across the CPR tracks."

"You mean this grub is for anybody that wants it?"

"Certainly. But I don't know how I'm to get mine home, since I have no conveyance."

"Well, now, why don't I get your load and take it home for you and come back for my share later?"

Everybody in Rattlesnake Park likes Mrs. Crosby, with the possible exception of Aunt Jane.

When Father drives his sleigh in behind a dozen or so others in the lineup, Sarah, who has tagged along, sees old Alfie Pugh standing in the open door of a boxcar with a five-pronged manure fork in his hand. Alfie is nothing but a two-bit homesteader, but he has that overbearing authority common to the English, who feel themselves a cut above the Irish and the Yankees who also settled the district. Lately, people have been saying that Alfie has been acting a little queer.

"Hop to it, you chaps," he is bawling. "Line up orderly and decent. Everybody takes his turn. Nobody rushes the line."

"We are lined up, Alfie. Let's get on with it. What's the hold-up here?" somebody hollers.

"My arse is frozen off and at this rate it's gonna be another hour before I get near the bloody boxcar," somebody else yells.

Alfie is obviously confused; by the time Father picks up Mrs. Crosby's share, he is in a positive tizzy; by the time Father returns for his own share, Alfie isn't certain what he has handed out to whom. When Father stops his team beside the boxcar and steps up into it, Alfie turns on him, the tines of the manure fork inches from Father's midriff. "You've had your share, Jamie MacKenzie. Get that rig out of here before I run you through."

"Alfie! What the hell? I just took Mrs. Crosby's –"

"Hop it, or I warn you –"

For, a moment, Father looks stunned, then with one lightning sweep of his forearm he sends the manure fork flying. "Listen, you little Limey bastard, I want my share, and you're not gonna stop me."

Alfie backs off, his watery blue eyes glowering. "Take it then. Take it," he yells. "But you're not to take one bite for that jailbird's brats that you're harbouring."

"That's right," Bill Raisbone, the Pool Elevator agent bawls, "like we told you at council, you're the big shot that took them kids, so you're the big shot that looks after 'em. You're not taking one bite out of our kids' mouths."

Besides a big mouth, Raisbone has a comfortable job and a regular salary. His daughter brings fruit to school to eat at recess. The smell of it drives Sarah wild with longing. Only yesterday she had watched Peggy take a bite out of an beautiful red apple, stare at it, make a face and toss the rest into the wastepaper basket, saying, "Don't you just *hate* it when you get a wormy apple, Sarah?"

Sarah would have done anything for that wormy apple, anything short of giving Piggy Raisbone the satisfaction of seeing her pick it out of the wastepaper basket to eat.

Father's face has turned the colour of milk. "Listen here, Raisbone," he says, "the council can maybe make it stick when they say I can't get relief from this municipality for Donald's kids, but Mrs. Crosby says the Maritimes sent this grub for anybody that needs it. I need it, and I'm taking the kids' share. You wanna try to stop me?"

Piggy's father drops his gaze, turns his back and spits in the snow. "Take it then, if you need it so bad, and get the hell out of here."

THAT NIGHT MOTHER SEEMS almost happy. She allows the kids half an apple apiece, gives another half to Sarah and splits the other half in quarters between Father and herself. Sarah wolfs hers, core and all; so does Ned, but Willie takes delicate little scrapes off of his with his top teeth, eyeing the other two and waiting between scrapes until the apple turns a little brown before he takes another. The smell of apple hangs in the air, so tantalizing that Sarah can scarcely bear it. Willie is smirking at her expression when Father reminds him that he still has to bring kindling in from the woodpile. He saunters outside, apple in hand, and saunters back a little later with an armful of stove wood and no apple.

"You never ate the rest of that apple in that time," Sarah accuses.

"I don't eat apples with worms in them," he says, deliberately dropping the wood so that it lands on her foot.

She hits him. Hard. It feels wonderful, even though he hits her back.

Father barges between them. "That's enough, Sarah! Cut it out." He turns on Willie, "You wasting an apple just 'cause it's got a goddamned worm in it?"

"I don't eat wormy apples and I'm gonna write and tell my dad on that Sarah too."

Father positively swells. "You *do* that, boy." He frog marches Willie outside and returns a minute later, the piece of apple in one hand and Willie by the scruff of the neck in the other. He slams Willie into a chair and hands him the apple. "Now, eat."

Down it goes, worm, wood chips, a suggestion of horse manure and all.

"Now, you get over there and write to your dad. And when you're done, I'm gonna tell him a thing or two myself."

"I don't wanna write to my dad," Willie mutters. "I wanna go to bed."

"All right." Then Father turns on Ned. "Now, listen, Mister, you wanna pee the bed 'cause you're too goddamned lazy to get up and pee in the slop pail, you just do that. But when you do, you're gonna melt snow and wash your own sheets. You got that?"

Ned casts a sidelong scared look at Willie. The two of them make down the winnipeg couches themselves and crawl into them without another word.

The house is almost comfortable and the north-wester has blown itself out by the time Sarah goes to bed. She stretches luxuriously, fingers the lump on her temple, and winces a little from a bloody wood scratch on her shin. But it was worth it. Worth ten lumps and ten scratches. She counts on her fingers. Only nine months till they turn Uncle Donald loose and those lousy kids'll be gone. I can hardly wait. She turns on her side, pulls her knees up under her chin, and drags the quilt over her head.

6. RATTLESNAKE FAIR

SARAH LIKES MR. LITT, THE NEW TEACHER. This year school is fun; Litt cuts problems into bite-sized chunks and cheers when you've chewed them. Like with the picture of wild roses that Sarah wants to enter in the School Fair. When she showed it to him, he said, "Fine, as far as it goes, Sarah. Now, why don't you push yourself a bit and abstract it? Something like this, see?" He sketched an iris on the board and beside it, a fleur-de-lis.

"Gee! You must be a real artist."

"Someday I hope to teach art at the university."

Sarah's eyes grow round. "At the university? Boy, oh, boy!" She only vaguely knows what a university is. No one she knows has ever gone to one.

Litt smiles. "I'll bring some of my work to show you, if you're interested."

Sarah is so flattered that she feels herself gulping and blushing. She is dying to tell him about the little nude Miss Hindman gave Mother before Mother left England. She knows the nude is the work of a real artist, but she doesn't know if it is quite right to talk to a man teacher about a painting of a naked lady.

After a three-day struggle, Sarah shows Litt her roses again.

He grins. "Knew you could do it," he says, setting the picture on the chalk rail for the class to admire.

Bessie Fetterling examines the roses from under her brows, scribbles a note and hands it across the row to Sarah. "Crayons yet? Thought you were in Grade *Six*, MacKenzie."

Sarah's face feels hot. All she'd had to her colour her picture was a few busted crayons. Now her effort seems tawdry and childish. At recess, she overhears Bessie telling Marjorie Strider, "Wait till MacKenzie sees *my* roses. They're gonna *slay* her."

"Bet you got a lot of neat stuff ready to enter in the fair this year again, eh, Bessie?" Marjorie fawns.

"Oh, yeah, some. Last year I won six dollars and forty cents in prizes, and this year I'll make – oh, I dunno, maybe seven or eight bucks."

Marjorie looks duly impressed.

Cheater! Sarah fumes. "Mummy" and "Daddy" do the work and you walk off with the prizes. But she doesn't say it. Nobody *says* it. These are hard times, and Bessie's old man is the big wheel in Rattlesnake Park.

On Friday afternoon, when Litt is about to dismiss the class, Bessie slips a stretched artist's canvas out of her school bag and lays it on his desk. He picks it up and frowns at it before he sets it on the chalk rail.

Sarah's breath catches. Abstracted roses! And painted in oils – *Mummy's* work! Sarah knows it, and she knows Litt knows it. His cheeks are the colour of beet juice. He clears his throat with a loud "Harrumph!

How does it happen you haven't been working on this picture in class, Bessie?"

"You never said we had to."

"You think it's fair to use an idea Sarah worked out?"

"Nobody owns an idea. Mummy says."

"I didn't know you were so proficient with oils. It comes as a pleasant surprise. Bring your paints to school. We'd all like to watch you work."

Sarah knows he is coming as close as he dares to accusing Bessie of cheating, but Bessie smirks as though he'd paid her a compliment. "Well, I don't know if I could paint with you guys watching me and anyhow, Mummy wouldn't let me bring my oils to school. They're kind of expensive and if anybody snitched them –"

Litt interrupts her with another loud "Harrumph!" He shoves his shirt tail into his breeches and abruptly dismisses the class.

LATE THAT AFTERNOON, Sarah is arranging a display of Irish Cobbler potatoes chosen from the pile Father dumped on the granary floor. She is still steaming mad. "He should have nailed her, Father. He shouldn't have let her get away with it."

Father's mind is not on the cheating Fetterlings; he has an enormous boil ripening on his backside. He sucks air goosily between his teeth, and eases the other cheek of his bum onto the sawhorse. "Well, Kid, you can't altogether blame young Litt. Teaching jobs is hard to come by these days, and old Fetterling is chairman of the board."

"But it's not *fair*."

"Oh, hell, Kid, lots of things ain't fair. Last winter I shoulda popped Fetterling in the snout for kicking Aunt Sally offa the relief roll when she bought that little bottle of wine to celebrate Christmas. That'd have been *fair*. But you don't go popping the reeve of the municipality in the snout when you gotta beg him to let you onto relief roll yourself." He shifts again and sucks breath. "Figure you could handle chores around here till this thing busts?"

A boil on his backside now! Wouldn't you know? She sighs. "Just have to roll out a little early in the morning, I guess."

Clancy, Skeezix's spring colt, blunders into the granary scattering potatoes in all directions. Sarah tousles his forelock. "Who invited you in here?" She backs him outside, makes a stern downward motion with one hand, and commands, "Down, Clancy."

The colt flops as though the legs had been chopped out from under him and lies watching her with one rolling walleye.

She turns to Father. "How d'yah like them onions?"

He laughs. "You got him so well trained he's muddled up, Kid. He ain't so sure he ain't a dog."

Sarah brings Clancy to his feet and rewards him with a few kernels of rye from her jacket pocket. "Well, I've been working on him since the day he was born, so.... You figure I'll walk off with first prize in the colt judging tomorrow?"

"Damn rights. That Fetterling kid'll have a pretty fancy colt, but the handbook says half the points go for handling and training. I'll lay you odds the only halter rope she touches is the one old Fetterling hands her just outside the ring."

"If we only had a calf worth showing –"

"Well, we ain't. Waste of time, you showing one of them pail-bunters of ours. You'd just as well be showing William Aberhart."

They both laugh. William Aberhart, the evangelist-preacher-turned-politican, is the premier of Alberta, but, in Rattlesnake Park, William Aberhart is the runty calf that belongs to the widow everybody calls Aunt Sally. William is always good for a laugh.

When Aberhart came to power in '35, a lot of folks had high hopes for him. He claimed that if he got elected there was nothing stopping him from handing out twenty-five bucks a month to every man and woman in the province. He was gonna get the economy rolling again. People believed him. Guys that hadn't had a new shirt in five years had orders made out ready to sent to Eaton's catalogue. Aunt Sally had her heart set on a fancy black dress with a pink cloth rose to wear at the waist. She never got the dress: nobody got the shirts either.

Last February, Aunt Sally's cow calved out behind Bill Mitchell's coal shed during a rip-roaring blizzard. When Aunt Sally found the calf, his ears and tail were frozen off and he looked like a goner, but she couldn't afford to waste anything, her living hand-to-mouth since she got kicked off relief. She packed him home, put him in a cardboard box behind the kitchen stove, filled his belly with sugar water, and the tough little beggar lived.

Not being long on respect, she christened him William Aberhart.

Since the only milk William gets is the little Aunt

Sally has left over after she's drunk her share and given some to Art Lawson's starving kids, William is nothing but one big belly with hide stretched over it and four skinny sticks of legs, but what he lacks in beauty he makes up for in spunk. The school kids rope him and try steer riding on him. (When Aunt Sally can't see them.) Nobody's ridden William yet.

The morning of the fair, Father is one big wince, lying on his belly waiting for his boil to bust. Mother helps Sarah load the wagon. She heads for the community hall, loaded down with baking powder biscuits, chocolate cake, a loaf of bread, garden stuff, plus a jar of sweet peas, a lamb, a turkey, and a gander, all in crates, and Clancy on a lead off old Dick's singletree.

Fetterlings' truck passes, kicking up a cloud of dust. Mummy and Daddy, and dear little Bessie, cuddled between them. They give Sarah a "shave-and-a-haircut-two-bits" toot on the horn.

Sarah spots a fancy Morgan colt and a beautiful black Angus calf in the truck box. And a ton of stuff I can't see too, I bettcha.

In the community hall, Sarah and Bessie rush past each other setting up exhibits. It burns Sarah to see Bessie's rose design hanging on the display wall. Hers, hanging next to it, looks washed out and kiddish by comparison. When she's sure nobody's looking, she rips it down and tears it up.

By the time she gets outside to start unloading her crated livestock, old Fetterling has all Bessie's livestock exhibits lined up and in place. Sarah is struggling with the crate holding the young gander. The gander, none too pleased with the handling, ejects a stream of green shit all over her blouse.

"Tough luck, Kid," old Fetterling titters, "but geese will be geese, eh?"

Sarah is mad enough to bawl. How am I going to show Clancy looking like this? she fumes.

"Maybe you'd have time to go and clean up at the artesian well before the colt judging starts, Sarah," Litt mutters, taking the crate from her and setting it in place. With her face burning, Sarah makes for the well. She manages to wash off most of the shit, but her wet blouse clings to her budding breasts. I'm not going to show a colt in front of the whole district looking like this. I'd sooner die. She races back to where she's left the wagon with the team and Clancy tied under a poplar tree, climbs into the box, skins out of her blouse, crouches out of sight on the floor of the wagon, holds her blouse up to the wind, and prays that nobody has spotted her. In fifteen minutes, the blouse is more or less dry, but the stains are still plainly visible.

"Good thing it's the colt they're judging and not me," she mutters as she buttons the blouse.

To pass time, she puts Clancy through his paces, then brushes his coat until it shines. Too fidgety to sit still, she gets the lariat out of the wagon and practices roping sage bushes, keeping one ear cocked towards the judging ring where Milligan, the District Agriculturist, a Fancy Dan decked out in whipcord breeches and English riding boots, is officiating.

She hears Litt hollering out the results of the poultry judging (a second for Sarah's gander and a third for her turkey), then calling for colts to be brought into the ring. By this time, half the farmers in the district, their wives, kids, grannies, and aunts, are crowded around to watch. Most of them don't work with horses

103

any more, but they all did once upon a time, and they all love horses.

First, the Jensen kids haul three wild colts around the ring that they'd just dragged in off the range that morning. The crowd hoots and Milligan grins and shakes his head. Cousin Cecil appears with a goosey little filly that kicks at Milligan when he tries to lay a hand on her. He is not amused.

Then it's Bessie's turn. She looks mighty cute with her little kilt swinging and that fancy Morgan colt stepping along behind. Milligan's eyes are shining.

When he's waved Bessie over to one side, Sarah puts Clancy through his paces. He behaves perfectly: she is so proud of him that she doesn't give a hoot about goose shit stains. But Milligan's eyes keep wandering back to that Morgan. He's waving Sarah aside when she says, "Can't I show you Clancy's tricks, Mr. Milligan?"

Milligan looks annoyed. "Tricks? Well, I suppose we could take a minute."

Clancy walks straight back without Sarah laying a hand on him, says his prayers, and plays "dead horse." Folks in the crowd cheer and clap.

"You've got quite a way with horses, young lady," Milligan says, "but I'm looking for good horseflesh, not cute tricks." He sorts out the blue ribbon, goes to Bessie, and with a little bow, hands it to her.

A hostile mutter passes through the crowd. They know all about the Fetterlings; still, nobody says anything. Sarah wouldn't have said anything either, except Bessie gives her this little "told you so" smirk.

"What marks do I get for training and handling, Mr. Milligan?"

"For training and handling?"

"Fifty points for the colt. Fifty points for training and handling. The handbook says. And the exhibitor has to do the training."

Milligan's face flames up. "You're saying Miss Fetterling didn't train her colt?"

Sarah's head feels all buzzy and her hands are shaking, but she says, "Ask her."

He turns to Bessie. "Well?"

"Yeah, *well?*" Aunt Sally echoes.

Bessie looks as though somebody'd stabbed her. Her little rosebud mouth is quivering. "Well, Daddy helped me a – a little."

"Yeah? How much is 'a little'?" Aunt Sally hollers. A hoot of laughter goes through the crowd. Bessie starts to bawl.

Milligan looks as though he's been backed into a corner and he doesn't know which way to jump. He turns to Litt as though he hopes Litt will bail him out.

Litt's face is awful white and muscles rope in his jaws; he shoves both fists so far down in his pockets that his pants sag and he looks right over Milligan's head.

"Comes down to one competitor's word against another's," Milligan huffs. "Since the Morgan is a far superior colt, my decision stands."

Sarah is leading Clancy back to the wagon. "Straighten out your goddamned face, MacKenzie," she mutters. But her goddamned face won't stay straightened. She's still working on it when Litt strolls up. For a while he doesn't say anything, just stands there making heel marks in the sand.

"Ripped up your art work, did you?"

"Well, it was *mine*."

"That's just the point. It was yours and you know it was yours, win, lose, or draw."

"But it was only coloured with crayons."

"Sarah, there are pictures hanging in famous galleries that are only coloured with crayons."

Now she is really having trouble with her goddamned face.

When somebody back at the ring starts bellowing that calf judging starts in five minutes, Litt nudges Sarah and points across to where William Aberhart and a bunch of his pail-bunting buddies are grazing by the artesian well. "I see you got a lariat with you." His expression is downright sly. "I just happen to have an entry tag here in my pocket." He cuts his eyes towards William and back again. "I don't think Aunt Sally'd mind, just this once. Do you?"

Sarah stares at him for a second before she catches on, then she bursts out laughing. Litt is one all right guy.

It's not hard to rope William, but hanging on to him is a case of "you and whose army?". She finally flattens the little son-of-a-gun and sits on him to hold him down. While she fashions a makeshift halter out of the lariat, Litt fills out the entry form in Aunt Sally's name and ties it under his chin.

From over at the ring somebody's hollering, "We're about ready to go, folks. Get your calves lined up."

"Drag William up close to the crowd and hang onto him till I give you the sign, Sarah," Litt says before he sprints for the ring.

When Milligan calls out, "All right, Miss Fetterling, lead your calf out whenever you're ready," Litt hollers, "Late entry here, folks. Can we make way, please?"

The crowd parts. William stands blinking at the opening, then it's like he's thinking, There's the Glory Road and I'm a-heading for Glory. He rips the rope through Sarah's hands and tears into the middle of the ring.

Bessie screeches, drops her calf's lead and blunders into William's path. William feints left; Bessie feints right. William feints right; Bessie feints left. Then William quits feinting. He's a-coming through! Oh, he misses Bessie. But only because she slipped and landed that cute little kilt of hers in a nice juicy cowflap.

William heads for the hills in one direction; Bessie's Angus heads for the hills in the other, with old Fetterling pounding after him.

"Well, it's *your* calf, Miss Fetterling. How come it's your *father* that's chasing it?" Milligan laughs.

Bessie picks herself up and goes bleating after her old man.

Aunt Sally lets loose with a whoop. Pretty soon everybody's whooping, including Milligan. Sarah spots Father in the crowd. He's laughing so hard he's crying.

So his boil's busted! He can darn well do the chores himself tonight.

When the dust settles, Milligan announces he's awarding William Aberhart a prize. "Gutsiest calf in the show," he says, bowing to Aunt Sally and pinning a blue ribbon on her coat.

Two days it took old Fetterling to catch that Angus calf. Nobody had time to give him a hand either.

Monday morning, when the prize money was divvied out, Sarah's share amounted to five dollars and a quarter. Litt winked at her too.

7. BREECH BIRTHS

SARAH READS THE POEM SHE WROTE FOR her Grade Seven English assignment again. Mushy! She is scarring through it with her tooth-dented pencil and turning to a fresh page when, deep in her gut, she feels that unpleasant little cramp. She freezes. *What if that bleeding business started when I was in school?* The thought appalls her.

Last night, when Sarah mentioned the cramps to Mother, she had said, "You'll be getting your monthlies soon, dear." And then added, very gravely, "You know, Sarah, girls are capable of having babies after they begin to – uh – menstruate. You – uh – understand, don't you? Well, about boys – ? Well, you must be very careful not to – well, *encourage* them. Men are not responsible for their desires. If you should ever allow – well, it would break my heart. And just imagine your poor old father's face if –" Then she added, "When I think of what Mavis Crosby did to *her* mother – and Mrs. Crosby such a wonderful churchwoman too."

Seems to me it's more like what poor old Mavis did

to herself, Sarah thinks, looking across the shabby schoolroom to where, in the Grade Ten row, Mavis Crosby sits in the June heat, hugely pregnant and puffing under the warm green cloak her mother made for her out of a blanket when she first started to "show."

One day last October when a wild chinook was blowing and all sounds were lost to the rushing, moaning wind, Sarah had been out hunting for cattle. She'd come upon Aunt Jane's Billy making love to Mavis Crosby beside the town's rubbish heap where they had found shelter next to an abandoned car. Sarah knows they never heard her ride up and she is just as certain that they never heard her ride away.

At first, it had been her secret, impossibly tender, impossibly romantic. But now...? At recess today Marjorie Strider had been practically smacking her lips when she said, "Mummy says Mavis could pop that kid anytime."

Sarah shivers. And she's only three years older than me. She picks surreptitiously at a scab on her bony knee. The scab starts to bleed; she spit-washes it with one finger. Aunt Jane says Billy's got to marry Mavis as soon as school's out. But I don't think he even likes her any more. A scared, sickish feeling passes over her. What if he won't?

After school is dismissed, Sarah gets Skeezix out of the barn and swings aboard. Dumb old Women's Auxiliary meeting at Aunt Jane's place this afternoon, she grouses. Wasting a day like this on Turkey dinners and church bazaars – what if I just didn't go? Ho! Would I ever catch it. Well, at least it's an hour or so before it starts, so I guess I'll go meet Mother.

She heads north to where abandoned homesteads have gone back to rangeland, their barbed-wire fences tangled and hidden under the prairie grass and their buildings now tumble-down and derelict.

After a dreary winter and a miserable, windy spring, a June day is like a gift from heaven. She slips off Skeezix's back and perches on a warm, lichen-covered rock. Wild roses and prickly pear are in bloom and the perfume of wolf willow wafts through the air. Far off, she can see Father's wheat field, still lushly green. He says they might get a little crop if they get a couple of days of rain in July. Since she was a little kid, she can't remember a real crop, nor rain in July, but it is June yet, and it doesn't hurt to hope.

When at last she sees Mother plodding towards her along the dusty trail, she rides out to meet her.

"Are you feeling all right, Sarah?" Mother asks anxiously.

"Sure, fine." Which is not exactly true. Several times she has felt that unpleasant cramp again deep in her belly.

"You haven't started your – ?"

"No!" Sarah cuts her off fiercely.

"Well, I only asked." Then the question that always makes Sarah cringe. "Was Mavis Crosby in school today?" Mother has a way of sucking bones where Mavis is concerned.

"Yeah. Yeah, of course."

"Good gracious, you needn't be so irritable."

When they arrive, a dozen or so ladies are already gathered in Aunt Jane's living room. As soon as Mother has greeted the company, Aunt Jane, whose eyes are suspiciously red, beckons her into the kitchen. Curiosity overcoming reticence, Sarah follows. She enters the kitchen in time to hear Aunt Jane say, "I told him his father must be turning in his grave, and you know what he said? 'So, let him turn.' That's what he said, if you can believe it. 'So, let him turn'."

Mother frowns at Sarah. "Make yourself useful. Go and greet the ladies as they come in. Aunt Jane and I need to talk."

Rebuffed and embarrassed, Sarah retreats to the living room.

Dorcas O'Conner, eighteen, safely married to the municipality's handyman and very pregnant with her first baby, is staring out the window. "Look who's coming!" she squawks.

"Old lady Crosby and that Mavis," Bunty Probert huffs. "Talk about nerve! Belly on her like a bloated cow and her still going to church and to school and whatever."

Dorcas giggles. "Looks like twins. Wonder what they'll name 'em?"

Irene Strider, Marjorie's mother (finger in every pie and nose in every chamber pot): "Maybe they'll drown 'em and act like it never happened."

Somebody titters. Glances are exchanged.

"Well, hey, you guys!" Irene brays, "It was only a joke."

Clammy sweat has erupted on the palms of Sarah's hands. Mrs. Crosby and Mavis have to knock three times before she can make herself answer the door and usher them in.

The widow Crosby has been a power since she moved to Rattlesnake Park. After the Depression took her farm, she piled all her good Nova Scotia furniture and whatever else she could salvage into a wagon, came to town, rented an old brick house with two spare bedrooms, arranged her well-oiled furniture about the rooms, and covered the floors with brilliant rugs she'd designed and hooked herself. Then she polished her good family silver, approached the two teachers at the school, and persuaded them to board in a genteel home.

That settled, she nowadays throws herself into the work of the Women's Institute, the Church, and the Women's Auxiliary. She manages to dress Mavis and herself from cleverly made-over hand-me-downs from "down east" relatives, feeds her household from the teachers' board, the produce of an enormous garden, and a small allowance the government grudgingly doles out to widows.

She is, at once, the ugliest and the most arresting woman Sarah has ever seen. Taken feature by feature, all save one, she is quite beautiful. Intelligent blue eyes, a fine figure, and a generous, laughing mouth. But then there is her nose, a monstrous hook which threatens to meet her chin and, as if such a nose were not enough, on its very tip is a large, brown, outstanding mole. People gossip about her appearance behind her back (Aunt Jane calls her " Beaky"), but no one has the temerity to be other than polite to her face.

Mother is one of her greatest admirers. "After they closed the Church in Manyberries, that woman drove here to Rattlesnake Park. Sixteen miles in a democrat. They could have gone to The United, right in the village, but no – the Church *means* something, Sarah, and don't you forget it."

Forget it? How can she? It weaves through her life like a thread in a tapestry. Every Sunday, Mother and she hoof it the three miles to the little grey church where they roast in summer and freeze in winter and chant and sing and pray, and every month they attend the Auxiliary meeting hosted by one of the Church ladies.

Now, seats are found for Mavis and Mrs. Crosby and the room is loud with inane chatter. Mavis regards the gathering with cool, pale-grey eyes, her one arresting feature. She is as aloof and composed as a Madonna, except that, from time to time, she sucks the contents of her sinuses back into her throat with a completely disgusting snort.

Sarah, staring out of the window to keep from staring at Mavis, is the first to see the Reverend Percy Bryce Beasley's rattletrap Ford drive up.

Pee Bee. And Mrs. Pee Bee not with him. She'd heard him telling Mother that "Prudence and I are expecting a blessed event at about the time of the birthday of our Lord." She wonders if Mavis's "event" is blessed too.

The Reverend Pee Bee, whom his church has found convenient to bury in "the colonies," is as poor as his parishioners, but genteely so. The hem of his shabby cassock is mended and his shoes are polished even though his socks peep through cracks in the leather. The ladies of his congregation, all except Mrs. Crosby, hold him in awe. Tough old grannies, who will cuss out a drunken son or a wayward horse so that they can he heard on the next section, whisper in Pee Bee's presence, but Mrs. Crosby talks to him just like he was anybody else. Some of the ladies whisper among themselves that they don't think that is quite proper.

He moves among his flock now, shaking hands and making stiff, unfunny little jokes. When he comes to Mavis, his face turns the colour of old brick. He takes one of her hands between both his own, pats it help-lessly, drops it as though it is too hot to handle, and passes on.

With the business meeting finished, Pee Bee begins his address in aid of missionaries in foreign fields, speaking in solemn tones about the trials of his broth-er "out there in Africa, labouring to the greater glory of God among the black heathen hordes."

Wonder if he tells his brother that he's "labouring to the greater glory of God among heathen hordes" of dryland Alberta farmers? She smothers a grin and shuts Pee Bee out while she toys with the name for the perfect horse she hopes to own some day, figures out how Bunty Probert cut the cloth to achieve the drape on the front of her blouse, and tries to avoid looking at Mavis, who is sitting, flush-faced, mouth slightly open, puffing under her green cloak.

Pee Bee starts a yarn about an old black woman (a mammy, his brother calls her, he explains apologeti-cally), who converted to the Church and in so doing became a person of such fine sensibility that she will not approach the communion rail until the white folk have finished their communion and returned to their pews, in case the chalice from which they all drink should be contaminated by her touch. The ladies are still making cooing noises of approbation when he intones, "And now, my dear sisters in Christ, let us bow our heads in prayer."

All do so except Mrs. Crosby and Mavis. Mrs. Crosby helps Mavis to her knees and kneels on the floor beside her. The two of them are perfectly composed, faces lifted heavenward, hands clasped in beseechment and corners of their closed eyes quivering in concentration. At a faint creaking of the floorboards upstairs, Mavis's eyes fly open.

Billy's up there. Peeking down through the stovepipe hole. I wonder if he can see Mavis's face? Suddenly Sarah understands what she overheard in the kitchen. She bites her lip hard and looks away.

WHEN SARAH WAKENS the next morning, she knows something has happened during the night. Out in the kitchen, she finds her parents at the table already drinking tea. They look awful. "Didn't I hear Aunt Jane here last night? And it seemed like Billy was – I think I remember him yelling?"

"Never you mind."

"For chrisake, Beth, the kid's thirteen years old. We can't keep her –"

"I won't have the sordid mess discussed in this house." She turns on Sarah. "Well, Miss, since you are up anyway, you had just as well go and find the workhorses for your father now."

By the time Sarah gets the horses home, she has only time to wipe around her mouth with a damp washrag, comb her hair, gulp a piece of toast, and skin into the overalls old Scotty Polson, the bachelor neighbour, had given her to make over. She rides like fury to make it to school on time. Mr. Litt has an uncomfortable way of making tardy students account for themselves in front of the whole class. Sarah hates to admit that she has to hunt work-horses. Even in these tough times, Father is the only farmer who still uses them.

She pounds upstairs to the upper level just as Mr. Litt clatters the handbell. As Sarah slips into her desk, she notices that Mavis Crosby's seat is empty.

The room prickles with tension.

Sarah realizes that everybody here knows something that she doesn't. Something beyond the restless desire for the summer's freedom bubbles beneath the surface of the well-ordered, sane class this morning. Mr. Litt allows false answers to review questions to pass with an absent-minded nod. Several times Sarah sees him staring through the window toward Mrs. Crosby's house – the only house in the village with a raked yard. His thumbnail gouges deep scars in the stick of chalk he carries in his hand.

Sarah's stomach is churning when she gets downstairs at recess. A knot of girls is clustered around Marjorie Strider who is burbling, "Twins. Breech births, both of 'em. They put 'em in a cardboard box and buried 'em under the trees up on Billy's Mom's place." She turns to Sarah with the air of one who has every right to know. "So, what'd your old man say when he got home this morning, MacKenzie? Reverend Beasley says it was him that dug the hole."

With a sick twist deep in her guts, Sarah remembers Mrs. Strider's joke at the Auxiliary meeting. Or was it a joke? Her mouth goes dry. "Shut your trap, Marjorie Strider. Mavis never had – Father did not dig – he wouldn't –"

"Did too. Mummy says. Reverend Beasley told her

all about it when he stopped at our place for gas. Was he ever *shocked*."

Sarah's upper arms go cold and heavy. She is swamped with weariness, colours fade from the day. As she stumbles towards the barn, Marjorie shrieks, "I suppose you're gonna tell us you didn't know that Billy lit out? Hopped a freight and swore he was never coming back."

MOTHER AND FATHER are sitting side by side on the davenport in the shabby little parlour with mugs of cold tea in front of them when Sarah gets home. They seem to have somehow diminished and aged.

"What are you doing here, Sarah? Did something happen at school?"

She gives it to them straight, just as Marjorie had given it to her.

"Breech births!" Mother sniffs. "The things you girls know these days. If any of you get into trouble, you have nobody but yourselves to blame."

Father slams his mug onto the table. "Christ, Beth, lay off. Does that kid look to you as though she *knows* anything? We shoulda told her the truth instead of –" He breaks off of a shaky sigh. "Now listen, Kid, at a normal birthing the baby's head comes first. You know that, eh? Well, in a breech birth, the baby gets twisted around and it's the bum that comes first." He makes a defeated open-handed gesture. "They was both dead when they was born." He looks at her shrewdly, eyes narrowing. "I think you'd better put that Strider kid straight on a thing or two."

"I'd like to rip her face off."

"Save yourself the trouble."

"But the story will be all over the country that you," Mother sobs, "that you and Jane and Mrs. Crosby – that wicked, wicked Mavis, bringing such a disgrace on –"

"Wicked? That *kid?*" A vein pulses in his forehead and his hands tremble. "You sound like that goddamned preacher, blabbering on about how he didn't *enjoy* rebuking the kid when she'd just had such an awful time, but it was his duty to uphold –"

"Well, it is his duty, painful as is may be –"

"He might try being a little *human*, then his goddamned duty might not hurt so much! It ain't a coupla drowned kittens buried up there under Jane's trees, y'know. And don't you start spouting his kinda shit to Sarah. I'm warning you, lay off." Sarah had never seen him so mad.

Mother doesn't spout anything to anybody, not for days and days and days. The first time she speaks to Sarah it is to remind her to appear at Mrs. Strider's after school for the Auxiliary meeting on Friday.

WHEN SARAH ARRIVES, Mother is already seated in Striders' living room, which is crammed with women who have never attended Auxiliary before, nor have they ever been to church. Mrs. Strider, very officious and very much the hostess, finds a perch for Sarah on a broad windowsill on the opposite side of the room from where Mavis Crosby is sitting, composed and silent as she minutely examines the chewed fingernails deeply embedded in her spatulate fingers. Strangely, she doesn't look much different from the last time Sarah saw her at school, except that she is very pale and she no longer wears her cloak.

Nervous conversations go on all about the room. Aunt Jane, looking evasive and shamefaced, is talking gravely to Mrs. Crosby when Pissy Pee Bee enters. The company falls into hushed whispers.

When Pee Bee starts holding forth about Africa, Sarah starts thinking about a coat Aunt Rose has sent from England, which she is going to try to make over into something fit to wear for the winter. She has gotten as far as deciding to remove the collar and rip off some braid trim from the shoulders, when some charged and peculiar tension in the room knocks her back into the present.

With the air of somebody who is about to die, Pee Bee is gulping and hesitating his way through a tale about some African tribe who look upon the birth of twins as an evil visitation. "But of course they are not to be condemned. Their lives there are hard and food is very scarce. Regretfully," he concludes in a shamefaced whisper, "it is the sad duty of the grandmothers to – to –" he stumbles a little and concludes, "to dispose of the little ones."

Aunt Jane's face is scarlet, Mrs. Crosby's purple, although she wears a fixed false little smile. A tremulousness peculiar to her at all times has intensified into a shakiness that is visible across the room. Mavis's cool grey eyes never flinch from Pissy's face.

Mrs. Crosby, the false little smile still on her face, crosses to Mavis, brings her to her feet and turns to face the room. "Reverend Beasley, we would be pleased if you would call at our home when the meeting is finished. Mavis and I have a complete layette, something that one does not prepare for unwelcome children. I'm sure you and Mrs. Beasley could make use of it." She bows slightly and, as stately as queens, she and Mavis turn and walk out of the house.

The room is frozen, open mouthed. Raging blood pounds through Sarah's head. She springs to her feet, dying to say something absolutely awful to Pee Bee. But when she looks at him, tears are streaming down his face and his shaking pink hands helplessly finger the heavy silver cross suspended from the rope about his waist.

She flees the house and wanders the prairies until almost dark. When she gets home, no one asks her where she has been. As she sits in the open doorway, staring out into the opalescent June twilight, she becomes aware of an unpleasant wetness between her thighs and that small ache again in the depths of her belly. When she looks down, there is a bloody spot on the crotch of her overalls. She starts when Mother says, "Sarah, dear, I've made some cinnamon buns. Wouldn't you like one?"

"Maybe. After a while." She is amazed that she can speak so calmly when she feels ready to explode. But if I could just turn the whole thing – Mavis and the curse and the damn fool Church and the whole shooting match – into some kind of a dumb joke, she agonizes. Oh, God! Some joke. And Mother's going to have kittens next Sunday, but I'm not going. I won't.

Suddenly, unaccountably, the giant's vow from "Jack in the Beanstalk" hops into her head. She grins, drops her voice to a guttural growl, and takes on Pissy Pee Bee's accent.

Fee, fie foe fum
I smell the blood of an Englishman

Be he alive or be he dead
I shall grind his bones for bread.

Mother stares at her with a shocked expression which slowly resolves into a shamefaced grin; Father throws his head back and guffaws.

Sarah laughs too, but hers is not laughter; it is uncontrollable and it hurts and she can't stop.

8. SEVENTEETH OF IRELAND

FOR THE FOURTH TIME SINCE SARAH STARTED churning the butter, Mother goes to the window, parts the winter-grubby curtains, and peers across the prairie. Sarah sighs, smothering exasperation. Fuss, fuss, fuss! Father'll come when he's good and ready. She ought to know that.

The sun, low in the western sky, washes across Mother's face, highlighting her furrowed brow as she squints, raising one hand to shield her eyes against the strong light. "I can't imagine what's keeping him. He knew we were almost out of water when he left this morning. There's not enough left in the bucket now to wash that butter when it comes." She turns fretfully to Sarah. "He wouldn't have gotten into trouble driving old Skeezix with Dick, would he?"

Serve the old bugger right if he did. Then she winces. Idiot! What would happen to Mother and me if he got really hurt?

"You don't think he might be in trouble, do you?"

Sarah keeps her eyes on the substitute churn, a Rodger's Syrup can, which she brings down against her thigh with a rhythmic chunk, chunk, chunk. "Ah, he's probably just playing checkers with old Mark." She changes the subject abruptly. "Couldn't we even afford a proper churn?"

"We could have afforded a number of things if your father hadn't insisted on buying you an Arab filly."

Sure. Any twenty-dollar cayuse would do for Sarah, wouldn't it, Mother?

"Now, Sarah, don't look like that. I realize you needed a decent pony. It's you that has to do all the riding for stock here since your Father...." She breaks off delicately; she never will say that Father hasn't been able to ride since he had that accident with the bull.

"Plus the small matter of Skeezix rolling over top of me and almost killing me."

"Oh, Sarah, I shall never forget it." Mother's hands flutter in agitation before she points to a spot in her midriff. "I could feel it, like a knife, right here when I saw you lying so still out there in the yard. And there was I, always thinking you were safe riding old Skeezix." Then she adds with maddening complacency, "Well, at least she's not likely to fall down when she's pulling the wagon."

Sarah bends over her task in case Mother should read her expression. Not fall down, maybe. Well, Father can't say I didn't warn him.

Last fall, after Father bought Lindy Lou for Sarah, he announced that he was going to relegate Skeezix to pulling the wagon along with ewe-necked, placid old Dick. Sarah was outraged. Skeezix might be a little nuts, Skeezix might be a clumsy old fool that rolled over top of her and almost killed her, but she

had ridden Skeezix practically from the time she started school: Skeezix was *her* horse and Skeezix was dear
to her heart.

"The old girl has earned her rest," she had stormed.
"She should be turned loose to run with the range
stock."

"Hell with that noise. She can damn well earn her
keep."

"Then I warn you, you'd better watch your step. Let
anything unusual happen, and Skeezix goes a little
nuts. You'd never believe the scrapes she's got me
into."

"Scrapes? With that gentle old plug you rode all
them years? Shee-it! I never heard about no scrapes."

Even now, ripples of rage make Sarah's movements
jerky when she pauses to pry the bulging lid off the
syrup can to allow a fart of sour gas to escape.

Her skirmishes with Father over Skeezix have gone
on all winter: Mother knows nothing about them.
Mother is going through "the change." She suffers
from "little attacks of nerves." Nothing must be
allowed to upset her. Now her eyes, wandering the
room, come to rest on the Thomas Trading Company
calendar. "Saint Patrick's day. Seventeenth of Ireland,
as your Father calls it." Indignation straightens her
back. "I know where he is. He's met old Pete
O'Donnel and they've gone to the pub to celebrate."

Father driving Skeezix when he's a little tight?
That's asking for it. Sarah thrusts the can into
Mother's hands. "Here, you finish the butter and I'll
go see what's up." Struggling to appear casual, she
dons a jacket, yanks on overshoes, checks her pockets
for mitts, and heads for the door.

Sunset throbs on the horizon as she races for the barn. Already the pools of runoff from the March chinook are covered with ice. When she opens the barn door the filly whickers. "Okay, Lindy, baby," she croons, fishing a rock-hard fragment of brown sugar out of her pocket and allowing the pony to lick it off her palm before she bridles it and leads it out into the farmyard, which, now stripped of snow, is a mess of rotten straw and cow shit.

Why can't that old bugger clean up this mess? she fumes as she mounts the pony. Wait till I'm eighteen. I'm going to get so far away from him and his stupid farm and Mother and her "little attacks of nerves." Boy, they get me down, they really do. And there's Father saying we're getting through The Depression "a damn sight better than most. We've got a roof over our heads and three squares a day."

Salt pork, turnips, and spuds all winter, with a little milk and butter thrown in – if the cows still happen to be milking. The roof leaks something awful, and he laughs and says it "don't rain enough to bother much anyhow." It's not him that has to make over the crappy used clothing the Church hands out. Party gowns straight out of the 1920s. Well, I'm learning to rip and snip and turn the bloody things into something more or less wearable anyhow, but –

The filly dances, tosses its head and jerks against the reins. Sarah controls it with a firm hand. The wagon ruts snaking across the prairie are treacherous with icy puddles. She guides the pony onto the short, frost-seared prairie wool and lifts it to a canter.

Twilight fades and the light of an enormous full moon sails beside them on a column of frost-crystaled grass. When they crest the hill that lies between the farm and the village, lights of houses half a mile away dot the night. Headlights of a farm truck across the CPR tracks blaze in Sarah's eyes and toy eerily with the tops of nearby sage bushes. Then she hears a wagon rattle and jounce over the iron-hard ground.

In three hundred yards, she comes face to face with Father and the team. Skeezix, neck stretched and wearing the goofy expression that says she's scared, drags old Dick along, leading him by a whole neck. Father is perched sideways on the loose plank deck roaring, "When Paddy came over the hill, his colleen fair to see," his voice jolting and receding in bursts timed to the jounce of the wagon. The lines, slack in his hands, flap along the wagon tongue. Water splashes from barrels sitting behind him on the deck.

"Pull up on your lines. Hold those horses down, Father."

"What say, Kid?"

"Pull up on your lines."

"Lines are all right. What the hell...?"

"You're going to have a runaway."

"Runaway, be damned. Been driving horses all my –"

The team heads down a knoll; the wagon runs up on their heels. Skeezix breaks into a gallop, dragging Dick with her. When the wagon jerks forward, Father drops the lines and claws for purchase on the bouncing planks. The teetering barrels slop water. One of the planks inches back on the bolster. The team do their damnedest to outrun the wagon thundering at their heels.

At a dead run, Sarah knees Lindy in beside Skeezix and grabs for her bridle line. Skeezix shies off, shoves

Dick out of his rut, and jolts the wagon onto rough prairie. Father clings to his plank like a hawk to a gopher. One wheel hits a badger hole. The barrels tip. Water flies in all directions. A deck plank upends. The rear bolster catches it, arcs it viciously towards Sarah and her mount, and misses by a whisker.

The filly explodes, bucking. Sarah, back cracking with the animal's every twist and arms cracking in their sockets, grips its barrel and reefs on the reins to drag its head up. It rears, teeters, threatens to go over on top of her. She gasps, grabs a hank of mane, bites her tongue viciously, and grips its barrel with all the strength in her legs. It lands on all fours, lunges in a circle, throws its head from side to side, and fights the bit. She drags it to a blowing stop. They are both winded, pouring sweat, shaking. The night thunders with the runaway, the filly's grunts, and Sarah's ragged heartbeat.

Two deck planks, at insane angles to each other, lie on the frozen grass. Father is nowhere in sight. Sarah heads the filly back along the path of the moon, comes upon another plank and a bundle of rags. She goes cold with dread. "Father...? Father...?"

The bundle untangles itself and heaves to its backside.

Sarah flings herself from the pony's back and drops to her knees, still clinging to the reins of her spooky mount. "Father, are you hurt?"

He cautiously flexes his arms. "Don't think so."

"Can you stand up?"

He rolls onto hands and knees, tries to get his feet under him, and collapses in a heap. "Dammit all to hell!"

Her heart chokes her. "You *are* hurt."

"Nah! Give us a hand here." He leans heavily on her, grunts, makes it to his feet, and tries a few wobbly steps. "Bruised up a little is all." He cocks his ear to the sound of the runaway and gives a silly, defiant little chuckle. "Quite a seventeenth of Ireland, ain't it?"

Sarah is weak with relief and, at the same time, furious. Stupid old bugger. I'd like to drown him. Making idiot jokes when....

That he might be acting out of pure bravado does not occur to her. Like a young Blackfoot, she springs to her horse's back. "You know what Mother'll think when she hears that team? I'll have to beat them home and tell her that you're okay."

As she streaks away, she hears the runaway circling off to the west, thunder under a cold moon. Abandoned farms lie in that direction. Scattered barbed wire everywhere –

Tom Moody had to shoot his team. Oh, Skeezix, I couldn't bear it if –

Mother, her face a working mass of apprehension, is waiting at the gate.

"He's all right, Mother. He's coming," Sarah gasps as the runway roars past the farm, angling across open range, headed for LePage's line fence. "I'm going to catch the team."

The filly stretches like a pronghorn in full flight. At first the wagon is loud in Sarah's ears; then there is only the hammer of Lindy's hooves. Under the brilliant moon, Sarah spots the team stopped at the fence. Whether they are cut and hopelessly tangled or merely standing, she can't tell. She hauls Lindy down to a walk and dismounts. She can feel the team's quivering terror transmit to the hand she lays on the barbed wire as she moves slowly towards them, speaking in a soothing croon.

Skeezix turns her head to the sound of Sarah's voice and gives a tentative, scared little whicker. Sarah inches closer, crooning wordlessly, willing them to stand, ignoring Lindy, who follows, rooting at her shoulder. When Dick begins to prick his ears in her direction, Sarah moves in, grabs Skeezix's bit, reaches under her neck, and snatches the cross line to Dick's bridle. As long as she hangs onto them both, she has a measure of control.

The tip of the wagon tongue, by some small miracle, has slammed into a broad tamarack fencepost, which has stopped the team dead, their chests against ripping barbed wire.

I don't dare back them up. Let Skeezix hear that wagon and she'll plough through the fence. There's the rifle and shells for it in the house. Could I? Oh, God.... Don't even let me think about it.

Still clinging to both lines, she snatches Skeezix's halter rope from the hame and, working one-handed, hauls the mare's head in until her nose is against the fencepost. "Please, Skeezix, for once in your life, don't get stupid and try breaking the halter rope. But how am I going to get to Dick to tie him up without letting go of his line?"

She solves the problem by easing under the fence and squirming along the far side in front of the team, belly to earth, juggling Dick's line from hand to hand past post and barbed wire, but when she starts to wiggle back under the fence, practically under Dick's nose, he whistles and shuffles his huge hairy hoofs in a panicky dance.

"Dick, it's me. Don't tromp the guts out of...Dick!" She gets a punishing hold on his bit ring, drags his head down and hauls herself under the fence and onto her feet. Dick shudders, gooses away from her and crowds the wagon tongue. At Dick's performance, Skeezix lets loose with a trumpet of terror, braces her feet, throws her weight against the halter rope, flings her head from side to side with all her might, and tries to break the rope.

"Skeezix, you silly old bitch, you! *Cut that out!*"

Skeezix lets up on the rope for a second then whistles another alarm that sends a shudder though Dick.

Sarah twists his bit until he spreads his jaws, grunting with pain. "Pay attention here, you." She grabs his halter rope, gets a turn around the post and hauls his head in so that he and Skeezix are snubbed, nostril to nostril, against the post.

Skeezix, wheezing as though she is choking to death, drops onto her haunches and throws her weight against the halter rope; she flings her head back and forth. Sarah, falling over herself, tears around the wagon, yelling, "Skeezix, you quit it, you old fool. *You stand!*"

Skeezix recognizes Sarah and, with a sound somewhere between a bleat and a whinny, comes to a stand, the fight drained out of her. She clacks her bit with her tongue, roots against Sarah's hand with her nose, and slobbers companionably against the sleeve of her jacket. Sarah slumps against her sweaty shoulder. "You fool, you, Skeezix. You bloody old fool." They are both quivering, steaming with icy sweat. But

Sarah knows it's safe now to unhook.

Fearfully, she begins to assess the damages. "Lines broken, a nick on Skeezix's nose, and two nicks on Dick's chest. That's all? Father's not hurt. And me...? Nothing. Well, my tongue hurts, but.... Funny. I wonder what I've done to it?"

Triumphantly, under a high moon, she heads back over the rigid, silent prairie; the three horses following at her heels breathe warm against her back. She stables them, rubs them down with the same rye straw which is their only feed, covers them with ancient, mouse-chewed horse blankets, and heads for the house, expecting praise for a job well done.

When she opens the door, she finds Father sitting on a kitchen chair, stripped to the waist, his face one great swollen bloody bruise. His glasses are missing and his torso is covered with wicked purple welts. Sarah is so shocked that she stands gawking, the open door in her hand, while Mother wails and dabs ineffectually at Father's face with the wet end of a towel.

"Ah, for chrisake, Beth, turn off the water works. Nothing's busted." He turns on Sarah. "Well, shut the bloody door. You trying to freeze us out?" He looks her up and down. "Ain't you got any more goddamn sense than to run off and leave a fella when he's had an accident?"

"You *said* you weren't hurt!"

"Do I *look* like I ain't hurt?"

"Don't you start in on that poor child. If you hadn't been out carousing with old Pete O'Donnel –"

"Carousing, hell! Three glasses of beer!" He rises painfully, hobbles towards the bedroom, and turns on Sarah again.

"I ain't driving that old fool of a mare no more. Knothead like that can kill a fella. In the morning, you kick her out to run with the range stock and fetch Danny in for me."

She nods, so shamefaced she can hardly look at him. Supposing he had been really hurt and I just rode away and left him? She starts shaking again. "As soon as I find Danny and get the lines fixed, I'll take him and Dick to get water and look for your glasses."

"Eee-yup. Well, take it easy with Dick. He'll probably still be a little goosey."

"Oh, you poor child," Mother wails.

Holy moley! She sounds like some dumb babe on Lux Radio Theater. "Little attacks of nerves" be damned. And Father blowing money on beer and getting into some dumb scrape with Skeezix. Just wait till I'm eighteen. Boy! Just wait till I'm eighteen.

She can hear the pig squealing down in the sty beside the barn. She knows that it hasn't been fed. "Haven't you even done the chores, Mother?"

"Chores?" As though she'd never heard the word.

Sarah snatches the milk pails and slams outside.

An hour later, when she is snuggled into her old straw mattress, the patchwork quilts rough against her face, a snort of laughter escapes. She claps one hand over her mouth and laughs until the bedsprings jingle.

Seventeenth of Ireland, eh? She wipes tears from the corners of her eyes. Well, anyhow, it's almost spring. And nothing's busted.

9. SHAGANAPPI SUMMER

SARAH HAS GROWN THREE INCHES SINCE January. Her shabby clothes are too tight; her breasts push embarrassingly against the thin fabric of her old blouses. Louts leaning against the post office nudge each other and leer when she passes. She slouches about, round shouldered, trying to hide herself, and yearns over pictures of bras in the Eaton's catalogue. Mother, who has never needed a bra, says, "Do stand up straight, Sarah. And for goodness sake, wash your armpits."

"I do," she protests. "Often." But she knows she still smells. And then there are the pimples. She sneaks to the little pocket mirror propped on the windowsill of her bedroom. Squeezing them only makes them worse, she knows that, but she can't seem to stop herself. And, of course, Mother catches her. "Do leave your face alone, Sarah. It's no wonder you are such a mess."

If I'm a mess, what do you think you are? Don't like me picking scabs? Well, I don't like you whining about how awful Canada is in comparison to England either. If England was so great, why didn't you stay there? But she never says it; Father has told her that Mother needs special consideration these days. She is still going through "the change."

But how long does this "change" go on? Two years now she's been talking about her "flow." I'm sick of her "flow" and her bloody rags. And I hate people like old Irene Strider cornering me. "Why don't your dad take your ma to the doctor?" Do they think he wouldn't if we had the money? Then, shivering and drawing into herself, she wonders, will I be like her when I'm old? "No!" she denies vehemently, "No, I won't. No, I will not. Never."

School is a happy escape. In spite of being odd man out, she is a top student. Litt says that her art work is outstanding. He encourages her talent and finds time to give her extra help.

Before Father married, when he could afford such luxuries, he'd bought a book of Charlie Russell prints. Sarah is in love with those prints. She spends hours copying pictures of cowboys and horses. Russell is her hero, but Litt encourages her to draw from her own observations. "Develop your own style, Sarah. You'll never do that if you copy other artists." She is not particularly pleased with the results of her struggles, but she would do anything to please Litt.

The real bright spot in her life is her little Arab mare. Mounted on Lindy Lou, she can imagine herself as a real cowgirl, although she has nothing to make her look like a cowgirl. Excepting the horse. No chaps, no Levis nor Stetson, and, worst of all, no saddle. Unlike the cowgirl heroines she reads about in *Ranch Romances*, she rides bareback like a young

Peigan. And as for the heroes she meets there with clefts in their chins, six-shooters on their hips, and names like Lance, or Monte, or Dusty – nary a one. But she has hopes, and the *Ranch Romances* allow her to escape Mother's dreary complaints. "No harvest again this year." "I detest the grease-and-sour-milk stench of that beastly cream separator." "That cursed wind again. How I hate it!" Her voice sometimes rises to that jittery note that Sarah dreads; that note that heralds one of her "little attacks of nerves." These little attacks can send her to bed to lie staring at the water-stained ceiling for days on end and leave Sarah to drag through the housework as well as her other chores.

She has no social life: the kids at school never invite her into their circles. She tells herself that she doesn't care, that she is happy riding the prairie alone hunting for livestock. Truth to tell, she never tires of the great rolling distances and the mighty arch of the turquoise sky with its drama of clouds and flaming sunsets, never tires of the brilliant desert stars. Never tires of running a bunch of antelope, flat out on horseback, just for the pure pleasure of watching them skim the sage flats. There is always something interesting to see. She can spend an hour lying on her belly, watching a litter of baby gophers; or crawling along a horse trail following a dung beetle shoving pellets of manure towards its burrows with its hind feet. She has seen a falcon dive on a jackrabbit, miss his catch, and come out of the dive, wings booming like a tiny thunderclap; she can work an entire evening with a pencil and a note pad, struggling to achieve the exact expression on the face of the coyote she's surprised sneaking up to the farmyard to steal chickens.

One hot June night, she is lazing along, trailing the cattle home for milking and admiring thunderheads whose depths will shimmer with heat lightning as soon as it gets dark, when she realizes that she doesn't feel well. Her head is aching and she is sure she is running a fever. Wouldn't be measles, would it? Oh, no! Marjorie Strider had them. Well, I'm not getting them. Waste two weeks of June in bed? Nothing doing. No way.

That's what she thinks.

In spite of the heat wave and her protests, Father nails a blanket over her bedroom window to block out the light, and leaves her to sweat it out. And sweat it she does; at times she is delirious. Her only comfort is the gallons of weak tea that Mother makes for her. During the worst night of her illness, Father and Mother take turns sitting beside her bed wringing out a washrag in cool water, laying it on her forehead, and trying to distract her from her misery.

Mother talks about England: the skylarks, the ancient churches, the apple blossoms, the hedgerows, and the primroses. But Britain is in the middle of World War Two. Sarah is much more interested in the reports she hears on the radio describing how the people are surviving German air attacks. That seems to her to be more the stuff of life.

Father talks about cowboys. "Well sir, Charlie McLaughlin's got more honest-to-God horse savvy in his little toe than all the fancy bronc twisters in southern Alberta chucked into a gunny sack. Funny, that. No way you can learn Charlie to write his name,

but let that little sucker get his hands on a green colt –
oh, he'll breathe into their nostrils and dust 'em out
with a saddle blanket. All that stuff, but...." He breaks
off, a puzzled expression on his face. "Then he just
sorta lays both hands against the little old pony and –
stands there. Never says nothing, but he swears he's
talking Horse. *Something* sure as hell happens. You
take the snuffiest pony and in most cases he'll be eating out of Charlie's hand in half an hour. Oh, there's
the odd one that'll give him a tussle, but he can ride
the hurricane deck with the best of 'em if he has to,
and when they've have had it out, Charlie just goes
back to talking Horse until the pony's listening."

"What outfit does Charlie ride for?" Sarah manages.

"What outfit? Well, that's what brung him to mind.
I hear he's got tired of bronc twisting and he's bought
the old Kisti place down on the river flats. Gonna settle down there and raise him some fancy ponies."

An honest-to-God cowboy not ten miles away?
Sarah pictures him, impossibly blonde and tall and
heroic, with that "look of eagles" about him. Will I
ever get to meet him? If only I wasn't so ugly – if only
I didn't smell so bad – if only.... But when the fever
eases and she falls asleep, she doesn't dream of cowboys, she dreams of Litt, whom she adores.

At noon, on the last day of June, she emerges from
her room, wobbly, pale, but determined. "I'm at least
going to school to get my report card."

"Grade Nine musta been a pretty good year, eh,
Kid?" Father teases.

She grins. "Not bad, I guess."

She heats water for a spit bath, then, using the

same water, washes out one of her faded old blouses. Hanging in the wind, it dries in ten minutes, but when she irons it, a disgusting, skunky odor rises the moment the hot metal touches the fabric of the underarms.

It's bad enough to be scabby and have these big ugly boobs, but do I have to stink? If I could afford one of those little jars of Mum.... It stops you smelling. At least, they say it does.

WHEN SARAH ARRIVES AT SCHOOL, the yard is filled with Bennett buggies, trucks, and old cars. Most of the community is here, all decked out in its shabby best.

"What's going on?" she asks Annie Bach, over the sound of the Tremain Family Dance Band tuning up.

"Didn't you know? Litt's leaving. Got a job teaching art at the university in Edmonton. Can you believe it? We're giving him a little send-off this aft."

Sarah makes her way to one of the desks which has been backed against the wall to clear a place for dancing, sits down, and fights to control tears. How could this have happened? George Litt, her friend, the guy she dreams about, the guy who will surely some day sweep her up and away, away from Rattlesnake Park and poverty and other peoples' worn out clothes. How can he *think* of leaving?

But everyone else at the send-off is having a grand time. Especially Litt. Sarah eyes follow him while he jokes with all the guys and dances with all the girls, and all their mothers. Then, wonder of wonders, he asks *her* to dance.

"I don't know how to dance, Mr. Litt. Mother

never allows me to –"

"You'll soon learn. C'mon."

She wants desperately to dance with him, but she stumbles over his feet and can't catch the rhythm. Marjorie Strider, in the arms of Luke Raisbone, Rattlesnake Park's most eligible bachelor, dances past. Luke is a catch. His father, the elevator agent, has made a buck or two. He was able to give Luke the down payment for Jack Corrin's wheat farm, when Jack keeled over, dead from a heart attack. And since wheat and its growers are "essential commodities," Luke is safe from the army. Marjorie smirks at Sarah's performance as they pass and whispers something to Luke. He eyes Sarah with a sardonic expression and, when she stumbles, throws back his head in a shout of laughter, white tusks gleaming.

When Litt leads Sarah back to her seat, she is so humiliated she hardly hears him when he says, "I have a few things you might be able to use to amuse yourself this summer, Sarah. I'll give them to you when I give you your report card."

She shrinks onto the seat; she can think of nothing but how foolish she must have looked when she was trying to dance. It shocks her to realize that, sometime over the past year, the other girls of her age have become young ladies. Marjorie Strider has blossomed from a gossipy little dimwit into a veritable butterfly. "Mummy" manages to dress her handsomely and allows her to wear make-up and curl her hair in the latest frizzy fashion. Marjorie could pass for a twenty-year-old. Since Christmas time, Luke Raisbone has been escorting her to the community dances.

Sarah has a feeling of being left far, far behind. She

sits, enviously watching the dancers. No one speaks to her, let alone asks her to dance. She keeps telling herself that she doesn't care; Litt is the only person that is important to her in this room, and soon he will be gone. Forever. Her eyes follow his every move.

Promptly at 4:00 o'clock, Luke Raisbone, who is acting as master of ceremonies, puts an end to the dancing with the announcement that, "The ladies tell me chow's on, folks, and George has a train to catch at half past five."

When the crowd settles down with its paper plates loaded with baloney sandwiches and slices of sugar-shy cake, Luke, in love with his task and with himself, launches into a tribute to the teacher. He praises Litt's humour, his willingness to coach the hockey team, and his fearlessness behind home plate when the pitcher "burns 'em in," concluding, "As for his teaching – wouldn't know about that. Never made her past Grade Eight myself, and I tried her three times." Loud laughter and applause. Luke scratches the back of his neck with that "look out, here comes a good one" expression. Everyone leans forward; Luke's a comical bastard. "Must be some teacher, though. Eee-yup," he says, holding the pause dramatically, "any teacher that can hold a kid's attention the way George Litt holds Sarah MacKenzie's has sure gotta have something on the ball, wouldn't you say?"

For a moment, Sarah can't believe her ears. Then she sees herself as everyone else must see her; gauche, ugly, smelly, and dumb enough to wear her heart in her eyes. She flees; a roar of derisive laughter and applause follows her out of the schoolroom, down the stairs and into the barn. She is putting heels to Lindy Lou when she hears Litt call to her. She doesn't look back.

She finds a grass-grown buffalo wallow on the lee side of a knoll out of the wind, goes down into it and cries. And to top it all, she didn't even get her report card. That brings on a fresh flood of tears.

THE CREAM CHEQUES from their half dozen cows are the MacKenzies' only source of income this summer. Since their pasture is eaten down to grassroots and poverty moss, Father is allowing the cattle to run on open range. Open, since farms on all sides have been abandoned. Sarah's task is to fetch the cattle home, night and morning. Sometimes she finds them in half an hour, sometimes she hunts for three. Other times, like tonight, she can't find them at all. At pitch dark she gives up and goes home.

"Where the hell you been, Kid? Jesus...." Father holds up the barn lantern and peers at her. "I was to town this afternoon. I hear there was some kind of a send-off for that Litt guy? Dunno how come, but he left your report card and some other stuff for you with Mrs. Thomas at the store." Then he grins. "Some report card, Kid. You can be proud of that one."

Sarah shuts herself in her room. She refuses to even look at the report card. She shoves it under the mattress so she will not be tempted. But she can't stop herself from ripping open the clumsy brown paper parcel that came with it.

Sketching pads, charcoal, brushes, a set of watercolours with plenty of use in them still, and a dozen or so half-used tubes of oils! There is a note, scrawled on the back of one of the pads –

Sarah.

It is not too early for you to be considering scholarships and bursaries for university. I will be sending pamphlets for you to study. Best of luck with your art. It looks promising.

G.S. Litt

Sarah keeps the note to herself and reads it again and again, heaping scorn on Litt and on herself. She hardens herself into what she hopes is a state of harsh cynicism, but Luke Raisbone's wisecrack and the laughter that followed her out of the school remains, a raw, picked sore that refuses to heal. She goes to ridiculous lengths to avoid going to town. When she is not washing dishes, scrubbing floors, or hunting cows, she is in her room, sketching or painting.

Mother, dull-eyed and apathetic, wanders between her rocking chair and her bed. If she notices Sarah at all, it is to find fault with her for picking her face.

"Whatcha working on in your room all the time, Kid?" Father asks, studying Sarah with a troubled expression.

"Oh, nothing. Just – drawing."

"Seems like a shame to coop yourself up all summer when you're gonna be cooped up in school all winter, wouldn't you think?"

Sarah can't quite control her face. She disappears into her room, flings herself on the bed, and stuffs a pillow into her mouth to muffle the sobs.

The next day, when Father returns from a mysterious journey to visit one of his cronies, he dumps an old saddle out of the wagon. "There you go, Kid. She's all yours."

Sarah pounces on the prize. "Where'd you get it, Father?"

"Swapped with Claude for that buggy harness we never use. Saddle ain't in great shape, but Claude chucked in a sheep's hide to line the skirts, latigo leather for rigging, and a new —" He breaks off as Uncle Cecil's truck rattles into the yard.

"I'm on the fly, Jamie, so I won't be stopping," he calls, tossing a pair of Levis through the truck window. "Just brought these for Tara Tenzie. We got them for young Cecil but they shrank in the wash, so if she can use them…." He casts a sardonic eye over her, removes the straw hat he is wearing, and tosses that to her too. "There you are. Now you can be a regular 'ol' cowhand from the Rio Grande.'"

So he's making fun of me again. What else is new? But with a pair of Levis, a hat that looks kind of like a Stetson, and a saddle, I'll look like a real cowgirl. And maybe…maybe some day I'll meet Charlie McLaughlin. And maybe…. But she doesn't dare take *that* any further.

She abandons her sketching and painting to spend her spare time in the tool shed stripping the saddle down to the frame, working grease into the leather until it is pliable, sewing sheepskin into the skirts, and fixing the rigging.

Now, all I have to do is to lace all the pieces together with new whang leather. Long thongs that will dance in the wind, she thinks. These I took out of the saddle are just nubbins that Claude's sheep chewed.

When she tells Father that she needs new whang leather, he takes a long time reaming out his pipe.

"'Nough to do a good job on that saddle's gonna run two, three bucks, Kid."

Two or three bucks? More than we get for a cream cheque! Why didn't I ask for two new bras, a half a pound of Mum, and whang leather besides? Why didn't I just ask for the bloody moon? Hell with the god-damned saddle.

She walks away and leaves the saddle in pieces strewn over the tool shed floor.

WHEN SHE IS FETCHING the cows home that afternoon, she sees Father out on the road allowance talking to some old guy driving a wagon pulled by a pair of black Percheron horses.

"Fetch your pony over here, will you, Kid?" Father calls. He grins at her as she rides up. "Feel like doing a favour for a friend of mine?"

Her eyes swing to the small swarthy man sitting in a wagon which appears to be held together with whitish strips of dry, green cowhide. A favor? For this old guy? What's Father talking about?

The stranger sits perfectly still, meeting her gaze with steady, grey-hazel eyes. "Miss, I'd take it as a real favour if you'd loan me that pony of yours for three, four days. I fetched me a coupla dozen old ponies from up around Pincher Crick a while back, and danged if they didn't find a spot where the fence was down last night and head for home territory. Tar and Buster here are the only horses I got to my name today, and they ain't too good for rounding up cayuses."

The nerve of the guy! And Father – he's the one that says you never loan your horse to anybody unless he's got two busted legs and he's bleeding to death.

Her heart is pounding, but she screws up her courage. "Sorry your stock got away on you, Mister, but I don't lend my horse to anybody."

His face darkens and he looks down at the fine roper's gloves covering his small hands. "Appreciate your concern for your pony and I admire you for it, but I think your dad'll tell you I take pretty good care of horses. I never fetched one home yet that wasn't sound in wind and limb."

"Sarah," Father's face is scarlet, "this here is Charlie McLaughlin. Didn't you know?"

Charlie McLaughlin! This little old guy is *Charlie McLaughlin*, the horse wizard? The – oh, brother!

Father's face has turned a little purple and his eyes are drilling holes into her.

"Well, if Father thinks…" she gulps. "Well, since it's you…." She immediately wants to bite her tongue. Am I crazy? I don't care if it is Charlie McLaughlin. The guy is a complete stranger.

"Appreciate that, Miss Say-rah." Charlie murmurs in his soft, western drawl.

Say-rah! He called me Say-rah. She'd never heard her name spoken in such a romantic way. If only he wasn't such an old guy –

After he has gone, she asks Father about the rawhide bindings on the wagon.

"Shaganappi."

"What?"

"Well, you see, Charlie's Pa was a squaw-man. Charlie spent a lot of time around his Ma's folks. Now, this shaganappi, Indians take a green hide and they knock the hair off and they soak the hide till she's good and soft, see? Then they take a knife and they start cutting her round and round in one long strip. Now, say they got a splintered wagon tongue, eh? They nail one end of a strip of shaganappi to the tongue and they wrap her round and round, good and tight, then nail down the other end. When that shaganappi dries, she shrinks and pulls that wood together tighter'n barrel hoops."

"How come you don't use shaganappi? There's lots of busted stuff around here."

He looks startled. "Damned if I know. Never thought of it, I guess."

After five days, Charlie returns leading Lindy, who is sleek, sassy, and none the worse for wear. "A right nice pony you got there, Miss Say-rah," he says as he hands her the lead rope. "Pleasure working with her. I think you'll find she'll stand a little better for mounting now, and I learned her to quit nipping when she's feeling peckish."

Sarah takes the rope absent-mindedly. Is this the little old guy she'd seen in the wagon? This hard-bitten character with a five-day growth of beard, mounted on a magnificent bay gelding, might have ridden straight out of a Charlie Russell painting. Every detail, except for the six-guns; the battered Stetson, the goat-hair chaps, the spurred boots, the coiled lariat tied to the right pommel of the saddle, the rifle in a scabbard lying under his left leg, and the whang leather saddle strings dancing and swaying in the wind. Honest-to-God cowboy. No fancy names or cleft chins here.

Charlie fishes a packet of tobacco out of his shirt pocket and takes his time "building a smoke" before he looks at Sarah from under his brows. "Your dad was telling me you done a nice job of fixing up an old saddle?"

"Well, it's not finished. I –"

"Never had no whang leather," he finishes for her. He plasters the cigarette onto his lower lip and reaches back into his saddlebag. "Just so happens I worked my own saddle over a while back, and I had a little whang leather left over."

Yards of the stuff! Beautiful pliant golden leather.

A good horse, a saddle with long strings, a pair of Levis, and a hat that looks a little like a Stetson – "ol' cowhand from the Rio Grande," eh, Uncle Cecil? Well, pee on you. I will be. And pee on you too, Luke Raisbone.

If it wasn't for these goddamned boobs....

She tries binding herself in a winter scarf, but that is too bulky. Besides, it's hot and itchy. She snitches one of Mother's embroidered flour-sack dishtowels and four big safety pins. The results are not spectacular and the contraption tends to slip. But at least it flattens the bloody things and stops them from bouncing. And what if I do stink a little? So does Charlie.

She would love to imitate his walk and his quaint, drawling manner of speech, but she knows that would make her look ridiculous. She yearns to know him better, to soak up his lore, to make him her friend. She could kiss Father when she overhears him telling Charlie that he is welcome to drop in anytime he is on his way to Rattlesnake Park for supplies. The following week he does so, but, to Sarah's disappointment, he pays no attention to her until he rises to leave; then he says, "That pretty little pony of yours close to hand, Say-rah? Dunno if you've heard, but there's sleeping sickness around. I gave my cayuses a shot and I got enough left for Lindy too, if you've a mind to catch her up for me."

"Appreciate that, Charlie," she says, playing it cool while her heart does flip-flops. While Charlie is inoculating the mare, Sarah is inspired to ask a couple of insightful "horse" questions. That evening, for the first of many, the two of them sit, knee to knee out in the pasture, talking "horse" and the wide-ranging talk of friends. It is almost dark when Charlie heads for home.

AT THE BEGINNING OF AUGUST, Father returns from town and hands Sarah a brown manila envelope. *Litt!* She recognizes the writing. She takes it into her room and stuffs it under the mattress with her report card.

For days on end, a crazy summer chinook tears out of the southwest. The air is choked with dust. Dirt grits between Sarah's teeth and forms muddy crusts in the corners of her eyes; even though the air is hot, she feels chilly. Father, who practically makes a religion of "trying to look on the bright side," says, "When that old alligator's mouth opens up and that son of a bitch starts howling in the summertime, I just wanna crawl under the blankets and pull 'em over my head."

But chores go on, chinook or no chinook.

Sarah is out hunting cattle. She has more to worry about than the chinook and the wind tangling her hair into knots. The end of August is approaching. She has managed to avoid going near Rattlesnake Park all summer, but she has never told Mother and Father that she is not going back to school. She dreads the confrontation. She is struggling with possible approaches when she rides up onto a bank that overlooks a deep pothole slough.

Down in the slough, so buffeted by wind and intent upon each other that they don't hear her, a coyote and a skunk act out a little drama. The skunk, tail erect in a threatening plume, squalls threats, stomps with his tiny kid-glove feet and holds his ground on top of an anthill which he had been excavating for grubs.

The coyote would settle for either skunk or ant grubs, but he's an old stager; he knows better than to rush a skunk. He circles, makes threatening feints, but never comes close enough for the skunk to wheel and blast him. Finally, the coyote backs away, pees on a rock, rakes dirt contemptuously in the skunk's direction, and trots away.

The skunk tests the wind with his nose, peers about with his nearsighted eyes, gradually lowers his tail and goes back to digging grubs as though nothing had happened.

After chores that night, Sarah goes to work with the oil paints on a board she salvaged from the end of an old apple box. When the painting is finished, three days later, rough though it is, she knows she's caught something true about skunks and coyotes and prairies.

Father is delighted. "By God, Kid, we gotta see about getting you some art lessons. I wouldn't be surprised but what you could make something of yourself."

"I doubt that my dear friend Isabel Hindman showed more promise when she was your age," Mother adds.

Sarah ducks her head. She thinks guiltily of her report card and Litt's pamphlets hidden under the mattress. Then she remembers the laughter that followed her out of the school that last day of June.

Late that afternoon, Charlie appears. As always, Father invites him to stay for supper. After the meal, while they are drinking tea, Father says, "Hey, Kid, how about showing Charlie that picture you painted?"

Sarah reluctantly props the picture against the teapot and holds her breath for Charlie's verdict. He builds a smoke purely by feel, his grey-hazel eyes going over the picture again and again. The wind-creases at the corners of his eyes deepen a little. "Deserves a frame, don't it? Gonna let me take it home and make you one, Say-rah?"

The day before school starts, Sarah is sitting in the shade of the house. She hasn't changed her clothes for days, her hair is tangled from the wind, she knows she smells awful, and she doesn't care. She doesn't see Charlie ride into the yard until it is too late for her to retreat.

He dismounts, reaches into his saddlebag, drops down beside her, and hands her the picture, now enclosed in a shadow-box frame which is, in itself, a work of art; willow twigs laced together with sha-ganappi strips cut as fine as shoestrings.

Sarah is flabbergasted. She knows it has taken him days of careful work; nobody has ever done anything like this for her in her life. She stares at the picture wordlessly.

"Tough little cuss, a skunk, Say-rah," Charlie says.

She looks up into his face.

A trace of a smile crinkles the corners of his eyes. "Tough little cuss. Nobody runs *him* offa his grub heap, eh?"

10. THE FOURTH PICTURE

SARAH WATCHES AS SUNSET FADES OVER the unfamiliar parklands of central Alberta and the train chuffs steadily northward. Across the aisle, a couple of rowdy young soldiers make kissing sounds, trying to get her attention. She would love to flirt with them, to be as silly as they are, but she ignores them, staring out of the window, her nose almost against the glass. Several times she sees farm kids trailing cows home for milking. Hundreds and hundreds of nights in this kind of light, she too has lazed along on her Arab mare bringing cattle home.

I miss Lindy something awful. And I even miss that old sandpile of a farm. How will Mother and Father manage there without me? And as much as anything, I miss Charlie. Can't write his own name, but he's so proud that I'm going to university. I know he couldn't afford to hand me that twenty dollars for "glad rags" either. Her throat aches with tears. If it hadn't been for Charlie, I would have quit school in Grade Nine.

She is startled by the elderly conductor. "Well, young lady, in a few minutes you'll be in the big city of Edmonton. Are you headed for a job of some sort?"

"No, the University of Alberta."

"Ah-h." He raises his eyebrows, taking in her shoddy homemade clothes. "So, what will you be studying?"

"I want to be a painter."

He smiles.

"Oh, she's gonna be a painter!" one of the young soldier mocks to his buddy.

"Wonder what she'll paint?"

"Nudes, I bettcha!" They both howl.

Idiots! Probably think nudes are dirty or something. Like some people in Rattlesnake Park. Aunt Jane still squirms when she sees that beautiful little nude Miss Hindman painted for Mother.

The conductor's eyes flick from her to the soldiers and back again. "Someone meeting you?"

"My landlady," she says stiffly.

"Better get your things together then. We'll be at the station in five minutes."

When she glances out the window she sees that the train is now passing row after row of houses, each enclosed in its own little yard.

So, that's the city. No place a person can go where somebody can't see you? I hate it already.

When they pull into the station, she eases her way down the steps with a shabby suitcase in each hand. The young soldiers push past, laughing and stiff-arming each other in the shoulder. Sarah sets her luggage down and stares about at the faces of people meeting the train. It suddenly strikes her that she has no idea who she is looking for. Mrs. Fuller has never described herself nor sent a picture.

What if she never comes? What if she's changed

her mind? What if she's forgotten? What if...?

The passengers have dispersed. A guy in a flashy blue suit with a watch chain across his belly smokes a cigarette and leans against the station. "How about you and me taking in a show, baby?"

White slaver! Oh, God. She grabs her suitcases and is heading for the safety of the station when a very pregnant young woman waddles through the door, stops, and assesses her. "Sarah? Sorry I'm late, but Myrtle bit the babysitter and I had to wait and settle them both down. Talk about the terrible twos! Myrtle's a terrible three as you'll discover."

"You mean *I'm* supposed to look after Myrtle while you – ?" Sarah gulps, her glance flicking towards Mrs. Fuller's belly.

"Oh, no. Myrtle will be going to her Grandmother while I'm in the hospital. You'll be alone keeping an eye on the house."

"What about Mr. Fuller?"

"South America. Engineer, you know. Won't be home until after the baby's born," she sighs. "Well, we have to make the best of things, don't we? Come along now, bring your things. You'll have to be up for registration early in the morning."

After a whirlwind ride back across the High Level Bridge spanning the muddy North Saskatchewan, they turn west into the area of well-kept older homes close to the university. Mrs. Fuller pulls up in front of a handsome brown brick and stucco house with Virginia creeper climbing over its walls. "Now, Sarah, if you'll tell the babysitter I'm waiting to drive her home...."

Sarah and the babysitter meet in the doorway.

Around a wad of chewing gum, the girl drawls, "Just one thing, Kid. You 'get' Myrtle before she 'gets' you. Otherwise, you don't stand a chance."

"Isn't she asleep yet?"

"Yeah, finally, the little brat."

Sarah, weary from her journey and the confusion of the past week, closes the door, leans against it, and stares about. Wow! This is a palace. I've only seen houses like this in pictures. What if I do something really dumb here and disgrace myself?

THE FIRST WEEK OF UNIVERSITY is almost finished. Still feeling lost, gauche, and unsure of herself, Sarah is sitting in the Arts Library looking through a book of prints of the works of Turner. The library, with its hushed atmosphere and oak-paneled walls, seems very grand; Miss Cleaver, the librarian with her "no nonsense, how can you be so stupid?" attitude, terrifies her, but she has managed to get a book she wanted and is musing through it when someone lays a hand on her shoulder. She looks up into the grinning face of George Litt. "Well, Sarah! You made it."

"Mr. Litt! I'm so gl –"

He lays a finger against his lips, "Sh-h! C'mon, let's go have a coffee. Then we can talk."

The university cafeteria, where Sarah works clearing tables every night, is almost empty at this time of day. Sarah is thrilled that Litt has asked her for coffee. She is gulping with nervousness.

I've got to make a good impression so he'll ask me for real date. I've got to.

But Litt dashes her hopes when he returns with a

tray containing two pieces of raisin pie and two cups of coffee. "I was telling my wife the other day that I hoped to see you this fall."

"Your wife?"

"Um-hmm." He takes his wallet from his pocket. "Three years now." With a flourish, he removes a photograph and hands it to her. "There she is. My Rose of Sharon and Georgie junior."

While Sarah stares at the pretty blonde girl holding a baby in her arms, Litt stirs sugar into his coffee. "I noticed you looking at some prints of the works of Turner in the library. Do you admire him?"

"Well, he was a great painter, I guess, but I like figure drawings too. Mother has a beautiful little nude done by a friend of hers, a Miss Hindman, that –"

"A Miss *Isabel* Hindman?"

"That's right. Mother and she were friends in England. Worked at the same boarding school."

"Describe the picture for me." His tone is so sharp that she is taken aback.

"Well, it's not very big. Maybe eighteen by twelve or so. Mother says she brought it in her suitcase when she came overseas. It's a nude, like I said. A young woman scuffing through drifts of apple blossom. Her face is turned slightly away and partly hidden by one hand, but her flesh absolutely glows and you can practically smell the spring."

"Do you think your mother would consider selling it?"

She laughs. "A peddler offered Father three hundred and fifty dollars for it when I was a little kid. That almost caused a divorce."

"She *does* know what it's worth then?"

"Worth? You really think it's worth anything?"

"If it is what I think it is. Catch me sometime when I'm not busy and we'll make a raid on the library. There's an article about a Miss Isabel Hindman who was killed in a bombing raid on London in 1943." He smiles at her and rises. "I'm sure you have studying to do and I have papers to mark, so…. Good luck, Sarah. See you around campus."

Me and my dumb crushes and him with his Rose of Sharon and his Georgie…. And what was he doing, blabbering about some picture that he hasn't even seen?

But in the scramble to keep up with courses, struggle with essays, clear tables in the cafeteria, and babysit, Litt and Miss Hindman's picture fade into the background.

In the meantime, she makes a friend. The first morning she enters the English class with a load of books in her arms, a pleasant looking young woman looks up and smiles at her. "Want to park yourself beside me?"

"Sure, thanks."

While she arranges herself and stows the texts she's bought for other classes under the chair, the woman, a tailored blonde with a beautiful smile, says, "New to the game, are you?"

"Green's the word."

"Like the first week I joined the WRENS. Wow! Didn't know whether I was on my head or my heels, but you'd be surprised how quickly it all sorts out."

"You were in the WRENS?"

"Overseas for three years. Wouldn't have missed it." She shrugs and makes a wry face. "Well, the Allies licked the Germans and the atom bomb put an end to the war in the Pacific theatre, so now it's back to the salt mines to upgrade my damned teaching certificate." She extends a hand, "Avril Thompson, and you are...?"

Sarah is awed by the friendliness of what seems like such a sophisticated woman and surprised to discover that they are enrolled in three of the same classes. At break, while they lounge about on the steps outside that first morning, Avril offers Sarah a cigarette.

"Oh, golly, thanks! I never...."

Avril lights up, cupping the match against the wind like an old cowboy, takes two puffs, and hands the cigarette to Sarah.

"Coupla drags takes the edge off things. Try it."

Not wanting to seem prissy, Sarah does so, coughs, makes a wry face, and hands the cigarette back. "Tastes awful."

"Give yourself time. Like I said, it takes the edge off."

Within a week, it becomes a ritual for the two of them to meet in the Tuck Shop after classes for coffee and a smoke. Sarah is a willing audience for Avril's wicked sense of humour and gift for mimicry. One rainy autumn afternoon, Sarah is working in the library when Avril drops into the seat across from her. "Sarah, could I borrow your notes from Philosophy this morning? I missed the class."

While Avril is intent upon copying, Sarah admires her curly blonde hair, which she wears in a bob, and her neat tailored suit. When Avril has finished with the notes, she rises, reaches across the table, and squeezes Sarah's arm with a strong, nicotine-stained hand. "Thanks, sweetie. I'm in a rush right now, but one of these days, let's find time to do something besides study."

"That'd be great."

Avril smiles, her eyes lingering on Sarah before she turns and marches out of the library, the metal clips on her heels clacking on the tiles. Sarah notices three sophisticated young "townies" watching with amused expressions. The way their heads bend towards each other, she knows they have been discussing Avril and her and she can't imagine why.

ALTHOUGH MRS. FULLER'S BABY is expected soon, she manages a full social life; dinner engagements, movies, and a bridge club.

Since Mrs. Fuller throws up her hands and declares, "I simply cannot do a thing with that child," it generally falls to Sarah's lot to put Myrtle to bed. To her relief, she discovers that the tiny terror can be quelled and held spellbound by stories about animals. As she tells Myrtle about creatures she's encountered and the animals on the farm, she realizes that she has treasures denied to an urban child. Myrtle will never go to sleep to the sound of coyotes singing wild in the dark, nor will she chase pronghorns flat out on horseback for the pure joy of seeing them run. She will never watch a rattlesnake swallow a gopher, nor see prairie chicken dancing in a lek in springtime. For her, the dark will be a fearsome place where strangers lurk; she will never wander free under the stars.

On the evenings when Mrs. Fuller is going out, Sarah disappears into her room with her books as soon as Myrtle goes to sleep. Sometimes she resents having to study so much. Must be great to sit for hours over a bottle of Coke in the cafeteria, flirting with some exciting young guy that's just returned from overseas. Or talking to some girl, for that matter. Avril and I would find lots to yak about if we had the time.

A heat wave hits Edmonton that October. All the library windows stand open and voices call to each other across the lawns outside. Sarah is reading Faulkner for an English course and finding the vocabulary challenging. When she has collected ten words which are unfamiliar, she goes to a huge dictionary standing on a lectern at one end of the library. Returning with her list and mouthing the words to memorize them, she is aware that a young blond fellow is watching her, a fellow almost as handsome as the dream cowboys out of her *Ranch Romance*-reading days. He is dressed in smart air force blues, wearing some insignia on his shoulder patch that she does not recognize. What she does recognize is that the colour of his uniform picks up the almost navy blue of his eyes.

Is *that* guy really watching me? When she steals a glance at him, there is no question. And he's caught me looking. She considers fleeing the library, but instead rises and turns her back on him.

He startles her by slipping into the chair beside her. "What are you reading?"

"*Go Down, Moses.*"

"Oh, yeah. Great stuff, eh?" He takes the book, marks her place with one finger and flips open the cover where she has written her name and address. "Well, Sarah MacKenzie, meet Clarence Cross. We're practically next-door neighbours."

"I didn't know they let guys that are still in the air force go to university."

"Was in the air force. Haven't quite got my walking papers yet, but in the meantime they're letting me attend the good old U of A."

"So you're boarding too? Have you got a good land-lady?"

"The best: my mother. Got time for a coffee?"

"Well, I – I guess so."

She discovers that he has been in a radar unit attached to the RCAF, that he has ambitions as a jour-nalist, that his family owns a contracting firm; heavy construction, which he loathes.

"Don't like construction? I think it would be excit-ing, building things."

"You wouldn't think it was exciting if you were working for my old man, plodding around in the rain with ten pounds of mud on each foot setting out flares before dark."

She hastily changes the subject. "So what was it like overseas?"

"I wasn't overseas. I got stuck freezing my butt off in Goose Bay."

"Labrador? Doing what?"

"Sitting in the dark reading screens to guide the fly-boys home." He shoves his chair back. "C'mon, let's go for a walk. It's too nice to be cooped up in here."

"Oh, there's an essay I have to...."

"Sarah, I put in two years at this dump before I joined up. There's always an essay. C'mon."

As they stroll through the university district, Sarah notices an older woman behind a white picket fence on the far side of a tree-lined street. She is cutting peony stalks and piling them into a wheelbarrow.

"Mom putting her flower beds to sleep," Clarence says. "She still works like a man in that yard."

Sarah looks from the flower beds to the house, glistening with new paint. Two enormous elm trees stand in the yard. The house itself is enormous, even by the standards of Mrs. Fuller's, which is daunting enough.

This Clarence guy may not be crazy about construction, she thinks, but if it were me, I could stand to set out a lot of flares with mud on my boots if I thought I could live in a house like that.

THAT NIGHT there is a flurry of activity about the Fuller household. Mrs. Fuller goes to the hospital, Grandmother collects Myrtle, and Sarah is left to hold the fort. When everyone has gone, she wanders through rooms she has never been invited to enter. Wow! Nothing busted, not a flyspeck on anything, and nothing stinks of sour milk. Wouldn't Mother love it? A grand piano in the living room. I wonder if Clarence's house is as nice? Probably nicer. Funny he didn't introduce me to his mother today. Maybe he doesn't like me.

But after classes the following afternoon, he is waiting to walk her home. When she takes her books from him at Fullers' gate he says, "Aren't you going to invite me in?"

She feels her face heat. "I...I don't think Mrs. Fuller would like...well, the neighbours might tell...."

He laughs. "Sarah, don't be a prude."

"Well, no funny stuff, okay?" she mutters, feeling ridiculous as she fishes the door key out of her purse.

As soon as Clarence enters the house, he spots the

piano. "Look at this, would you?" He slides onto the bench and runs through a few thunderous Hammond Exercises. "Great tone. In tune too." And, as delicate as moonlight, he launches into "Claire de Lune."

Sarah is captivated, breathless. She has never known anybody who could really play classical music. She does not move until the last note sounds and Clarence smiles at her with his beautiful, even teeth. "That, Miss Sarah, will cost you one cup of tea."

Every night, while Mrs. Fuller is in hospital, he plays for her. She is caught between loving his music and some strange undefinable reservation about Clarence himself.

IT IS EVENING, three weeks after Mrs. Fuller has returned from hospital with her new son. Sarah, returning from work, is about to enter the house when the door opens in her face and Mrs. Fuller, decked out like a fat little sausage in a smart black cocktail dress, says, "Oh, I'm glad it's only you, Sarah. I was afraid Mr. Fuller might have arrived early."

"I didn't know you were expecting him."

"Surprised me. He is a most impetuous man. He's laid on a party at the MacDonald Hotel tonight with his partners and their wives to celebrate his home-coming. But how can I go anywhere looking like this?"

"Got a sewing machine? I can fix that dress in a jiffy."

"Really?"

"I'm a pretty good dressmaker. How much time do I have?"

"Maybe half an hour."

164

"Then you'd better do your hair and get your make-up on."

Twenty minutes later Sarah takes the dress upstairs with the seams eased, two darts removed, and the garment pressed. As Mrs. Fuller turns in front of the mirror, beaming at her own reflection, the downstairs door opens and a jocular male voice calls, "Bertha, my proud beauty, your carriage awaits you."

She dons a mink stole, picks up gloves and purse from the bed, and indicates the clothes closet. "There's some rather nice things in there I'm never going to wear again, Sarah. I don't have the self-discipline to starve myself into them. Help yourself."

"But, Mrs. Fuller –"

"Anyway, my husband says I deserve a new wardrobe, having produced his son and heir."

"You mean it?"

"Indeed I do. You can take anything, excepting of course the shoes and furs. And what you don't want, I'll send to the Sally Ann."

After Sarah has changed the baby and settled him down with a bottle, she tiptoes back into Mrs. Fuller's bedroom, careful not to waken Myrtle, and opens the closet door. Still not quite believing her luck, she chooses a classically simple ruby-coloured dress that she thinks might do good things for her dark hair and eyes, tries it on and slowly turns in front of the full-length mirror.

Golly! I'm…I'm kind of…kind of…well, not cute, not pretty either, but…. No, I'm what they call striking. Kind of. And I never knew I had such a great body. What was it I heard those guys say in the cafeteria when they watched that Margaret Woodfern that's supposed to be such a heart-throb walking away? "Stacked." That's it. She laughs. That's what I am. Stacked! Now, if I knew what to do with my hair....

She loosens it and lets it tumble over her shoulders and down her back. I don't know anything about perms and curlers. Mother'd never stand for me primping, as she called it. I wonder if Mrs. Fuller would have any ideas?

As it turns out, Mrs. Fuller has an excellent idea. "Suppose we give you a few wisps to soften your face a bit, blunt the ends, and sweep it all into a thick black ponytail? No trouble to look after and, with the strong bone structure of your face, it'll look wonderful."

When Sarah comes into class the following Monday morning, dressed in a smart sweater set, a good skirt, and her spectacular hairdo, heads turn. Clarence comes up to her. "My goodness! Who have we here?"

"Don't you like it?"

"Yeah, I guess it's all right. Just a question of whether it's you or not."

Sarah is bewildered and a little hurt. Other fellows who have never noticed her before are looking at her with admiring glances. That afternoon she is not particularly pleased when Clarence appears after her last class to walk her home. She supposes that he wants to apologize for his rudeness, but he does nothing of the sort. At Fullers' gate he pauses. "I've been working on a new Mozart I want you to hear."

"Working on a new Mozart and going to university? When do you find time to study?"

His face flushes. "Do you want to hear it or not?"

"Well, the Fullers are home. I can't just...."

"Suit yourself." And he strides away down the sidewalk.

Of all the unreasonable.... "To hell with you, Buster," she mutters. "What did you expect me to do, barge into Fullers' and tell them their lives have to stop while you play their piano?" But by the time she is settled down with her books, she is thinking, poor guy probably worked his head off to impress me and here I go implying that he is neglecting his courses. I'll ask Mrs. Fuller if I can't invite him in tomorrow night.

When she does so, Mrs. Fuller says, "He's welcome to come in if he'd like to play." After a moment she frowns. "This isn't that Cross boy from over on 87th Avenue, is it?"

"You know him?"

There is the briefest pause. "I know the family."

"What...what about the family?"

"Oh, well...." She looks evasive. "Rather...uh...spirited. The old man looks upon himself as a great success story. He boasts that he landed in Edmonton with thirty-two cents in his pocket at the turn of the century."

But she doesn't like the Crosses, Sarah realizes. I wonder why?

SINCE REMEMBRANCE DAY falls on a Friday, it will be a long weekend. Sarah decides to go home and surprise Mother and Father. Maybe she'll find time to ride down to see Charlie too, and tell him about her adventures in the big city. Always, in her letters home, she sends some little message for Mother to read to him when he appears at the farm.

Bus fare is cheaper than train fare, Sarah discovers, and there will be a bus passing through Rattlesnake Park heading for Edmonton on Sunday night. She plans to catch it and be back in time for classes Monday morning. Feeling very attractive in her new clothes and the bit of discreet make-up Mrs. Fuller has encouraged her to wear, she buys her ticket, hurries out to the bus, and mounts the steps.

She holds out her ticket and offers some inane remark to the handsome young driver who is sitting studying a clipboard. At the sound of her voice, his head snaps up and she finds herself looking deep into a pair of shining, Celtic-blue eyes. After a long moment he takes the ticket, his fingers brushing hers, and murmurs in a husky voice that hints at deep emotion, "There's a seat for you right here behind me."

He removes his jacket from the seat and she slips into it. He smiles at her in the mirror, a bit of gold glinting in his front teeth as he closes the door, salutes some fellow standing beside the depot, manoeuvres the huge vehicle out of its parking bay into the stream of traffic, and asks, "So, what's in Rattlesnake Park?"

"Just going home for the weekend."

"Checking up on the boyfriend?"

"I don't have a boyfriend," she admits, it never having occurred to her to lie.

They are almost out of the city when he murmurs, "You didn't tell me your name."

"Sarah MacKenzie." She feels her heartbeat pick up.

"Good name for a black Celt."

Thrilled, she touches her dark hair and studies the

back of his muscular neck with the fringe of dark hair appearing under his cap. "And so is Jock MacDonald, speaking of black Celts," she says, seeing his name displayed on a clip above the mirror. "Have you been driving for Greyhound long?"

"A year or so before I joined the air force. Just got out a couple of months ago. Believe me, I'd sooner be pushing this baby than flying kites across the North Atlantic."

I'll bet he was stationed in Goose Bay. Wonder if he knew Clarence?

"So, what was it like, flying the Atlantic?"

"Dark. Cold. Hairy as hell the odd time and boring as hell the rest. But the leaves in Britain were great. Oh, those London lassies! Wild little beggars. Game for anything. Once, at the end of the war, I even got over to Copenhagen. The girl I was with dragged me to the opera and, you know, it wasn't bad? Actually, I kind of got a kick out of it."

Those "London lassies" were probably no older than I am, she thinks jealously, And what was I doing all the time they were flipping around with good looking air force types? Hunting cows and talking to an old half-breed. Boy! Life just whizzing past me before I've even lived.

When she slides her foot along the ledge beside his seat, yearning to be closer to him, he takes the foot in his hand and squeezes it tenderly. "You really don't want to go to Rattlesnake Park tonight, Sarah, do you?"

"I...I don't?"

"I'm taking this load through to Banff, then I've got a day's layover."

Her heart is choking her. "Oh, I couldn't. I...."

"Sure you could." His grip tightens deliciously on her foot. "You want to, I know you do."

"It doesn't matter what I want. I don't do that kind of thing."

He laughs. "Jeez! I didn't know there were girls like that around any more."

Good grief, I sound like such a silly little priss. The guy's right, of course. I know half the girls in university are sleeping around with their boyfriends, but not little Goody Two Shoes Sarah MacKenzie. She doesn't do that kind of thing.

Her weekend at home is miserable. Father is dull and predictable. The old farmhouse is drafty. Sarah is outraged by the greasy binder canvas Father has hung on two spikes in front of the living room door to stop the draft and the strips of dirty rag he has stuffed into the cracks around the windows. At night, mice skip about the floors. Lindy is off somewhere running with the range horses; Sarah never does see her. The snow is too deep to go looking for her, and she never gets to see Charlie either.

Mother questions her closely and suspiciously about her associates, particularly about her friendship with Avril. "Be careful of her," she warns. "After all she's an older woman, and she's been in the armed forces."

"Careful of what? She's just a nice friend and we enjoy studying together."

"That's all very well, but –"

"Mother, I'm not nine years old. You're not telling me how to pick my friends."

Mother is cool for the rest of the visit. Sarah is glad

to get back on the bus. When she changes in Calgary, Jock is standing at the door of the new bus taking tickets. "Well, Monkey Face, how was the weekend?"

"Don't ask."

"Told you you should have come with me. Move my jacket there and sit in behind me, okay?"

He keeps that jacket there in case he sees some girl he'd like to make a little time with. Well, I'm not playing his game.

She checks through to the back of the bus, but all the other seats are taken. She finally removes his jacket and slips into the seat, planning to be very cool and haughty with him, but he is so entertaining and funny that she melts. When he lets her off the bus in Edmonton he says, "Well, coming with me next weekend?"

"Oh, I can't. There's exams to...."

He steps in close to the side of the bus and beckons. When she comes into his arms, he kisses her with open-mouthed urgency. She feels his cock harden against her thighs and she goes wet with desire. She cannot refuse him.

She leaves the depot, stumbling towards a streetcar, and barely escapes being hit by a truck. The driver curses her and roars away blasting his horn. She doesn't care.

She scarcely remembers going to classes. All week she lives in a fog of lust and desire. On Friday night, she buys a ticket before she goes out to Jock's bus, which she has spotted standing with its door open at the parking bay. When she hands him the ticket, he takes it, winks, shoves a slip of paper into her hand, and murmurs, "There's a seat right there behind me, babe." From time to time, as the bus trundles along through the snowy, early dark, he tenderly squeezes her foot. By the time they arrive in Banff, Sarah is so soggy with desire that she can barely make her way up the steps and across the lobby of the hotel where Jock has written that she is to ask for a room reserved for Eileen Taylor.

The hotel room is chilly, rather barren. She is thankful to step into a hot shower, one ear pricked for Jock's arrival. She is finishing towelling herself when a discreet tap sounds on the door. When she opens it, Jock draws her to him in an open-mouthed kiss. The serge of his uniform is rough against her skin. "H-mm!" he murmurs, "clean and damp. Just the way I like 'em."

He sweeps her up, carries her to the bed, then strips off his clothes. His erect cock seems enormous, but when he comes to her, he does not try to enter her at once; instead he kisses her lightly before he tongues and nuzzles her breasts. As her nipples rise and harden, she hears herself moan with desire. He noses down her belly in a series of fluttery little kisses, then, to her amazement, his tongue finds that tiny button which has always seemed to her too sensitive to touch. After the first shock of embarrassment, she melts to the caressing tongue as wave after wave of unexpected pleasure shudders through her. When he enters her, she embraces him with arms, legs, and lips while he brings them both to climax.

She is so far off on some dizzy star of ecstasy that it is not until he is snoring beside her that she realizes that he did not use a safe. She doesn't think he did, at least. Not that she really knows what a safe looks like.

For two days she is desperate with worry until she

gets her period. Then she makes up her mind that next weekend, when she goes to Banff, she is going to insist that Jock use a safe. She phones him to tell him so. He groans and giggles. "Kind of like washing your feet with your socks on, Monkey Face, but if you insist."

For two weekends she sneaks off to Banff, lives in a fog of lustful ecstasy, studies scarcely at all, and earns two bare pass marks on mid-terms. When she tells her boss at the cafeteria that she is going to take the third weekend off, he threatens to fire her.

That jolts her into reality.

This will never do. I've got to phone Jock and tell him I'm going to hit the books this weekend.

"You're taking this university stuff awfully seriously, aren't you?"

"No, but you don't understand. I've always want-ed…I've worked for years. I can't just.… Well, I've told you I'm here on scholarships and if I don't keep up…."

"Okay, babe, don't get in a tizz. There's always the weekend after. See you then."

But on Friday night she can't stop herself from going down to the depot to speak to him, to see him, just for a moment. It is a bitter night with a north wind swirling snowflakes through the frozen streets. She sees his bus, standing with its door open, but at first she does not see Jock. When she does, she real-izes he has another girl crowded in beside the bus and is making ardent love to her.

She slinks away down Jasper Avenue, jostling and being jostled by people hurrying home with squinted eyes and mufflers hiding their faces. She is too upset to think of taking a streetcar; someone might ask her why she is crying. She turns south onto 109th Street so that the wind is at her back, plods past the legislative buildings, half-blinded by tears and snow, and heads across the High Level Bridge with the bitter wind whipping snow into her face and her hands and feet freezing. She creeps into her room, crawls into bed, and cries herself to sleep.

At midnight she wakens. The house is still, sleeping. She turns on the lamp and looks at herself in the mirror. Her eyes are swollen and her face blotchy. Serves you right, you bloody fool. You'd better thank your lucky stars that at least you know you're not pregnant. But... I'm nuts about the guy. I don't know how I'd ever.... Everything would be...bare without him. Bare...nothing to look forward to. Nothing to.... She stares out into the swirling snow and listens to the wind faintly rattling the shutters. At last she comes to a decision. I'm not going to see him again. I don't care how crazy I am about him. He's not treating *me* like a whore. And then, reluctantly, Clarence wouldn't treat a girl like that. If he was your guy, he'd be *your* guy.

She pitches into work to redeem herself and starts whenever the phone rings, certain it will be Jock. She has a speech prepared for him, but she never has to deliver it; he never phones.

Not that she lacks for male company. Clarence is always at her elbow. Several times they go to movies and sit eating popcorn in the dark. Often, after classes, he invites himself into Fullers' to play the piano.

"You must practice a lot to keep up that standard," Sarah probes.

"Couple of hours a day and then a couple of hours writing."

"Essays?"

"Oh, God, no. Short stories. That's where I live."

"Short stories? For publication?"

"In time, I hope."

When he invites her home for Sunday dinner in late February, she is both pleased and alarmed.

He isn't getting serious about me, is he? He's nice and everything, but, well, I don't know. He just doesn't.... Kissing him is like kissing my brother, if I had a brother. I wonder if he's ever had a girl? He never even tries to get me into bed. Oh, God, Sarah, he's twenty-five years old. What guy that's been in the air force hasn't had a girl?

The Cross house, grander than Sarah imagined, overflows with two married sisters, Sophie and Robin, and their families, as well as the brother, Ben, his wife, Maggie, and their three children. Sarah discovers that all the men in the family, excepting Clarence, work for the elder Cross and they all treat the old man with careful deference. He scarcely speaks to Sarah, aside from nodding in acknowledgement to Clarence's introduction. The mother is a brittle, austere woman with a nervous, mirthless laugh. The sisters fuss over Sarah, seat her in the most comfortable chair in the living room, ask anxiously if she is warm enough, ask her if she is enjoying university, want to know where she comes from and what her parents do.

Well, let them have it straight. "My folks are dryland farmers. Poor as they come. My father still farms with horses, but he pays his debts and he never cheats a soul." She is annoyed with herself for sounding so defensive. She notices the old man's eyes on her, narrowed, a little sneaky smile playing around his mouth.

"Bless their hearts," Robin simpers. "You must have had a very hard childhood."

"Depends how you look at it. I had a pony from the time I started school and I had time to really know the prairies. Not everybody does."

"But what's there to know about the prairies?" Sophie asks, "One time we were driving back from Saskatchewan and I thought I'd die if I didn't see a tree pretty soon."

"You'd just have to live there a while and learn to look."

"Not me. Not...." Sophie breaks off as Clarence appears, a sheaf of typewritten pages in his hand. "Oh, oh!" she covers a laugh with her hand. "You're in for it, Sarah."

Clarence gives Sophie a dirty look and hands the papers to Sarah. "Thought you might like to read this story."

Her education in Literature is scant. The school library in Rattlesnake Park was practically non-existent. The only short stories she has read, outside of the school texts, are the ones that appeared in the farm periodicals and pulp fiction like *Ranch Romances*. As she struggles through the story, she realizes, This thing is awful. I can't say why it's awful but I know it is.

She glances up to see Clarence's sisters on the edge of their chairs awaiting her verdict while Clarence paces up and down the room. When she can put it off no longer, she sorts the papers and squares them on the edge of the coffee table.

"Well?"

"I can see that a lot of work's gone into it. But...it's probably too deep for me, Clarence. I don't get it. What does your prof say?"

"I don't need a prof to tell me there's the makings of a writer in me."

"Oh, Clarence," Sophie brays. "Why don't you forget all this writing nonsense? We've all told you, if you had any sense you'd stick with your music. You could always teach if you really don't want to go into Cross, Cross, and Associates.

"Mind your own bloody business," Clarence erupts. "What do you know about Literature? You've never read anything deeper than the *Ladies Home Journal* in your life."

"*Ladies Home Journal,*" Sophie bristles, "what's wrong with...?"

"Clarence, if you weren't so goddamned stubborn," Robin begins, "you'd –"

"Make you a bet, Clarence," Sophie cuts her off. "A thousand bucks says that you can't get a story accepted in the *Ladies Home Journal* in the next six months."

"Who'd want to get a story accepted in a piece of shit like the *Ladies Home Journal?*"

By now, things are completely out of hand. Clarence shouts insults and blasphemy at his sisters and they shout insults and blasphemy back. At first, Sarah is horrified; she has never seen such a display. She fully expects the sisters and their families to storm out of the house. She is amazed that the husbands do not come to their spouses' defense. Finally, she realizes that everybody is enjoying the battle. For them, it is high drama; it doesn't matter in the least that neighbours on either side must be able to hear every word.

"Are you forgetting Clarence has a guest?" Mrs. Cross tops them, wading into the fray. "Shame on you, all of you. Come along now. Dinner is ready."

Sarah, wishing herself anywhere but where she is, is assigned the seat to the right of her host. The old man does nothing more than grunt a monosyllable to a question she puts to him about construction, but to her relief, the two brothers-in-law and Clarence start a lively argument over the relative merits of the works of Hemingway and F. Scott Fitzgerald, whose work, it appears, none of the rest of the company has read.

What a weird bunch, Sarah thinks, after Clarence has walked her home. And the worst of it is, I think Clarence really likes me. Well, I don't care how hand-some he is, I'm going to give him the brush-off. This is ridiculous.

For a week, she makes excuses and spends all her spare time with Avril, then he corners her. "I take it you didn't like my family?"

"I don't know your family well enough to like them or dislike them."

"Then it's me."

"Clarence, look, finals are coming up in a month and a half. I don't have time for anything besides my two jobs and my studies."

"All right, you made your point." He turns and walks stiffly away under the bare maple trees with a last few shivering seeds clinging to their boughs. His every movement tells her how hurt he is. She wants to call to him, but she does not do so.

IT IS A FRIDAY NIGHT, the middle of March. There has actually been a thaw. Tulips poke their noses above ground in front of Mrs. Fuller's windows. Sarah is lonely and weary from studying. When the phone rings, she skips downstairs to answer it, hoping against hope that it might be Jock. "Yes?" she says breathlessly.

"Sarah?" Avril's voice is friendly and warm. "Let's knock off and go to a matinee tomorrow. My treat. Pick you up about one."

The following day the two girls choose the back seat in an almost-empty theatre and, well supplied with popcorn and licorice, settle down to watch *My Friend, Flicka*.

When the goodies have been demolished, Avril slips one arm around Sarah's shoulders. She thinks nothing of it at first, but a few moments later she realizes that Avril is watching her and not the show. Puzzled, she casts a questioning glance at her.

"That old cowboy buddy of yours calls you Say-rah, doesn't he? Beautiful name for a beautiful lady. I'm going to call you Say-rah too."

Sarah is embarrassed. "Well, thanks, but I don't think Charlie –"

Unexpectedly, Avril takes her face between both hands and kisses her with a kiss so passionately hungry and at the same time so tender that Sarah teeters between the desire to respond and the desire to flee. After a moment she tears away and stumbles out into the bright sunlight of the afternoon, confused, a little frightened, and terribly ashamed. To her relief, Avril does not follow. What would I say to her if she did? Maybe there's nothing in the world wrong with it…two girls…For a minute there it sure didn't feel like there was anything wrong with it. I shouldn't have been so.... Oh, god, poor Avril.

At their first class on Monday morning, Avril is already seated when Sarah enters the room. Avril looks pale and sad. "No hard feelings, Sarah, okay?" she says. "And do me a favour." She lays her forefinger meaningfully across her lips and pleads with her eyes.

Sarah knows she is blushing furiously. "Yes.... Well, no.... Well, of *course*." Sometime during the lecture, she is impelled to glance back. Avril is still watching her with a pained, wistful expression.

SARAH HAS WRITTEN HER LAST EXAM. Now she is scuffing along a cinder path, a short cut to the Tuck Shop, filled with reservations about meeting Clarence. But he was so pleasant when he phoned and invited her for coffee that she would have felt boorish refusing; besides, she wants to celebrate. Without ever seeing her marks, she knows she has no reason to worry about scholarships for next year and she is looking forward to returning to the farm until university summer session begins. She is shocked when Clarence appears in ordinary civilian dress. Somehow, he is not nearly as handsome, nor are his eyes as blue.

"So, how were your exams?" she asks when they are seated at a table with Cokes and dishes of ice cream in front of them.

"Only wrote a couple."

"I thought you were dying to graduate and get into journalism."

"I'm dying to get my novel published, that's what I'm dying to do."

"I didn't know you were writing a novel."

"You betcha. Tore it off in a couple of months. I've been too wrapped up in it to bother with a bunch of Mickey Mouse courses."

She concentrates on her ice cream and avoids looking at him.

He lays a brown paper parcel on the table between them. "How about reading it for me?"

She recoils. "Me? Oh, Clarence, what do I know about…?"

"You feel qualified to judge my music, why can't you judge my writing?"

"I don't *judge* your music, I just like it."

"You didn't like my short story," he accuses.

"I didn't ask to read it. You put me on the spot."

"Thanks for the vote of confidence." He springs up, throws five dollars on the table, snatches his novel, and stalks through the crowd, leaving her staring after him.

Remind yourself to run the opposite way whenever you see that character coming, she fumes, rising and slinking out of the Tuck Shop, hoping nobody she knows has been watching.

That evening she has just finished clearing the last table at the cafeteria when George Litt bursts through the door. "Sarah! Your landlady said I'd find you here. I was afraid I'd left it too late and you'd gone home." He drops onto a chair and takes a magazine out of his coat pocket. "Sit down here a minute, will you? I remember mentioning this article to you the first week University started, but…." He breaks off, thumbing through pages until he finds the place he is looking for and slides it, fully open, across the table to her.

She stares at prints of three nudes, all posed by the same model. Something about the face is tantalizingly familiar. In one, the model lazes on a divan, her glowing body warmed by firelight while she looks pensively through a window at a suggestion of bare winter trees. In another, she lies as though asleep in a summer field of ripening barley, and in the third she reaches lazily to pluck an apple in an autumn orchard. The article is headed by the provocative question, "Who owns the fourth nymph that completes Isabel Hindman's year?"

My god! Mother was the model. Sarah stares at the prints, trying to cover her dismay. I can't believe she was ever that beautiful.

"So?" Litt is studying her keenly.

"Mother is Spring. Apple blossoms…. Miss Hindman must have given her the picture sooner than paying her modeling fees. But this article seems to imply that it's worth money."

"About ten or twelve thousand dollars, if your mother wants to part with it. Miss Hindman's work has become very popular since her death."

Sarah can only stare at him. Ten or twelve thousand dollars is more money than her parents have ever seen.

"Take the magazine with you," he says, rising and buttoning his coat. "Show it to your mother. If she decides to sell, let me know. I'll see she gets a fair price."

Sarah reads the article three times. Her hands are shaking when she stands up to leave. I'm afraid to tell Mother. She treats that picture like the crown jewel. But surely for that kind of money… They could have an artesian well, a truck…and electricity in the house. A new lease on life!

SHE HAS BEEN HOME FOR A WEEK. Save for an ongoing niggle with herself as to when and how to broach the subject of Miss Hindman's picture, she has fallen back a century into the routines of her girlhood, into the slow, comforting rhythms of the earth. University seems long ago and far away. She is content to carry water out to Father who is struggling to finish sowing his fields, to ride for stock, and to do chores. At every opportunity, she sketches, swift little scenes to record details of whatever prairie creature she happens to encounter. The days, unusually warm for so early in the season, are sweet with new grass and meadowlark song.

She is sitting on a knoll under the full wash of a May moon; Lindy is grazing nearby, reins trailing. Every sage bush glistens with dew. The night is still, save for the murmured conversations of thousands of migrating birds passing overhead on their way to their northern nesting grounds. She hasn't heard from Clarence. Doesn't expect to, doesn't want to. But she can't forget Jock.

Why couldn't I have been his special somebody? she mourns. Why *couldn't* I have been? Why couldn't he have been just some decent guy? Well, at least I'll never have to lie awake wondering who he's sleeping with when he's away from home. But that doesn't stop my damned heart from hurting.

When she finally rises to catch Lindy and head for home, she realizes that Charlie has not appeared for his weekly visit. "Don't you think it's funny that we haven't seen him, Father?" she frets when she enters the house.

A troubled look crosses his face. "Damned funny.

I've been so busy with spring work I never thought...."

"I'll ride down tomorrow and see what the old badger's up to."

She is heading Lindy down the long river hill the next morning, where, below on the Belly River flats, she can see Charlie's "spread," a mud-and-wattle shack, a couple of slab barns, pole corrals, and a forty-acre alfalfa field. In one of the corrals, she recognizes the three horses Charlie always keeps close to hand. Tar and Buster, his work team, and Spider, the magnificent bay gelding he rides. The moment she appears the horses spot her. They crane their necks over the poles of the corral, jostling each other and calling to her in hoarse, frantic voices.

A shiver passes over her, stirring the hair on her arms. She lifts Lindy to a lope. When she reaches the corral she is horrified. The horses are gaunted, hollow-eyed skeletons, so weak that they stagger against each other when they move. The poles of the corral are chewed to shreds.

Starving! And dying of thirst. What's happened here? Where's Charlie?

When she opens the gate, the horses stagger past her, flounder down the river bank, wade out belly deep in water, still thick with ice pans, bury their noses to the eyes and drink as though they can never drink enough; cough, choke, and drink some more.

Only then does Sarah notice the faint, pervasive odour of death.

She stares for a long time at Charlie's shack, dreaming in the warm May sun. It is all she can do to force herself to go near it. When she turns the doorknob, a dozen bluebottle flies rise from a horrifying thing dressed in Charlie's mackinaw that is lying on the floor. Sarah jerks the door closed and backs off, retching.

An hour later, when she chokes out her story to Father, who has just come in from finishing his fields, he says, "Somehow I ain't surprised. Charlie's pretty stove up from his bronc twisting days and this last while he's been complaining about a bad pain in his chest." He squeezes her shoulder with a work-hardened old hand and shrugs. "Way she goes, Kid. Happens to all of us. Now, if you wanna go round up some of the boys from the Masonic, I'll head over to the graveyard and get started digging Charlie's grave."

The burial is finished; the windswept graveyard is again sweet with the scent of sage and distance and the Masonic has finished its graveside service. Mother and Sarah are the only mourners. Sarah stares at her parents standing beside the mound of raw earth on the far side of the grave.

"Happens to all of us," he says, and they're older than Charlie, Sarah thinks. Fix up that farm, supposing Mother would agree to sell the nude? I must be crazy. Fix it up for what? Old Greedy Guts, the Mormon bishop, to buy for a song?

But they could sell him the land. He needs the Aldridge quarter to complete his empire. He'd give them a fair price just to get his hands on it and he'd haul the old house into Rattlesnake Park to boot. Then they could hold out until they got their old age pensions. If they were careful. Old age pensions! Enough to just keep them from starving after a lifetime of poverty and hard work. When I think of how the Fullers and the Crosses live....

The next morning, after Father has gone about his

chores, she screws up her courage to tell Mother what George Litt has said about the painting's value and to show her the magazine she has kept hidden in her room.

Mother looks for a long time at the picture of the artist, a bespectacled, severe looking woman with grey hair swept into a chignon at the back of her head.

"Dear Isabel," she breathes. "Somehow, I never thought she'd grow old. She was always so full of...." She catches herself, her eyes meeting Sarah's. "I'm not selling the picture, you know. And you're not to tell your father. It's all I have left of Isabel, and it's mine."

Sarah averts her gaze. She has seen exactly the same expression on Avril's face the first time they met after their disastrous encounter at the matinee.

11. RATTLESNAKES' WEDDING

THE GREYHOUND PULLS INTO RATTLE-snake Park at 1:30 in the morning. Sarah stumbles off, half asleep, and waits while the strange driver retrieves her suitcases. As she watches the bus pull away, she mutters, "Why couldn't it have been Jock driving tonight? I thought that if I showed him my ring, he might ask me to send it back. Ask me to give him another chance." But as the ruby tail-lights fade in the distance, she sighs, "Oh, Sarah, who do you think you're kidding?"

With a suitcase dragging from each arm, she heads home to the farm, three miles north. She falls in love all over again with the August prairies, sweet with dusty sage and dreaming under moonlight. Then, with a pang, she realizes how seldom she will see the prairies once she marries Clarence.

WHEN SHE ARRIVED in Edmonton that July evening seven weeks ago, the night before summer session started, she walked across to the Tuck Shop to see if any of her classmates were about.

She had scarcely settled herself at the counter when Clarence climbed onto the stool beside her. "Mind if I join you, Sarah?"

She shrugged. "If you like," she said, noting that his left hand was swathed in bandages.

"Look, I'm sorry I acted like such a horse's ass on that last date. I really am." His expression was troubled, contrite.

She gave a small embarrassed laugh and indicated his bandaged hand. "Looks like you've had an accident?"

"Chopped off two fingers." His voice was trembling.

"Two fingers?" She was horrified. His music – What about his music? He must be dying inside. I'd be dying if I'd been a pianist and one of my hands was mangled so that I couldn't…. "Oh, Clarence, I'm so sorry. I'm so…. It hurts even to *think* about it. How did it happen?"

"Trying to make a buck working construction for the old man."

Tears stung her eyes; she longed to put her arms around him and comfort him. "Well, it won't stop you going into journalism, anyhow," she blurted. "There must be lots of good newspaper reporters out there that just hunt and peck."

"And I intend to be one of them. I'm getting on with *The Edmonton Journal* in September."

She stared at him. "Not finishing your degree?"

His expression was grim. "The old man is none too pleased with me. I gotta get out of that house."

"None too pleased with you? Your father?"

"Figures he can bully me into joining his lousy construction firm now that I'm a lame duck." His face turned obstinate and grim. "Well, there's no bloody way."

She helped him stir sugar into his coffee and waited for him to elaborate, but he did not do so. For a long time he stared at the coffee swirling around inside his cup, then looked at her from under his brows and muttered, "I've given up any damn fool idea I had about making a living out of writing fiction too." He shifted uncomfortably on the stool. "Submitted that novel I wrote to a publisher. Friend of the family, actually." He laughed. "You were smart not to read it. Christ! Did he give me a raking over."

"You think he was wrong?"

"No, I gotta face it. He was right." His snort was wry. "Nothing like a guy getting his nose rubbed in a good hard dose of reality, huh?" He rose, fished some change out of his pocket, tossed it on the counter, and offered her his good hand. "Whew! It's a hot night. Let's wander down to the Legion for a beer."

"I'm not twenty-one until next March. They wouldn't let me in."

"I play piano for the Legion on Saturday night." He winced. "Well – used to play. They're not going to ask questions about your age when you're with me."

As soon as they entered the lounge, they were surrounded by veterans, young and old, all tight, and all brimming with sympathy for Clarence's injury. Beer materialized like magic. Time and again, Sarah listened to accounts of Clarence's accident. "My own damned fault. Ben warned me not to shove ply through that saw with my bare hands, but there I was, trying to save a little time. Somebody hollered at me.

Just that second not watching what I was doing, and…."
He held up his bandaged hand.

"How long before you'll be playing piano for us
again?" somebody named Alfie asked.

After a long second, Clarence muttered, "Alfie, I'm
never gonna really play for anybody, ever again."

Alfie's red face turned scarlet. "Jesus, that's tough,
kid." He shook his head. "I never heard anybody that
could do a job on Scott Joplin's "Maple Leaf Rag" the
way you can – could. Nobody," he muttered, backing
away.

Clarence's face quivered and his eyes shimmered
with tears.

"Why don't we go?" Sarah whispered around the
knot in her own throat.

"Yeah, I…. Yeah, thanks, Sarah."

He walked her back to Mrs. Fuller's through the
almost dark of midnight, while all around them the
air was filled with the cries of nighthawks swooping
on moths fluttering around the street lamps. At the
door, he took her in his arms and kissed her tenderly.
"You're really great, Sarah, you know that? I hope I'll
see a lot of you this summer."

THAT HE DOES. There are long, long walks by the
river, long, long discussions about the meaning of life
and hasty, unsatisfactory lovemaking when they get
the chance.

I guess it's only because he's nervous, Sarah frets, but
two minutes and it's all over. I don't think he knows it
takes a girl time to…. Jock did. He could keep going for
a half an hour and…. Oh, god! When I came…. When
we both came…. She whimpers, remembering the

pulsing, tugging ripples of climax that seemed to leave her very bones flooded with warm milk.

She is both flattered and uneasy because Clarence's sisters, Robin and Sophie, make a fuss entertaining in her honour. Before dinners, served on Royal Doulton and eaten with Georgian silver, scotch whiskey flows freely. Sarah limits herself to two drinks and notes, with some puzzlement, that people in Clarence's family never offer whiskey to him. The sisters call him "baby bro," pet him, inquire solicitously about his chopped off "fin-ders," and mourn that he can no longer play. Sometimes Sarah sees the old man watching him with slightly narrowed eyes, his lipless mouth a tight, straight line.

The dinners are an ordeal. Sarah is never certain which fork to use and, although the Cross's friends are supposed to be the "best people," she is never at ease with them. Their talk is all about money and investments, trips they have taken, or trips they are about to take. Mexico, London, Geneva, and the Greek isles. The woman named Myrna always to turns to Sarah and says in her most syrupy tones, "You really must go there sometime, dear. You'd simply *adore* it."

Fat chance I'll even get to Vancouver, let alone…. That dame gives me the heebie-jeebies. Father's old buddy, Charlie, was my kind of friend. He was only an old half-breed bronc buster, but with Charlie I knew where I stood. With this bunch? Do they like me? Don't like me? Are they making fun of me, or what?

Most Sundays the whole Cross tribe, plus friends and acquaintances, form a caravan to drive out to a beach cottage on Pigeon Lake, the senior Cross's Cadillac leading the way. The elders drink and laze about in the sun while the younger ones swim, sunbathe, and tow each other around on water-skis. Such days seem slothful to Sarah. Even on their summer picnics to the river with Mother and Father when she was a kid, she had had to spend half the day picking saskatoons or chokecherries for canning before she was allowed to swim.

After weekends of sloth, the weekdays are a scramble. There are her classes, scholarship standards to maintain, and every spare moment Clarence at her elbow, attentive, humble and quick to anticipate her slightest wish.

When she senses that he is becoming serious about her she sits, night after night, on the edge of her bed, smoking in the dark and arguing with herself. One side of her says, If I had any sense I'd dump him before this goes any farther. Another side says, But he treats me like a queen and the poor guy's had one tragedy in his life this summer already. Her heart wrenches with pity when she remembers him staring wistfully at the beautiful pianos in the Cross homes. Pianos which, Sophie tells her, were bought so that Clarence could play whenever he visited.

"And how he could *play*," Sarah mutters. "I'll never forget him playing 'Claire de Lune.'" So, she lets things drift.

But now, standing with the prairie night all around her, she asks herself, Was it only because I felt sorry for him when he asked me to marry him? Or was it because his father promised us half the value of a house for a wedding present?

She turns on herself. "No. No, Sarah MacKenzie, it was not!"

Well, okay, so he's not so great in bed, not compared with Jock, but that'll straighten out when we're not sneaking around in hotel rooms or in the back of his dad's car. He'll learn. Guys do learn, don't they?

But how do I explain a wedding date less than a month away to the folks? Oh, God I wish I'd written to them. What'll they think of Clarence? What will Clarence think of *them?*

Once clear of the village, she sets the heavy suitcases down to rest her arms, holds her extravagant diamond up, and squints at in the moonlight.

No girl in Rattlesnake Park has got a ring like this. Mother's never had an engagement ring of any kind. Nor much of anything else. I feel guilty about leaving them, but if Mother sells Miss Hindman's picture and they let the Mormon bishop have the farm, they could retire. Leave the old sandpile to the jackrabbits. And as for Clarence – he is a nice guy and he loves me. What more could a girl ask? For a long time she stands, listening to a pair of coyotes in the far-off distance. Jock MacDonald, that's what. But I'm never going to have him, so....

The following morning, when she gathers the courage to show her parents her ring and the rich ivory satin she's bought to make her wedding dress, Mother bristles with disapproval. "I don't like the sound of this one bit. How are the two of you going to live on the pittance you say *The Edmonton Jounal* pays a cub reporter?"

"There are my scholarships. We'll get by."

"Don't jump into things, my girl. Marry in haste and repent at leisure. Remember, the Church does not countenance divorce. You make your bed, you lie on it."

Sarah does not point out that she has not been near the Church since she was thirteen; that her generation does not bend unquestioningly to its laws. And yet…and yet…no woman of her acquaintance has left a marriage. In her world, such a drastic step is never considered except in the direst of circumstances

"And what about children?"

"Oh, Mother, don't be primitive. Nobody has kids these days unless they want to."

"So I heard Bessie Fetterling say at her wedding shower." Mother trowels on the irony.

Bessie has been married five years. She already has three kids and another on the way.

A baby right away could really throw a monkey wrench into the works. "I have been to see a gynaecologist, Mother. I'm sure he knew what he was doing." I hope to God he knew what he was doing.

Father doesn't say much of anything, but Sarah senses his reservations. This concerns her more than Mother's ranting. Father keeps taking his cap off and punching his fist into the crown, while his forehead washboards up into his hairline. His face is deeply lined and old. "Well, Kid," he mutters, "it's your life, but go into her with your eyes skinned. Marriage can be one hell of a rough road if you make a mistake."

His words rouse niggling doubts that Sarah can't quite face. What I need is to get busy so I don't have time for stupid arguments with myself, she tells herself. I'm going to get started on my wedding dress.

When she checks out Mother's old sewing machine, it knots thread, misses stitches, and drips oil. She decides to borrow Aunt Jane's Singer. While she is hooking the horses to the democrat to go and get the machine, she tries to picture Clarence struggling with the tangle of traces and britching and laughs out loud. "Oh, be fair," she mutters. "You know he's never been around horses." But she can't help but compare him to Jock, who handles those huge buses with an easy grace that borders on insolence. Jock would figure out how to harness a team. Nothing flat. She sighs. Yeah, I know he's a crud with the morals of an alley cat, but.... Well, Clarence will learn. Guys *do* learn.

And who do you think you are, Miss High and Mighty? A little farm kid that was lucky enough to get scholarships for university. You happen to have a good eye, a sense of composition, and a way with a paintbrush. All very well for profs to go on about how talented you are. You're a long way from being an artist. As for supporting yourself? You couldn't, not for years. Maybe never, not unless you could get on the faculty to teach. But now you are dreaming.

She pauses guiltily. Clarence would have a fit if he knew what I was thinking. He says my job is to make a home for us. Thinks I'm kidding when I say I'm going to finish my degree. Well, he'll find out I'm not.

Once started on the wedding dress, she concentrates on it completely. It must be absolutely perfect. She cuts and fits and bastes and stitches and tries to field Mother's questions. "Well, yes, of course Clarence's family are nice to me. Why wouldn't they be?" A nice home? "Well, yes. I guess they're well-to-do. His father owns a construction company." She shies away from mentioning the wedding present.

"A construction company and Clarence is taking a

job as a cub reporter at *The Edmonton Journal?*"

She glowers at Mother, a pair of dressmaker's shears in one hand and yards of satin cascading to the floor in the other. "Moth-er, the poor guy hates construction and I told you what happened to his hand."

"Presumably he wouldn't have to work with a pick and shovel."

"Why should he have to work at construction at all if he doesn't want to?"

Mother stares at her from beneath raised brows, sighs gustily, and begins clattering the cream separator together.

Sarah hands tremble as she bastes piping into the waist of the wedding dress. She stabs herself with a needle. As she waits for the bright blood to stop welling, she tries to divert her misgivings by admiring the gussets set into the underarms.

That old girl that taught us Home Economics in high school used to say, "The dressmaker that has mastered the gusset is on top of her craft." Maybe I should be designing clothes instead of struggling with easels and oils. People always have to dress; they don't have to buy paintings. But I'd need a sewing machine and I'd need to advertise and rent a work space. I already own the easel and the oils for painting.

Going to be a clutter, me painting in that poky little apartment we rented until we find a house. Place'll stink of turpentine and Clarence hates it. Well, he'll just have to get used to it. He'll change his tune if I sell a few paintings. God knows, we'll need the money.

Her wedding dress takes a week of hard work, but when it's finished it's beautiful and it fits her perfectly.

"Clarence's sisters were surprised when I told them I was going to make my own wedding dress, but I'll bet neither of them had one nicer than mine," she tells Mother as she turns to admire herself in the mirror.

"No, indeed. That's the kind of dress that's laid away in tissue papers and kept for daughters to wear at *their* weddings," Mother says wistfully, as she goes to study the flyspecked Thomas Trading Company calendar on the wall beside the sewing machine. "You must be getting excited."

Sarah's breath catches. Where did the time go? Tomorrow night Clarence is coming to meet the folks.

She glances about the old farmhouse that is little better than a glorified shack and is ashamed of it. The place always has a faint odour of sour milk, and of Father's stinking pipes. Poorly fitting screens do little to keep out flies and in the living room there is a broken window covered by a piece of cardboard. Father has never got around to fixing it.

What was I thinking of to invite Clarence here? Oh, Sarah, don't be dumb. If you're going to marry him, he's *got* to see it, sooner or later.

Rattlesnake Park has been long asleep the following night when Sarah stands outside the little restaurant-depot waiting for the bus. When it pulls to a stop and the driver steps out, Sarah finds herself face to face with Jock.

"Well, Monkey Face!" He flicks the end of her nose playfully with his forefinger and grins, the light catching that bit of gold in his front teeth, "Wondered when you were gonna show up."

Clarence is halfway down the bus steps with his suitcase in his hand. "Keep your paws off my fiancée, MacDonald."

"Fiancée?" As alert as a weasel, Jock's eyes snap from Sarah to Clarence and back again. A slow, sardonic grin spreads across his face. "Well, I'll be damned. You learn something every day."

Sarah feels a trifle hysterical. "You two know each other?"

"Old war buddies. Good old Goose Bay, eh, Cross?" Jock examines the two of them with an expression of cool amusement before he scampers back up into the bus. "Good luck, Monkey Face." The door closes, the air brakes release, and the bus is gone.

"Where does MacDonald get off calling you Monkey Face?"

"Oh, I've ridden Greyhound back and forth to university. You get to know the drivers."

"How well do you know MacDonald?"

"Well enough so that we kid each other a little, that's all." She manages to sound offhand, but she is grateful for the darkness that covers her expression. "C'mon, grab your suitcase. The democrat's just around the corner."

"Democrat?"

"I told you, the folks don't own a car."

He laughs. "This'll be something to tell the grandchildren. The week I spent with Grandma on the farm."

Suddenly, she is angry enough to drown him. "I warned you, the farm's nothing but an old sandpile and there's nothing to do there beyond the usual round of chores. No electricity, no running water, and the bathroom's a stinking biffy out in the yard."

"Oh, hey, Sarah, baby, if you can stand it, so can I."

We'll see, Clarence, baby, we'll see. But if you turn up your nose....

But to her surprise, he seems delighted with the farm. He treats it all like a huge adventure, couldn't be sweeter. Mother is entirely captivated, particularly since almost the first thing his eye lights on is Miss Hindman's little nude.

"Mrs. MacKenzie, that is a little treasure. I don't recognize the artist, but I was dragged around to enough galleries when I was a kid to know something good when I see it. My mother has some pretty nice paintings, but nothing of that quality."

Just look at Mother's face. Talk about saying the right thing.

Father spends a lot of time fiddling with his pipe and his tobacco pouch. He is watchful and polite with Clarence.

The following afternoon Sarah takes Clarence down into the pasture to meet Lindy Lou. "Isn't she beautiful? Gentle as a lamb with plenty of Arab spunk. I'll miss her something awful when I have to leave her, but I know she'll be happy here running with the range horses," she says as the mare comes to her, whinnying softly and rooting at her with her nose. "Okay, baby, here's your treat." She takes a handful of chop from her pocket and allows the mare to lick the last morsel from her palm and from between her fingers.

Clarence touches the mare's neck gingerly. "Pretty, all right."

"Have you ever ridden a horse?"

"Only Shetland ponies a guy was renting for rides

at the Edmonton Exhibition. I don't think riding is my thing."

When the two of them leave the horses and stroll away, hand in hand over the autumn prairie, they are arrested by the sharp, warning buzz of a rattlesnake.

"Look at him!" Sarah exclaims. "All coiled, loaded for bear, and his old tail going a mile a minute. Kind of beautiful, isn't he, with all those diamonds parading down his –"

"C'mon, Sarah! Let's get away from the thing." Clarence's voice is trembling and his face is white.

"He wouldn't hurt us unless we were silly enough to tease him."

"I can't stand snakes. When I was a little kid, Ben used to catch me and tie garter snakes around my neck."

"Ben did? He's ten years older than you are! Where was your mother?"

"Too busy licking the last wound the old boy'd inflicted on her to bother with me. And the girls were too busy fighting with each other."

"Clarence, that's –"

"I'd just as well tell you right now, my dad and I had a real knock-'em-down-drag-'em-out row just before I came down here."

"A row? What about?"

"Figured he had me under his thumb, finally. No son of his was living on some girl's scholarships and the starvation wages they pay a cub reporter. He was gonna take me into the firm. Make it Cross, Cross, Cross, and Associates."

"But would it be so awful, working for the firm, Clarence?"

"I'd sooner be dumped into a nest of rattlesnakes

than to be dumped into that goddamned firm. The way Ben and those brothers-in-law have to brown-nose and toady to the old bastard would turn your stomach."

"But the girls are always saying what a close-knit family —"

"Close-knit? Shit!"

"Oh, Clarence, I'm so —"

"The old man told me I wouldn't last two years in the newspaper game, nor in any other game either." He breaks off, his face twitching with hurt. "Look, I'm not telling you this to make you feel sorry for me; I'm trying to tell you that from here on in we're pretty well on our own. Well, except for the house."

"That's more than most young couples ever have, Clarence. I'm sorry you're on the outs with your family, but to tell you the truth, I'm never comfortable with the way those girls crowd me into corners."

"There's something else you'd better understand, Sarah. It's not going to be long until my split with the family is going to be all *your* fault."

"My fault?"

He shrugs. "That's just the way they operate."

SARAH LIES AWAKE, while outside the crickets of August fill the night with their tuneless love songs. The old farmhouse has no such luxury as a spare room. Clarence is asleep on the living room couch, next to Mother and Father's bedroom. Sarah is drifting towards sleep when a howl rips the darkness. Then Father's voice, "What the hell...?"

Sarah rushes barefoot through the house and into the living room. "Clarence! What on earth...?"

Her eyes, keenly adjusted to the dark, behold him, crouched on the edge of the couch like a trapped and terrified wild thing, pointing to a fold in the blanket. "Snake! Son of a bitch! See him?"

She finds the kerosene lamp and a match to light it. "There's no snake, Clarence. You're dreaming. Wake up."

He slowly comes back to himself while Sarah, along with Mother and Father, stare at him.

"Jesus! Sorry for the snafu. Musta been a nightmare. I could have sworn that fold in the blanket was a snake lying right across my chest."

"Are you all right now?"

"Yeah, sure. Just go back to bed."

Sarah lies awake a long, long time, staring into the darkness.

WHEN UNCLE CECIL and Aunt Frances come to call, Clarence is charming. He bows over Aunt Frances's hand and holds chairs for her at the table, asks Uncle Cecil's opinions about the way the country is being governed, and listens solicitously to his answers. When they rise to leave, Uncle Cecil says, "Prince of a fella you got there, Tara Tenzie. You better take care of him. They don't come along every day."

Implying, of course, that I'm lucky to catch any fellow. But she smiles sweetly and says, "Oh, I think we can manage to take care of each other, Uncle Cecil."

When Sarah returns Aunt Jane's sewing machine, Clarence comes along. Aunt Jane, offhand and rough-tongued, offers them tea in cracked mugs. Sarah knows she disapproves of Clarence. She is not surprised. Aunt Jane has been a life-long Cassandra wherever Sarah has been concerned.

The day finally comes when Sarah sees Clarence onto a Greyhound bus bound for Edmonton. He embarrasses her by kissing her again and again and declaring that he can't wait until their wedding day while Luke Raisbone and Jimmy O'Connor stand by, nudging each other and grinning.

When the bus pulls out, Sarah stares at it growing smaller and smaller in the prairie distance. She feels curiously light and free, like a kid with a whole summer holiday stretching ahead.

THAT AFTERNOON SHE RIDES LINDY down to the bluffs above the confluence of the Belly and the Bow, where they join to form the South Saskatchewan. She wants to see the rocks that mark the old tipi circles again and wonder at the mysterious giant outlined on the prairie there in stones. She rides home through starlight, through air pungent with sage and alive with songs of coyotes in the hills. She is prairie-drunk, desperate to store it all within herself. On a night when there is no moon, she sits on a knoll watching northern lights gathering at the zenith like stealthy ghosts. Suddenly they come to life, dancing gauze, silver, rose, and apple green, sweeping around her.

Like the wedding veils of ghosts.

She mounts her horse and flees.

The day before she has to catch the bus for Calgary, she comes upon a flock of meadowlarks staging for migration. The sweet carols of their springtime now are gone; their single note is a questing whistle, filled with unease.

She seeks out the mighty lone poplar that she used

to pass on her way to school, stands with one hand against its trunk and whispers, "It'll be all right. I'm going to *make* it all right." But tears spring to her eyes and she leans her head against the rough bark. I can't back out now. I can't. I'd look like such a fool.

Two days later she is standing in front of the full-length mirror in a hotel room while Mother twitters around her, admiring the wedding dress and fussing with the veil.

My wedding dress is beautiful, I am beautiful, and my life with Clarence is going to be fine, Sarah rattles off in her head. And is still rattling as she marches down the aisle on Father's arm to join Clarence at the altar.

Outside, the sun throbs towards its setting and, beyond the city, the prairie night beckons. Beckons…. Her heart stutters and, for the briefest moment, she toys with the notion of tearing away down the aisle and out of the church with the wedding dress hiked above her knees. Instead, she looks up to smile into Clarence's face.

He stares straight ahead, eyes blinking rapidly.

She starts to tremble. She doesn't remember repeating anything the priest says, but she knows she must have. She is staring at a thin gold band on the third finger of her left hand. She starts when the nervous, gawky stranger standing beside her bends to give her a self-conscious peck on the lips.

They are on the train, headed for a week's honeymoon in Banff, when he says, "I never told you. I didn't get that job as a reporter. They're going to start me as a proofreader."

"Oh? What's a proofreader?"

"Thought everybody knew that. It's the fellow that checks copy to catch stupid mistakes. There's lots of guys that do it for a living."

She doesn't quite dare ask him what his wages will be. "But they *will* give you a chance as a reporter, won't they?"

"What if they don't?" It is a flat, hostile challenge.

She doesn't answer.

Once in the hotel room, he takes a mickey out of his suitcase, pours a hefty dollop into each of two waterglasses, tops them with water, and hands one to Sarah.

He raises his glass. "Mrs. Clarence Cross!"

Does she imagine it or is his tone slightly mocking? A trifle piqued, she raises her own glass, "Mr. Clarence Cross."

"Okay, kid, bottoms up." He gulps the contents of the glass in six huge swallows, and offers her a prim, old-maidish kiss.

She throws her arms around him. "Uh-uh. Let's kiss for real." The moment her tongue touches his lips, he recoils as if he'd been bitten. "Sarah! That's dirty stuff."

"Love isn't dirty. Love is wonderful. Let's enjoy." She is unbuttoning his shirt and running her hands over his bare chest.

"Seems to me you know an awful lot about it for a new bride."

The flame of hot desire that was rising in her flickers and wavers. "Meaning what?"

He shrugs one shoulder. "Nothing, but –"

She backs away, staring at him. "Clarence!"

"Oh, hey, I didn't mean…. Like you say, let's enjoy."

And he begins undressing, laying his clothes fussily over the chair.

When Sarah comes out of the bathroom, he is already in bed, cuddled down in flannelette pyjamas. He covers his eyes against her nakedness. "Sarah, you hussy, you're going to catch cold."

"No, I'm not and neither are you. Off with 'em." And she begins stripping off the pyjamas while he lies there, giggling helplessly.

He has scarcely entered her when he comes. "Oh! Jesus. Sorry about that, wifey. The whiskey's getting to me. I should have known better than to…." And he collapses on top of her, dead asleep.

DAWN CREEPS INTO THE ROOM. A movement beside her starts her awake. She finds herself looking into the face of a wild creature crouched on one corner of the bed, staring at her with an expression of absolute terror. Years later, she will still wonder whether he had been asleep or whether he had been awake.

"Clarence, you're dreaming. It's all right." She draws his head down against her shoulder. He snuggles there, not speaking, not moving, while she stares into the strengthening dawn.

PART TWO: AGE

12. VOYAGE TO THE FAROES

SARAH WAKENS, FEELING.... SHE SNORTS. At eighty, she can't be quite certain how she feels. And she *is* eighty. Today. Her granddaughter, Beth, has promised to join her at the lodge for supper. Promised to bring toffees – Sarah's favorite fruit, as she likes to joke. These days she eats toffee and candy kisses without guilt. And yearns for Beth's real kisses.

She hauls herself to a sitting position, cursing her slowness, cursing burrs grinding in her joints. "Get up you damned old cow. Up! That young attendant, what's-her-name, will be in here nagging in a minute."

A voice in the corridor. Sarah, trying to hurry, reaches for clothes scattered over the chair.

Clean panties. Nice. Now, to find my bra. Why do these damn fools insist that I take off my bra at night? I've slept in a bra all my....

She pauses, seeking a dream that lingers tantalizingly, just on the edge of consciousness, while she peers at a stretched artist's canvas resting on an easel in one corner of her heavily-curtained room. Two weeks ago, she had prepared the canvas, but she cannot seem to start the painting.

"What I want to paint is in that dream. I'm sure of it," she mutters. "If only I could remember…."

A chilling thought flits through her mind. Or could it be that I've lost my skills?

"No." She heaves herself from the bed to the chair. "Nothing doing. I may be a little slow, but…. One of these days…."

Maybe I should tell Beth, talk about the dream a bit. That might help me remember. But she might laugh at me. She's not the kind that's interested in dreams.

Beth. Named for my mother. It seems like only yesterday that I invited her out to the West Coast for a month's visit, and she's been here thirteen…? No, fourteen years.

The day when Sarah had decided to invite Beth to visit had been an eventful one in a series of uneventful days, of uneventful years, really. Since her retirement from the University of Alberta, there had been her studio, some dealings with her agent, and aside from a few newly-made casual friends, nothing but the sea and the sky, her little house and her garden.

❦

THERE HAD BEEN RAIN THAT YEAR, just before Christmas, a week-long downpour. Fir branches sagged, streets ran rivers, but Sarah had come to like the West Coast climate. When she entered the shopping mall, another elderly woman was shaking out an umbrella. "Beastly country!"

Sarah was amused.

What you need is an honest-to-God old Alberta blizzard, sister. Something to howl about, she thought, as she hobbled towards the bank to cash her pension cheque.

The line-up inside the bank was so long it doubled back on itself. Coats smelled of wet wool and people fidgeted, studying their pay cheques, lips moving involuntarily. Sarah banked her own cheque, kept back twenty dollars to do her for the holiday, and headed back out into the mall. At the door of the expensive jewelry shop where she had bought Beth's watch, she hesitated.

Cost me a penny or two, that watch. She frowned. Did it have a second hand or not? I'm sure it did, but.... Well, there was another exactly like it in the store, so....

The clerk smirked and batted her eyelashes. "That watch? Don't you remember, dear? I sold you one exactly like it a couple of weeks ago. You had me send it to your granddaughter in Halifax."

"Never know, *sweetie*. I just might want that one for myself."

The clerk did have the grace to blush, and Sarah was pleased to see that the watch had a second hand, but the incident had made her a trifle unsure of herself.

Just outside the jewelry shop, she almost collided with an old man. To her amazement, she realized it was her ex-husband's brother, Ben. She hadn't seen him since the night she walked out on the "lovin' cup" twenty years before. He looked lost now, out of his element, cranky.

Doesn't recognize me. Should I speak to him? Well, why not?

When she called to him, he stopped and looked at her with a puzzled expression.

"Ben, it's me. Sarah."

He blinked at her. "Sarah? What're you doing in Nanaimo?"

"I retired here after I left the university in 1986."

"Five years ago? Be damned." He backed away, wiping one corner of his mouth with the back of his hand.

"More to the point, what are you doing here?"

"Passing through. Maggie wanted to do something different this Christmas, being as none of the kids were coming home, so she's dragging me out to drown at this place they call Long Beach on the Pacific side of the island."

"Maggie's in the mall, then?"

"Went to get her hair done or her toenails painted or some damn thing." He was evasive, uneasy; she knew he wanted to escape.

"Care for a cup of coffee?" She regretted the invitation before the words were out of her mouth.

Seated at the small table with cups of hot coffee in front of them, they were both awkward and embarrassed. Ben raised his cup in a mock toast. "Merry Christmas."

Well, at least you don't try to pretend that it's a "lovin' cup" these days, do you, Ben? she thought as the kiosk faded into background and she was helplessly awash in a time, more than twenty years ago, when her world had come apart.

It was a week after her son's funeral…. Her beautiful, talented Josh. She was working in the studio he had set up for her in the new duplex, forcing herself to struggle with a surreal concept that she planned to use with her senior class when university session started the following week. The exercise was so demanding that it mercifully blotted out thought.

At a step behind her, she turned to find Alan, her twenty-year-old, hesitating in the doorway. She had been worrying about him. He was not dealing well with his younger brother's death. She wanted to go to him, to put her arms around him and hug him, but Alan was not the hugging kind. He never had been, even when he was a little boy.

"Not working today, Alan? Are you all right? You're very pale."

"Mom, I've got something to show you. Come out to the street."

When she rounded the corner of the duplex, she saw a new red Mustang parked at the curb.

"Blew every cent in my bank account. I've never *been* anywhere, Mom. Josh had never been anywhere either, and now he's…. I'm heading out, Mom. I *gotta*. I'm heading out."

"Heading out? Where?"

"Just – heading out. Anywhere. I dunno. I can always get on with some city's engineering crew if I'm broke. Old Steve gave me a real good recommendation. I'll write, Mom. I'll send post cards." He flung his arms around her, gave her a hasty smack on the cheek, then raced for the car. Before she could collect her wits to call to him, the Mustang had roared around a curve in the street and was gone.

"Just like that?" she cried. "No warning. No –" Then she stopped herself. "Well, let's not make a *thing* of it, Sarah. It's not as though *he's* dead."

She heard the slight rustle of the venetian blind behind her and turned to see Clarence, peering through a crack between the slats.

That stupid kid never told his father he was leaving! As though Clarence can't think of enough reasons to sit around, nursing that broken thumb and feeling sorry for himself….

She cleared the steps in two jumps and yanked the door open. Clarence stared at her, bags beneath his eyes, a four-day growth of grey bristles on his chin. Behind him, Rubinstein was playing *The Appassionata* on the stereo. "Did Alan borrow somebody's car, Sarah?"

"No. Alan bought the car and Alan's taken off. Where, I don't know, and I don't think he does."

"Taken off? Taken *off*? And he never even told me good-bye?"

"He barely told *me* good-bye." She caught a whiff of his cheesy, unwashed flesh. "When did you last bathe and shave?"

He held up the thumb wrapped in a dirty grey bandage. "I don't know if I'm supposed to get this wet."

"Not supposed to get it wet! It's a broken bone, not a wound. Did you go and have it X-rayed like you were supposed to?"

"Well, no, I –"

"Work a little harder at it, why don't you, Clarence. You might be able to stretch that broken thumb into a month when you squat around here doing nothing and feeling sorry for yourself."

"Sarah, you don't know –"

"Two days ago you promised to get hold of Denny Grogan's wife and get this bloody duplex on the market. Have you done it? No, I'll bet you haven't."

"Sarah, I just feel –"

"Well, I 'just feel' too. Believe it or not. You'd have a little less time to *feel* if you got off your ass. Try painting that pigsty of a suite downstairs that Eric left after we threw him out. Or are you waiting for me to do that too?" She marched down the corridor into her studio and slammed the door so hard that she could hear dishes tinkle far away in the kitchen. She worked until the light was gone, concentrating fiercely to keep from thinking. When she quit, she became aware of muffled footsteps passing her studio, up the corridor and down the corridor again.

She opened the door. Clarence brushed past her as though he did not see her. "Didn't even say good-bye," he muttered. "Didn't even say good-bye."

God! He acts like he's.... What if he...? I shouldn't have jumped him. She followed him to the living room.

"Look, Clarence, Alan's only a kid, and he's had a terrible shock too. He's probably not thinking straight. He'll be back."

Clarence didn't even glance at her. "Didn't even say good-bye," he muttered, pacing exactly around the outside perimeter of the living room rug, down the corridor and back again, staring straight ahead, with bulging, unblinking eyes.

"Clarence, I'm sorry I blew up. Come and sit down. I'll get us a cup of –"

When she tried to take his arm, he warded her off with the same gesture he had used to ward off the girl who had broken his thumb.

Apprehension knotted her solar plexus. "Clarence, please. I'll get you a tranquilizer. You're —"

He gave no sign of having heard as he took up his pacing and muttering again.

THE FAMILY DOCTOR was an old friend. "Get him over to emergency, Sarah. I'll meet you there. Sounds like we'd better pop him into hospital for a few days and keep an eye on him."

When the doctor met her anxious questions out in the hospital corridor after Clarence had been admitted, he said, "Too early to tell. Sometimes people snap out of these things in a few days, and sometimes…." He left it on a shrug. "Been coming for a long time, I think. Some of us deal better with stress than others. You're one of the lucky ones."

ONE OF THE LUCKY ONES, EH? You didn't know I swallowed a handful of 392s that night. Never expected to wake up. But I did. Brown puke — I don't know where it all came from. For days I could touch my skin and not feel the touch. I could see; I could hear; I could think; I could even drive. And God knows, I could hurt. So what do you do with that much pain? What else but work? Teach all day, then crawl into my studio and paint until….

"Interpreter of the prairie soul," the critics said. "Bold imagination." "Startling use of colour." "Deeply moving and disturbing concepts." "Powerful images, painful in their intensity." "Fire and ice of the prairie spirit."

Bullshit!

They never saw the canvasses I slashed with an

Exacto knife; never heard me curse while I sat alone in the dark and lit one cigarette from the butt of another. Never saw me stinko. But never so stinko that I didn't have one ear out for the phone, in case Alan called.

THAT SHE HAD EVEN ENTERED the exhibition where her work won such praise was something of a fluke. A friend of hers, Anne Cameron, was mounting an exhibition; she needed Sarah's work to complement her own.

As the two of them were removing the few canvasses that had not sold, after the exhibition closed, Anne said, "Wow! Was *that* an exhibition, or what?"

"I hardly remember what I entered. The canvasses were barely dry, but the money will come in handy. All new furniture for the bungalow I settled on. A surprise for Clarence when he gets out of hospital."

"How is he?"

"They say he'll be home by Christmas." She couldn't stop herself from going stiff and awkward when Clarence was mentioned. He was so flaccid, so indifferent.

She'd put the duplex up for sale the day after he'd gone into the hospital. To her great relief, the real estate agent brought her a decent offer two weeks after the place went on the market.

When she went to the hospital to ask Clarence to sign his consent to the sale, she found him toying with the piano in the mental patients' lounge, crippling through a little of Bach's *Goldberg Variations*. Ordinarily, he never touched a piano when anybody he knew could hear him. When Sarah spoke to him, he sprang away from the instrument as though she'd caught him in an indecent act, turned and shuffled away down the corridor to his room.

She followed him diffidently, sat on the edge of the chair, and told him about the offer on the duplex, while he lay on his bed with his hands behind his head, staring at the ceiling, his face as impassive as stone.

"Clarence, you…you have to sign the papers."

He snatched the pen from her and scribbled his name without even reading the document. When she began telling him about the bungalow that she'd found, trying to make it sound attractive, which indeed it was, he rolled over on his side with his back towards her and muttered, "Do what you want."

As Sarah closed the van door on her three unsold paintings, Anne said, "You know what we need, Kid? A good stiff drink. C'mon."

"Can I take a raincheck? I make a point of being home at suppertime, in case – well, in case Alan phones."

"How long since he's been gone?"

"Three months."

Anne patted her shoulder, her expression both embarrassed and troubled. "Oh, I think he'll phone. Probably any day now."

You don't think any such a damned thing. You think he's gone for good and I'm beginning to think so too.

She headed for home through a bitter early December night, as cold and shiny as the "steelies" the boys used to play marbles with when she was a kid at school. She put her van in the garage, plugged in the block heater, and let herself into the new bungalow.

Not a patch on our old house, she thought, but it's paid for and there's a dandy room for my studio. Clarence's family will turn up their noses, of course, but they won't be around often, and I don't care what they think.

She fished a can of beef stew out of the cupboard, opened it, and was about to put it on to heat when the phone rang.

Alan? She was annoyed to hear her voice pitch upward with anxiety when she picked up the receiver. "Yes?"

"Mom?"

For a moment she didn't answer. Relief weakened her knees; she eased herself onto the padded bench beside the breakfast nook.

"Mom?"

"Alan! Are you all right? You're not in trouble of some kind, are you?"

"Trouble? Oh, gosh, no. I'm great."

"Where are you then, if you're so great? That is, if it's fair to ask."

He giggled nervously. "Oh, jeez! I guess I should have phoned, eh? I just kept putting it off."

Shut up, Sarah. Don't say something you'll regret.

"Hang onto your hat, Mom. I've got some news."

"Let me guess. You've been elected Prime Minister and your wife has just presented you with twins."

She could hear him gulp. "Well, not quite. But Mandy and I got married this afternoon."

"Look, Alan, is this your idea of a joke? Who is Mandy and where the hell are you?"

"Halifax."

"Halifax?"

"Yeah. Got on with the city here and I'm doing good. I rented a room from Mandy's mom and…well…." Muffled giggles and the sound of the receiver being jostled, then Alan, "I wanted her to say hello, but she's too shy." More scuffles and giggles, then, "So, how are you getting along, Mom? How's Dad?"

She took a deep breath, fighting for calm. "Things are more or less under control at the moment. If you want to send me your address, I'll write and tell you about it sometime." As she hung up the receiver, she could still hear him calling her name.

THE NIGHT BEFORE CLARENCE was to be discharged from hospital Sarah was trimming the Christmas tree. She was standing with the little angel that had always graced the tree's top spike in her hand when the phone rang.

"Sarah!"

Clarence's older sister. "Oh, hello, Sophie." She managed to keep her voice neutral, pleasant.

"Clarence says he's going to be discharged. You naughty girl, you never told us."

"Well, I…I suppose I should have," she floundered, "but…."

"Never mind. Have we got a surprise for you."

The back of Sarah's neck tightened. "Oh?"

"The whole family is meeting for a 'lovin' cup' tomorrow night to welcome Clarence home. We've got a suite reserved at the MacDonald. Caterers, the whole bit laid on, so you don't have to do a thing but deck yourself out in your best bib and tucker and appear with a smile on your face."

For a moment, Sarah couldn't find her voice. "I'm

sure you mean well, Sophie, but Clarence will have to be kept very quiet. With the medications he is on, I've had strict orders not to let him touch liquor. I haven't got a drop in the house so that he won't be tempted."

"That's no reason the rest of us can't have a little drinky-poo."

"If you all have a drinky-poo, he'll want his share. No liquor, or we don't go."

"Well, if those are the conditions," Sophie sniffed. "We'll expect you, dressed for dinner, at seven."

When Sarah and Clarence walked into the suite of rooms the Crosses had hired for the evening, the place was overflowing with relatives and near relatives of the clan. Although there was no liquor in sight, it was plain they had all been drinking. The whole family descended on Clarence with hugs, kisses, and repeated endlessly what a heartbreak it must have been for a guy to lose a son, and then, on top of everything else, to have the other one just walk out of his life. It was enough to send *anybody* around the bend, by God, and that's the truth.

Some time later, Robin cornered Sarah. "Say, I wanted to ask you – I read something in one of those publications from Alberta Culture that somebody with your name had been exhibiting pictures with that Anne Cameron that's supposed to be the best artist in Alberta. That wouldn't be you, would it?" Her tone implied the great unlikeliness of such a possibility.

"Why wouldn't it be me?"

"But they were talking about real far-out stuff that was selling for thousands of dollars."

"Oh! Some of it."

Robin's eyes widened. "Well, gee, I wish you'd invited us to the show. We don't mind bragging that we've got somebody famous in the family."

"One good exhibition doesn't make me famous."

"But you're going to quit teaching now, aren't you?"

"I like a steady pay cheque. Exhibitions are a some-time thing."

"Ah, let Clarence support you. I've never worked a day in my life."

Doesn't she know that Clarence will be lucky to get a job as a janitor now? Doesn't she know it's *me* that supports *him*, and that I have done for years?

While she was trying to think of a tactful way of escaping Robin's clutches, she realized that she hadn't seen Clarence for some time. "Do you know where Clarence is, Robin?"

"Ben said that he was going to get him alone so that they could have a little heart-to-heart."

Clarence and Ben having a heart-to-heart? That's one for the books.

Fifteen minutes went by. Sarah was becoming uneasy, suspicious. She interrupted a long tale that Sophie was telling about how she had acquired the fashionable evening gown she was wearing, by saying, "I'm concerned about Clarence, Sophie. Do you know where he is?"

"Just talking in Ben and Maggie's private lounge." There was something smug in her tone, something that indicated that she knew something that Sarah didn't.

"I'd better check on him. It's time for his medication."

She found Clarence and Ben sitting side by side on

an elegant tapestry sofa, each holding an empty whiskey glass. Ben looked up at her with the defiant expression of a street urchin. Clarence wavered unsteadily and blinked at her with reddened eyes.

She turned on Ben. "You've been feeding him whiskey!"

"Coupla little drinks. Hell!"

"A 'coupla little drinks' could send him back to the hospital."

Clarence was on his feet staggering towards her. "Loosen up, old woman. C'mon, Ben, us guys are gonna have a little party. Yaa-hoo!"

"Ben, you'll have to help me get him home."

"Home? Jeez, Sarah, the guy's just having a little fun. No harm. Long as he doesn't drink any more."

Sarah stood by, outraged and helpless while Clarence staggered from woman to woman, making lewd advances, and rampaged among the men, making threatening gestures and flinging every indignity or slight he thought he'd ever suffered back into their faces.

"Look, Ben, we've got to get him home, and you'll have to stay with him until he settles down," Sarah insisted. "If he doesn't, we'll have to take him back to the –"

"Back to the booby hatch?" Clarence snarled. "You go to hell, you castrating bitch. Big artist these days, eh? Hot stuff. Selling real estate – buying real estate. Come up in the world a step or two, haven't you? First time I brought you home you didn't know which fork to use at the dinner table, so don't try throwing your weight around now."

The room fell silent, rigid with anticipation.

Maggie hid a titter behind her hand; the brothers-in-law studied their toes and smirked; Robin, Ben, and Sophie stared at Sarah with bright-eyed malice. Clarence gagged, and was sick all over a Persian rug.

Sarah stepped away from the mess. The company shimmered before her through a red haze of rage. She stifled an urge to pitch the Waterford goblet in her hand through the plate glass mirror above the mantelpiece. But when she spoke, she was amazed at how quiet she sounded. "Well, all right, you Crosses, that about does it. I've packed your 'baby bro' on my back for twenty-five years. Now you can take over."

Clarence started to yell. She could still hear him yelling as she checked her pockets for car keys and wallet, zipped her down-filled coat, and waited in the corridor for the elevator.

Half an hour later, she was pushing two suitcases out of the door of the little bungalow. As she paused on the steps, dragging the clean, cold fire of a -32 degree night into her lungs, she turned and cast her eyes back over the house. "There you go, Clarence, baby. It's *all* yours. I don't give a damn what you do with it."

WHILE ANOTHER SCHOOL BAND took up its place in the mall, and made a ragged start on "Frosty the Snowman," Ben said, "I wish Maggie'd get a move on. They tell me that road west of Port Alberni's a windy bugger. I wanna get over it before dark."

"It's not an Alberta highway, but it's safe enough. Just slow. You haven't told me any news about the family."

"Nothing to tell. Same old sixes and sevens."

Something his mother used to say when she wanted to be evasive. He is a great deal like her now, even down to that nervous, mirthless laugh.

"The last time I heard of Clarence he was working at some all-night gas station out on the Edmonton Trail," she ventured. "He surely wouldn't be there now?"

"Nope."

"You haven't seen him lately?"

His face was beaky, mean. "Not lately. He died last year around Christmas time."

The little kiosk, the people in it, and the coffee-cult paraphernalia lining the walls, wavered for a moment. "I had no idea."

"Nobody had your address, so…."

"What would have been the point of telling me?"

"Well, you'd have surely come for the poor bugger's funeral?"

She considered for a moment and then said, flatly and truthfully, "No."

Ben looked shocked.

What did he expect? That I would burst into tears? Say I was sorry? Not that I blame Clarence. Not any more. Things just…happen. He was probably more sinned against than sinning. I could beg that kind of quarter for myself. If I were the begging kind.

She took a careful sip from her cup and stared at people rushing past in the concourse. They were rain-soaked, miserable. Tired kids, hauled along by impatient mothers loaded down with shopping bags, howled with dreary hopeless voices. The mall was garish. Lights of all colours blinked and winked and flashed. Christmas trees glittered with gewgaws and tinsel. A band from some high school played "Rudolf, the Red-Nosed Reindeer." Sarah had heard it on the radio fifteen times that day while she'd been working in her studio. From time to time, some guy stopped, spread his arms and hugged another, exclaiming, "How are yuh, you old bugger? Merry Christmas." They came out of the clinch, made vague remarks about getting together over the holidays, shuffled their feet and passed on, faces again taking on an anxious, harried expression.

Worrying already about January bills. Well, no more of that for me. A roasted chicken breast, a salad, a couple of beers, and, aside from cards from Beth and Alan, that's Christmas.

She rose and dropped three dollars on the table. "Have a pleasant time out at Long Beach, Ben. I hope you brought your rain gear. The ocean is wonderful when it storms."

As she moved away, she noticed he was looking after her sourly, probably wondering if she had been somehow making fun of him.

THE CAR WAS FOGGED UP INSIDE. Rain sluiced down the windshield so fast the wipers would hardly clear it.

I should go home, she thought, but the sea *is* wonderful when it storms. I'm going down by the beach and listen to the waves.

When she rolled down the window, mist dewed her face. Somewhere out on the strait a ship was bawling in the fog. Gulls at the edge of the sea hopped breakers and bleated protests. Waves crashed, hissed and retreated, crashed, hissed and retreated.

Both the kids – gone. And Clarence – what a thing.

Well Alan isn't really *gone*, but I see him so seldom. Once when Beth was born. That was three years after he'd left home. Then again when Beth was five. Strange little sly thing with her big grey eyes.

I'd planned to stay in Halifax a month that time, she remembered, but Mandy and I lasted exactly one week. I couldn't see myself going back to Edmonton after I'd traveled all that way, so I headed for Newfoundland.

The Rock. What a place! Those seas, and the humpbacked whales I watched from the cliffs. Sea birds, and the great icebergs, drifting, deadly. And so beautiful.

That was the time I knew that sometime I wanted to live beside the sea. But not in Newfoundland. Newfoundland in July is one thing; Newfoundland in February is another, and I figured that a continent between me and Mandy would be just about right.

Well, I never saw her again, and the last time I saw Alan and Beth was at her funeral, shortly after I'd retired.

Poor Beth, awash in tears. Hard, losing your mother, even if your mother happened to be Mandy.

Rain slashed across the windshield, obscuring the view. Realizing that she was shivering, she made sure the car was in neutral, set the parking brake, then turned the engine and the heater on.

No Christmas card from Beth and Alan and tomorrow's Christmas Eve. I count on it, but if I were to meet Alan on the street, I'm not sure I'd know him. And as for Beth – eighteen, or is it nineteen that she'd be now? A young lady.

I never know what to send her for Christmas, but I

think she'll like the watch. It's a good one. I'd have turned handsprings if my grandmother had sent me anything like that when I was young. Oh, there'll be a letter thanking me – very formal, very correct. And very dull. It's as if the kid has no juice in her. Sarah laughed. But then, maybe she thinks there's no juice in me, either.

Supposing I were to invite her here for a little while, pay her fare after she's finished that secretarial course she's taking? Oh, Sarah, don't be crazy. What does sixty-five do with eighteen? Even for a month?

For a long time, she sat as though in a trance, while grey veils of rain swept across the sea's face and waves crashed on the rocks as the tide came in. She was startled when a huge, grinning black lab reared up and planted his forepaws on the window edge. He had a stick between his teeth and he was begging her to throw it for him. A red-faced young man appeared. "Barney, get down!" He grinned at Sarah uncertainly. "Sorry about that, Ma'am."

She laughed. "Don't be. He's a lovely dog. If I wasn't so gimped up, I'd get out and throw the stick for him."

The creases of concern left his brow. "Whenever he spots anybody he thinks he can con, the crazy bugger'll take a chance." He held his hand out for the stick. "Gimme." The dog instantly complied. "Now heel," he commanded, before he saluted Sarah and said, "I'm going down to see if the old otter's still holed up in that pile of driftlogs before I toss the stick for him. So long." His grin was very white, very friendly.

At least he didn't say, "Merry Christmas," she thought, as she watched him hop down the rocks and stride along the sand with the dog scampering beside him, looking expectantly up into his face.

For a moment she envied him, wished that she could stride along with him, then she shook her head. "No, I don't, not really. I wouldn't be twenty again. Not for all the emeralds in Bolivia. But you're here in my head, my young friend, and tomorrow I'll start setting you down on canvas, you and Barney and the sea. You'll make a nice addition to my West Coast Exhibition next spring."

As she cautiously turned the car around, preparing to head back up the hill, she came to a sudden decision. "I *will* send Beth the fare." She grinned. "Why not take a chance? She might be fine."

◆

PEOPLE ARE MOVING OUT IN THE CORRIDOR. Sarah knows she has to hurry. She frowns when she finds a ketchup splash on the front of the blouse she was about to put on. "Old slob! Dribbling like a baby –"

And she is suddenly five years old. The summer Father and Mother and she moved onto the Aldridge Quarter. She is running to greet Grandpa; she's seen his buggy coming.

She remembers his horse's name. Queenie. And she remembers that a grasshopper, flying crazy in the wind, had somehow managed to get down inside her shirt. While Grandpa was fishing the thing out, she noticed that he was dribbling spit down the stem of his pipe. She was revolted.

She cringes. I couldn't bear it if Beth…. Oh, she *knows* people get old, she *knows* they get –

Furiously, she bunches the blouse and stuffs it into the laundry bag.

Beth – I'm so thankful that she came out to the West Coast. Loves it here, she always says. Sarah snorts. Loves the men, anyhow. She's lived with three of them. Mother would be scandalized, but Beth's had more sense than to put all her eggs into one basket. Trouble is, since she's broken up with that Howie what's-his-name, she keeps talking about some job with an oil outfit in Calgary.

Worry knots Sarah's brow and her hands are trembling.

❧

THE MORNING SARAH went to meet Beth's plane, she was nervous about highway driving. Lately she had had some nasty little "turns" that left her weak and dizzy. She was thankful to get off onto the side road leading to the Nanaimo airport.

She pulled into one of the passenger pick-up slots in front of the terminal and settled down to wait, staring across the landing field to where shedding alders dropped their leaves in the grey September stillness.

She checked her watch. Half an hour yet. She sighed nervously. "Oh, what's the matter with me? She's only a granddaughter, for God's sake, not the Queen of England. Not that I'd curtsy to her either."

Two young fellows hopped out of a pickup and slammed the doors. One jerked his head in Sarah's direction and said, "That old doll's talking to herself." They both laughed

I like to talk to somebody with a little sense, buddy,

Sarah quipped in her head, then sobered. But I've got to watch that when Beth's around. I don't want her thinking I'm cracked.

To pass time, she started going through mail she had collected that morning. A load of flyers that she shoved impatiently aside, a periodical on the arts in Canada, a couple of bills, and a letter from the curator of the Edmonton Art Gallery.

Now, what would he have in mind?

She ripped the letter open, perused its contents, then sank back into the seat with the letter in her hand, staring unseeing at people coming and going from the terminal.

A retrospective of my work at the end of November.... Been working on it with your agent for months.... Wanted it to be a surprise.... Wants me to suggest which paintings I still have should be included.... Has already made arrangements to borrow many others from their owners.... Be honoured if I'd attend.

Well, I'll be damned. Got to the retrospective stage, have I? But I don't feel old. Not most of the time. Of course I'll attend. I'd be foolish not to. Provided they accept some of my current work. Those last three abstracts are the best things I've ever done.

She remembered the effect of every brush stroke, the bare horizons slashed low across the canvasses and, above, the suggested infinity of prairie skies, or skies above the sea.

It might be a good thing to have Beth here, she decided. If she's finished that business course, or whatever it is that she was taking, she should be able to write a decent letter. It's going to take a bit of chasing back and forth to Vancouver to make arrangements with my agent if I want to include those latest pictures. Beth can be my legs.

Trouble is, I don't know the girl. Can I trust her? Letters and phone calls don't tell you much. I could never stand her simp of a mother. What if I can't stand Beth? Or she can't stand me? How do I know that's she's not some stupid little druggie and I could have the cops on my doorstep next week?

Oh, cut it out, you old fool. She'll only be here a month or so. You've had hundreds of kids in your classes and you certainly weren't scared of them.

But her apprehensions will not be quieted. Or maybe we won't have anything to say to each other. Alan and I never did. Not that we fought. I just felt I never knew the kid. I could never reach him, and he was gone by the time he was twenty. Would I even recognize him if I saw him now?

She removed the keys from the ignition, worried them in her hand, and muttered, "Would he recognize *me?* Almost six years – that's a long, long time."

Looking over her shoulder through the window, her heartbeat picked up when she saw the plane approach from the distance. It landed, turned, and taxied back to the loading area, looking like some oversized mosquito.

Sarah struggled out of the car and entered the terminal, which was filled with people, every eye fixed on the passenger entry door.

When the door burst open, several burly fishing, logging types barged through, followed by a family with four howling kids, two "cute young things" very conscious of any male eye that might roam in their direction, some businessmen with briefcases, an old lady in a wheelchair pushed by an attendant, and finally, a middle-aged man hobbling on a cane, accompanied by a tall girl.

That girl reminds me of somebody, Sarah was thinking. Then, with a sharp intake of breath – *Josh!*

She was still staring at the girl when the man came towards her. He grinned at her uncertainly, gaps missing between his tobacco-stained teeth. "Mom?"

"Alan?" She gulped, and struggled to readjust her thinking. My God, *he's* middle aged. *He's* not far off old.

He grabbed her with his free arm, hugged her against his beer belly, and said, "Thought we'd surprise you."

"Well, you certainly did that."

She was ashamed to realize that she was not at all pleased to see him; rather, she felt quite panicky.

"Have you had an accident?" she asked, indicating the cane.

"Busted leg. It's coming along all right, but I won't be able to work for a while, so I thought I'd come out with Beth. Look, if putting me up is going to be a problem I could always get a –"

"Oh, no, no. I have room. It's just that I wasn't expecting…. Well –"

She turned to the girl, who was watching them with eyes so grey and calm that Sarah was reminded of Athena, Homer's goddess of the grey eyes.

Guardian spirit or nemesis? she wondered, taking the girl's unlined hand in her old wrinkled one. "I'm glad you could come, Beth. You are very like your Uncle Josh, you know. I'm sure your father has told you that."

"Really? You mean, the one that was killed?"

The distance in the girl's voice shocked Sarah. It was as though she was speaking about some event so far in the past and so devoid of emotion that it might indeed be some legend out of Ulysses.

"Well, at least you know."

"Daddy told me about it on the plane."

"Just *now?*" She swung around and looked at Alan.

He avoided her eyes and began snaffling bags off the carousel and piling them onto a luggage cart. Once the luggage was stowed in the trunk, he turned to Sarah, puffing a little from the effort, and held his hand out for the car keys.

"Now, how do you think I get around when you're not here, Alan?"

His face reddened.

"It's a strange town to you," she said, by way of apology. Then, as she climbed behind the wheel, she told herself, Cut it out, you miserable old crow. So he *was* a stupid, thoughtless kid. Aren't most of them? She dredged around in her head, trying to think of something to cover the moment, fought her voice down to a calm, low register and said, "So, you've finished your secretarial course, Beth?"

"Top marks too," Alan put in.

"They call us executive assistants, now, Gran."

"Do they now? So, I take it you can write a decent letter?"

"Yes, Ma'am." The girl was grinning.

Well, she'd got some confidence anyway, Sarah thought, as she turned off the highway to avoid heavy traffic and cut back onto leafy side streets and back roads, with their startlingly beautiful views of the little mountain on the one side and, on the other, glimpses of water and the coastal ranges across the strait.

Beth, who was taking it all in, said, "Is this ever a neat little town. And you say there's hardly any winter here, Gran?"

"Nothing that you'd call winter."

"Wow! Do you think I could get a job here? It might be fun to stay a while."

"Oh, Christ, baby –" Alan began.

"Daddy, don't start."

"A job?" Sarah pondered, "Well, as a matter of fact I'm friends with a young lawyer. She was telling me she'd be looking for a temporary secretary in a couple of months, since her regular will be taking maternity leave. Do you think you could handle the job?"

"I'm a quick study, Gran."

Sarah snapped a look at her. She was beautiful, with her huge grey eyes and her clear skin; a good deal like Josh and, at the same time, a little like her mother. But with twice the poise and three times the brains, Sarah guessed.

"How'd you like to do a little job for me until Karen needs you? The Edmonton Art Gallery is arranging a retrospective of my work. I'm not sure I'm up to the trotting back and forth and all the letter writing and phone calls it's going to take. Standard secretarial wages suit you? Travel expenses, and of course you can live with me."

"Gran, that sounds great!"

"Baby, you can't leave me," Alan groaned, "I dunno what I'd do without –"

"Oh, Daddy, I've got to leave home sometime. You did. We all do."

Sarah snatched a glance at him in the rearview mirror. His eyes met hers for the merest second, then flinched away.

I hope he's not going to stay long, she fretted. I'm afraid this is going to be a rough visit.

But, as a matter of fact, it was not. Not in the way she had feared, anyway. Alan was content to putter around the yard or to channel surf the TV, looking for sporting events while he drank beer, burping softly to himself and smoking one cigarette after another.

"Wouldn't you like to go out to Long Beach for a couple of days, Alan?" Sarah offered. "You could take my car. The Pacific's great."

"The Atlantic's great too, Mom, if you like oceans, and I see that one all the time."

"There's a wonderful place up on the Port Alberni highway. Cathedral Grove, they call it. Old-growth timber. Monster trees, mostly Douglas fir. Some of them were seedlings when Columbus discovered America. We could drive up there next Sunday."

"A bunch of old *trees?* Nah. The Blue Jays are playing on Sunday, and I don't wanna miss the game."

"Well, how about Victoria? We could drive down and have afternoon tea in the Empress one day."

He crooked his small finger and held up an imaginary teacup. "I can see me now."

After Beth had gone to bed, Sarah slipped into her bathrobe and crept out to join him where he sat, staring at the TV. Whenever she tried to talk to him, he fidgeted and said, "Yeah. Well, I guess it's about time to hit the sack, eh?"

Isn't he *ever* going to talk to me? she fumed. There have been several of these nasty little "turns" since he and Beth came. What if I never see him again?

She and Beth, on the other hand, had developed a rapport. The girl's cool demeanor forbade familiarity, but she was, as Sarah guessed, extremely intelligent. Whatever needed doing she did with no-fuss efficiency – drove skillfully, tossed appetizing meals together, did beautiful secretarial work (making Sarah's computer hop through paces that she had never known were within its capabilities), wrote copious numbers of letters, and handled phone calls about the upcoming retrospective with poise, tact, and good sense.

But when it came to art, to Sarah's great disappointment, the girl seemed blind to anything excepting its monetary value. She gave a perfunctory glance at a number of brilliantly executed abstracts, and asked, "How much would these be worth, Gran?"

"Oh, probably twelve or fifteen thousand apiece for these two. This one should go for quite a bit more."

"Like what?"

"Twenty-five, thirty, maybe."

"Wow! Just for a little bit of canvas, and a few smears of paint."

Sarah winced. You little Philistine, you! she thought. But she managed to keep her mouth shut.

Beth, unaware, probed. "So, I guess you must be rich, eh, Gran?"

"Hardly. Everything beyond what I need goes into scholarships. That's how I got through university, scholarships and bursaries, and now it's pay-back time."

The girl shrugged resentfully. "Well, it's *your* money, I guess."

"There'll be something for your dad when I'm gone.

And for you, the house, the car, some of my unsold paintings, and –" She gestured towards Miss Hindman's nude.

Beth cast a glance at the nude, then looked dismissively away.

Sarah was amused. Never spotted the *real* money.

THE END OF OCTOBER HAD COME, that strange season between summer and what passes for winter on Vancouver Island. Frequently, Sarah wakened to grey light and the sound of rain pattering on the shakes, days when sea and sky merged in pewter stillness.

She was becoming increasingly nervous about the retrospective. She had been warned that the press would be out in force to interview her. Ordinarily that would not have worried her, but last week, while she was working in her studio, a shiver had passed over her, and her mind had gone curiously blank for what seemed like a long time. That "little turn" was much worse than others. She came to herself, slumped in a chair, cold and trembling. It was some time before she could gather the strength to get to her feet. She didn't tell Beth or Alan, and she was certainly not going to tell that snotty young doctor who kept warning her to cut salt out of her diet.

Beth further upset her the following morning by announcing that they were going on a shopping spree to Victoria. "We'll get you decked out like the Queen of Sheba for the retrospective, Gran," she said. "Some smart-looking suits and a couple of really smashing outfits for the dinner and that fancy wine and cheese 'do' when you'll have a chance to mingle."

"That's all I need, to stand for an hour or so with

my broken back trying to make intelligent conversation while a bunch of jackasses make silly remarks about my work."

"Gran! Why are you so grouchy? Are you feeling all right?"

"Yes, I'm feeling all right," she snapped, and was immediately ashamed. "Oh, Beth, I'm sorry. But couldn't we go to Victoria some other day?"

"We could put it off till Friday, but we'll have to go soon in case we have trouble finding something suitable for you to wear, or in case it needs altera –"

"Yes, yes, I know." She fended Beth off with the flat of her hand and disappeared into her studio, but she made no attempt to paint. For a long time, she sat, staring at nothing, her forehead propped on the tips of her fingers and her eyes welling tears.

What if it happens again? What if it's really bad next time?

The Friday when they finally went to Victoria was a gorgeous day. Sarah felt fine. The sea was adream in autumn haze, there were still a few brilliant maple leaves on the trees, and the mountains dozed in gauzy distance.

In an upscale store, almost immediately, Beth found two graceful caftans, one in a deep ruby shade, the other black, formal, which she dressed up for Sarah with chunky, fake jewelry. The caftans hid Sarah's bulges, set off her silver hair, which Beth had arranged for her in a smart chignon, and were such a perfect fit that they required no alterations, but she baulked when Beth suggested a pair of high-heeled shoes to go with them.

"You want me to break my neck falling flat on my

face in front of the whole art community?"

"Oh, Gran!"

"Nothing doing, Kid. Those simple flat black slippers are the very thing."

"But Gran, they don't really go with formal dresses."

"Neither do I."

They both laughed, and suddenly, they were friends.

Ever since Alan arrived, Sarah had repeatedly asked him if he would not like to attend the retrospective, offered to buy his plane ticket and accommodation for him at the same hotel where she and Beth would be staying.

"Nah, I've seen your stuff, and I never could stand that artsy-fartsy bunch you hung around with."

"Well, how about visiting some of the family in Edmonton then, or looking up some of your old buddies? Or you may want to go and see your father's grave."

"You gotta be kidding. Nah, I'll just stay here and keep an eye on things. Be meeting you at the airport when you get back. You know I'm pulling out on the same plane that fetches you and Beth home?"

BETH AND SARAH LANDED at Edmonton International late in the afternoon on the last day of November. A bitter, brutal day. Snow wraiths fled across the frozen tarmac, driven by a cruel north wind. As soon as the plane's door opened, cold charged into the aircraft. Sarah had forgotten how much she hated it. "Why didn't I have sense enough to wear my down-filled? I've kept it all these years, just in case –"

"Don't worry, Gran, we'll soon be in a nice warm car. The Dean of Humanities will be here to meet us, and the curator of the galley too. Royal treatment."

Sarah was suddenly unsure of herself. Shy. She had worked alone so long since her retirement that social occasions, even casual ones, were something of an ordeal. She hadn't had any new clothes in years. Hadn't needed any. She wondered if the good suits Beth had insisted she buy were appropriate. She was not at all sure about the chignon into which Beth had piled her hair. When she'd looked in a mirror, she reminded herself of the picture of Miss Hindman in that magazine Mr. Litt had given her to show to Mother all those years ago. It amazed her that she should look like the well-known English painter who had once been Mother's lover.

While they were waiting for the other passengers to disembark, Sarah tugged irritably at the girdle that was cutting into her side. It had been years since she'd worn one. She dreaded the lecture that she was scheduled to deliver to students in the Art Department the following afternoon. What if she had one of her nasty little "turns" in the middle of that, or at the formal dinner that was laid on for tomorrow night? She dreaded, most of all, seeing again some of her paintings which had been borrowed from their owners. Would they be as good as she remembered, or had she been only fooling herself?

But to her surprise, everything worked with amazing smoothness. Once into the swing of things, she found herself talking with humourous authority about her work and listening to others' opinions with alert deference. She even managed to eat at the formal dinner without dropping a speck of food onto her caftan.

She was standing at the wine and cheese "do," alone for the moment, sipping a glass of wine and looking at the little sage impression she had given Mother and Father after her first exhibition.

When I'd painted that little picture, I knew I was on my way, she thought, grinning; then she remembered Father's sister, Aunt Jane, asking if people really paid money for stuff like that.

Next to the sagebrush sketch was the picture of the trapped coyote she'd done almost forty years ago. She had intended merely to glance at it and then move on, but the coyote's eyes would not let her go.

She remembered that she had been working on that picture just before her thirty-ninth birthday, at a time when she had been so busy with her career and her family that she hardly had time to think.

EDMONTON WAS IN THE MIDDLE OF A COLD SNAP, every chimney belching smoke. She went to the window and watched Josh and Alan joining some chums on their way to school. She waved to them. Neither waved back.

What teenager wants his buddies to see him waving good-bye to his Mommy? she thought. It wouldn't be "cool." She was about to turn away from the window when she saw Clarence backing his eight-year-old Chev out of the driveway.

I thought he'd left twenty minutes ago. Must have had trouble getting that old beater started. Or did he forgot to plug it in again? Look at that face. Glum. Glum. Glum. And he's been sitting up at night, drinking beer and listening to his old piano records lately. Something's gone wrong at work. Would he be getting ready to quit the insurance company? Well, he's stuck it out for three years. That's a record. And before that there was journalism, then there was landscaping, then there was Clarence's Speedy Delivery Service, and then there was that used car outfit – God! Eighteen years of it. Well, if he quits, there's always my job at the good old university.

Oh, knock it off. He was decent about me bringing Mother in to live with us after Father died and he's okay with the kids. When he happens to remember that he's got kids.

She sipped from a cup of tepid coffee, dumped the dregs into the sink, stowed the mug in the dishwasher, and went to the mirror to apply lipstick and put the finishing touches on her hair. When she had finished, she turned in front of the mirror and frowned at her reflection.

Need to knock ten pounds off my butt. A middle-aged spread for an instructor in the Department of Arts and Design? Won't do, Professor Cross. Won't do.

She had slipped sketches she planned to use with her class into her portfolio and was reaching for her purse when the phone rang.

Now who? Well, it could be the curator of that new gallery wanting to arrange a showing of my latest oils, so –

She lifted the receiver. "Yes?"

"Sarah Cross?" A female voice, stiff, with a nasal twang, tantalizingly familiar.

"Yes."

"May I speak to your mother?"

"I don't think she's up yet." Who is this? I should

know that voice. "You realize Mother is very deaf?" She waited. Silence. "Well, if you'll hold a moment, I'll check."

A tinkling laugh ending with a small catch of breath.

Cousin Gwendolyn! Well, if she can play coy, I can play dumb.

When she opened Mother's bedroom door the old lady peered at her, mouth slightly ajar.

"Someone on the phone for you, Mother."

The old head snaked forward, anxiety intensifying the expression. "What's that?"

"You're wanted on the phone."

Mother rose from her half-reclining position against a pile of pillows and hurried with tiny bare-footed steps to the phone on the desk in the hall; a musky smell of old flesh and stale urine drifted in her wake. She lifted the receiver with both hands, stared at it, then put the mouthpiece against her ear.

"It's upside-down, Mother."

She made a hundred-and-eighty-degree turn to face Sarah. "What?"

Sarah took the phone from her and placed it in the proper position.

"Yes?" Mother's voice quavered upward apprehensively. She strained to listen, brow knotted, then turned to Sarah with a pathetically hopeful expression. "Sarah, I do believe it's Gwendolyn, but I can't make out what she's saying."

Oh, damnation! Now I'll have to invite Gwendolyn here. Well, the house is reasonably tidy today, and I don't have to *be* here, she thought, as she took the receiver. "Gwendolyn, is that you?"

"Your mother knew my voice."

"Look, I'm sorry to seem abrupt, but I'm late for classes."

"Still taking art lessons?" Cool, amused.

"No. I'm teaching at the university."

"Really? Well, isn't it nice that you're making something of this art business after all these years?"

Sarah rolled her eyes. Gwenny-baby, I love you too. "You understand, I can't be here today, Gwendolyn, but Mother's anxious to see you."

"I came up especially to see her."

Minutes later, Sarah was easing her car into the flow of rush-hour traffic and thinking, There are benefits to working for a living besides a regular pay cheque. Imagine being stuck with Gwendolyn for the day! Wonder what she's like now. Belle of the ball, she used to be. Statuesque blonde with frost-jade eyes. Learned how to wiggle her ass early and married the richest lawyer in Medicine Hat. Shyster, but he's got the dough.

At half past five that afternoon, she was locking the door of her office. It had been a long day. Two classes, three students protesting their marks, plus a faculty meeting. Half an hour later, she was pulling into her driveway, looking forward to comfortable slippers and a quiet bottle of beer.

She found the door locked. When she went around to the back, she found that door locked too. She fumbled through her purse and realized that she didn't have a key. At her second ring, she heard somebody brush against the door, checking the peephole from the inside. "Sarah? Is that you?"

Gwendolyn! Oh, damn! I was sure she'd be gone

hours ago, she thought, as a skeletally thin woman opened the door and said, "I hope you're not sore at me for locking you out of your own house, Sarah, but with so many perverts running around these days, I always think it's better to be safe than sorry."

Sarah mustered a more or less civil greeting and hung her sensible tweed coat next to Gwendolyn's sapphire mink. As she kicked off her shoes and stepped into a pair of sheepskin slippers, Gwendolyn said, "The boys said to remind you that they had hockey practice after school and Auntie's having a little nap. Isn't she precious? She insisted that I stay for dinner, since George will be at a stag tonight."

Sarah was a trifle desperate. She had no idea what she and Gwendolyn would find to talk about, and she had nothing in the house fit to serve a guest for dinner.

"And, oh, yes," Gwendolyn added. "Clarence phoned. Said he'd be a little late."

And a little tight, I have no doubt. I hope he doesn't come stumbling in here before I get rid of you. Well, since I'm stuck with you.... "Would you like to join me in a bottle of beer while I catch my breath, Gwendolyn?"

"Beer? Oh, I never touch the stuff. You know it's very fattening?"

"Well, perhaps you'll allow me to indulge in my iniquity?" She removed a bottle from the fridge, snapped the lid off, and went into the living room, which reeked of tobacco smoke. Gwendolyn perched daintily on the couch beside her, eyes roaming the room.

Sarah was conscious of the stain on the rug that she could never get out where Alan had spilled a bottle of

Orange Crush, the sun-faded chairs, and rips the cat had made in the skirt of the couch.

Gwendolyn opened a silver cigarette case and offered it to Sarah."

"No thanks. I quit last year. So far, I've made it stick."

"Wish I could. I've tried everything. Spent a fortune on hypnosis and revulsion therapy and goodness knows what else, and just look at me. Two packs a day, still. And it's getting so expensive. Of course, George doesn't begrudge the money. He's a regular doll. Nothing's too good for his Mummykins, and he gets along so great with Cecil and Lloyd. They go goose-hunting together and pronghorn-hunting too when it's in season. Just like brothers. They bought snow-mobiles last year and they had more fun running coyotes when the snow got deep."

And I wonder what else they share, Sarah thought sardonically, as she carefully peeled the label off the beer bottle and tried to hide her distaste.

Coyotes. I must have painted the little one I saw in the granary a dozen times, but…. Something eluding me. Something – I don't know what.

While Gwendolyn prattled from inane remark to inane remark, Sarah studied her covertly. What lay beyond that facade? Everything about her shrieked money. Beautifully styled hair, still silver blonde, but artificially so now; subtle perfume, manicured finger-nails, a cunningly fashioned silk blouse, and a tailored mohair skirt. The only things that didn't fit the picture of a pampered and adored female were the eyes that never quite met Sarah's and the way she picked at the cuticles of one hand with the nails of the other.

Gwendolyn broke the silence with a nervous little laugh. "My, you're a sly puss, Sarah, letting me go on about your painting this morning, and here you're a professor. Had shows of your work and everything. Auntie showed me reviews she'd cut out of the paper.

"Maybe you heard that George is building a gorgeous new home for me overlooking a bend in the South Saskatchewan? Thirty-four hundred square feet. The architect says we should decorate with the work of prairie artists. Good for business, you know? George has stuff lined up, but I get to choose a couple too. I wanted to look at your stuff this afternoon to see if there was something I could use, but Auntie couldn't find the key to your studio."

Sarah turned away to hide her rage. You bitch! That's why you stayed. You want to look at my work and tell me there's nothing good enough to hang in your goddamned house. Well, screw you, baby. Screw you.

She took a deep, careful breath. "Teaching has taken all my time this year. There's nothing finished that I could show you."

Gwendolyn's face coloured. "But Auntie says that you're always painting someth –"

"'Auntie' *says* lots of things, and there's lots of things that 'Auntie' doesn't *know*." She set the empty beer bottle on the coffee table and picked up the phone book. "We're low on grub around here tonight. Kentucky Fried suit you?"

"Kentucky Fried – oh, I never touch the stuff. It's so...."

"Well, supposing I make you a pot of tea, and you can watch us eat?"

"I'll just go back to the hotel if you'll call me a cab."

Her voice was stiff with insult.

Sarah shoved the phone book along the coffee table. "Be my guest."

THREE HOURS LATER, supper had been eaten, the boys were in bed, and Mother had stopped puzzling as to why Gwendolyn had left without saying good-bye. Clarence had not come home, but Sarah no longer worried about him. She poured herself a strong mug of coffee, made for the garage which was her studio and her refuge, set the unfinished picture of the coyote on the easel, stared at it and sipped coffee.

Something I'm missing. Something about the eyes, I think.

Working from deep instinct, she mixed colours and applied paint with a few swift strokes.

It was finished. It was right; she knew it.

"But why does it bother me?" she muttered when she stood back to look at it.

WHEN SHE LOOKED INTO THE EYES NOW, shame jolted her. What I was really painting was Gwendolyn! She flinched and steadied herself with the cane that she'd begun to use lately when she became too tired.

Beth hurried across to her. "Something wrong, Gran?"

"No, no! I'm fine. Do you think you could get me another swallow or two of that red wine?"

As Beth turned to do so, Sarah moved on to her painting of the lone poplar, which she had lent for the retrospective. Her heart lifted with pleasure. So there you are, you old beauty, still alive in my painting. I can almost hear your branches thresh and wind rustling your leaves.

She took a sip of the wine that Beth had brought her and turned to *Venus*. The painting had elements of caricature, of cartoon. Viewed close up, it appeared to be a picture of a pot-bellied, louse-eaten horse with a white blaze on its forehead. A sorry-looking creature with a drooping head and a drooping lower lip. A ragged little kid was combing the beast's ratty tail, but when the viewer stood back, the cartoon incorporated itself into a ghostly suggestion of a magnificent Arab with fire in its eyes and its tail flowing on the wind.

Sarah resisted the temptation to touch the painting, removed her glasses, and blotted at the tears.

She was entering another gallery to look at her latest work, her prairie abstracts, which her agent had told her had already been sold, when she glanced across the room. An old man, dressed in a pair of casual pants and a heavy, intricately-knit Arran sweater, was watching her from the doorway. His Celtic-blue eyes were faded now.

AFTER THE "LOVIN' CUP," Sarah had rented a bed-sitter with a north skylight in one of the highrises in Edmonton's university district. A simple workaday place, cluttered with painting paraphernalia and half-finished works, and furnished with shabby things Mother and Father had brought with them when they'd come to live in Edmonton. For Sarah, it was merely a place to work and a place to hang her hat.

Whenever she could get away, she spent time in her camper on painting expeditions out in the foothills of the Rockies. Jock, the Greyhound driver with whom she'd had an affair when she was a student, frequently joined her. They had only recently met again after many years.

Jock had exquisite taste in Scotch whiskey, equally discerning judgment in his choice of beefsteak, and was capable of such lovemaking as Sarah had only dreamed of all the years of her marriage.

He was sympathetic about the loss of her kids, but she knew he really didn't understand. About Clarence, he merely laughed and said he couldn't figure out why she hadn't dumped the silly bugger years ago.

Sarah was thankful that he never pushed for any change in their own status. Seemed not to want it. Certainly, she did not. His visits were wonderful, but she couldn't really see herself introducing him to her colleagues.

She never discussed her professional life with him, and when they were apart, she had become adept at shutting him out, unless they had some assignation planned.

One afternoon, between classes, while she was sitting in the faculty lounge, drinking coffee and leafing through some professional publications, she came upon an ad for a term's exchange teaching with a university in Australia. Her training and expertise fit the qualifications. On a whim, she applied.

She was not counting too heavily on getting the position. She had told no one except the dean of her faculty. "Hope you get it, Sarah," he'd said. "A change of scene would do you a world of good."

When a phone call came, asking if she would be prepared to take up her duties for the upcoming term, she heard herself agreeing to do so.

Not until she burst into her apartment that afternoon, breathless and a little discombobulated, did she realize that she had never told Jock about the application. Since she knew that he would be in Edmonton between buses in an hour's time, she phoned Greyhound and asked that he return her call.

When he did so, she could tell that he was uptight. She never phoned him at work. "What's up, babe? Something wrong?"

After she'd told him her news, there was a long pause. "You did this without even talking it over with me?"

"Jock, it's only for a few months. And it's not as if we are —"

"All right. I guess I know where I stand. Good luck, Sarah. I hear those great big sunburned Aussies make pretty good studs." He slammed the receiver back into its cradle so hard that it made her wince.

"Studs! You bastard, you! Well, *right!* Right on. What *did* we ever do besides screwing? When did we ever have an intelligent conversation? And you wouldn't know a Matisse from a Picasso and you couldn't care less. To hell with you."

Then she cried for a long time.

She had thought about writing to him when she returned after her term in Australia, but she had never done so.

Now, she remembered the nights, after love-making, when they had lain out on the foothills under the great wheel of the stars, watching the little brown bats against the sky. She took a step towards him, but he shook his head slightly, made the old-fashioned "OK" sign, circling thumb and middle finger, and faded into the crowd. She could scarcely speak around the choking fist in her throat when Beth came up to her.

"The crowd's thinning out, Gran. Do you think we should make our exit now?"

RAIN WAS THREATENING when they landed in Nanaimo the following morning. Sarah was exhausted, and she dreaded saying good-bye to Alan.

Oh, cut it out, you old fool, she scolded, how do you know you'll never see him again, and anyhow, what did you ever have to say to each other?

Alan was weighing his luggage in at the ticket counter when they entered the terminal, a big stolid man, earnest and dull. After the attendant handed him his boarding pass, he spotted Sarah and Beth.

"Well, how'd it go?" he asked, coming up to them.

"Fine. Gran was a regular star."

"Oh, yeah? That's nice." But Sarah knew he hadn't really heard. His eyes were searching Beth's face. "I hope you're going to get this West Coast bug out of your bonnet pretty soon and come home, baby."

"Daddy, I like it here. You never can tell, I just might stay for good."

His face sagged with pain. Sarah turned away, tears for him brimming in her eyes.

❧

AS SARAH MAKES HER WAY across her shadowy room and opens the closet to look for a clean blouse, Marcie, the young attendant, enters the room. The doors clash.

"Breakfast, Sarah."

Sarah would like to scream, "Damn it to hell! Did no one ever teach you to knock?" She would like to tell Marcie that no one, outside of her own family, has called her Sarah since she became department head at the Faculty of Arts.

But how can you scream at someone whose task it was to change your diaper every three hours the last time you'd had that bad turn? And how can you be sure you won't have a bad turn again?

Marcie negotiates the doors and cheerfully enters the room. "Let's get a little light on the subject, Sarah." And as she pulls the curtains back, "See the harbor, all blue and shining in the sun. Came out especially for your birthday, didn't it? A-hah! Thought we'd forgotten, didn't you? There's a cake for supper and your granddaughter will be...."

"Tell me something I don't know." Trying to pretend she's not pleased.

But Marcie's a nice girl. Really she is. Beautiful, too. I believe Miss Hindman would have considered her a great model.

Marcie is looking at the pictures lining the walls. "Your paintings are lovely, Sarah. When are you going to start working again?"

"When I'm damned good and ready."

Marcie's voice is kind. "If you think painting is beyond you, we could take the easel down. It *does* crowd the room, and Matron thinks the smell of turpentine isn't good for –"

"Beyond me? Who says? You tell Matron that I'm paying for this room, and I'll decide when –"

"Now, Sarah, you know what they say," Marcie

teased. "'Use it or lose it.'"

"Balls!"

"Language, Sarah!" smothering a grin.

"Shit, balls. Fuck and damn." There you go, Miss. Grin at that.

"Oh, all right. Cranky, cranky. Breakfast in ten minutes." And she is gone.

Tears spill onto Sarah's cheeks as she examines the three paintings she could never bear to sell. They are so beautiful she can't believe now that she ever did them. She never knew what this one represented, but she knows how it makes her feel. Strata of…something. She remembers her driven state while she painted it; no rest until she had that touch of ice-green turquoise exactly so. And this one of a child, a girl who seems to materialize out of barren rock – A dark-haired child with an indistinct face bending towards what might be a wild rose. And here is her favourite, the magnificent lone poplar rearing indomitable against the prairie sky.

IN THE SUMMER OF 1955, during the break before she had to start teaching university summer session, she returned to Rattlesnake Park to combine one of her prairie-painting expeditions with a visit with Mother and Father. On this trip, she planned to paint the poplar that grew on the east side of the road allowance a mile north of town. Father said he remembered the tree as a well-grown sapling at the turn of the century when he'd arrived in Rattlesnake Park, a kid with his homesteading family. Now, Father was an old man and the tree was a giant, a miracle on those bald-headed plains. Sarah was determined to paint an oil that would do it justice – some impression as powerful, as simple, as the tree itself.

Always a restless sleeper, she'd wakened at dawn. Rather than lie and worry about money, since the second of Clarence's business ventures had failed, she rose, pulled on jeans and a wind shell, laced her hiking boots, collected camera and sketch pad, let herself out into a gorgeous summer dawn, and headed north down the dusty gravel road where, riding old Skeezix flat out, she used to thunder past Kenny Krebs plodding back and forth to school.

"Wouldn't kill you to give the poor kid a lift, would it?" Father had once suggested.

Sure as hell would kill me! If you knew what Kenny Krebs tried to do to me....

Not that she'd tell. Never. And after all, she had been peeing in the school barn.

When she reached the tree, she laid one hand against its rough bark and looked up into its branches. "So, here you are, decked out in your new leaves again, the only truly beautiful thing in Rattlesnake Park"

She remembered once, the spring when she'd been eleven, she'd ridden up and caught Kenny Krebs breaking branches off the tree and piling them over something on the ground. "Just for the hell of it," he'd said, when she accosted him.

"Leave that tree alone, Kenny Krebs."

"Fuck off."

"*You* fuck off, you snot face, or I'll run Skeezix over top of you."

And after our little altercation in the school barn, he was scared I'd do it too.

But, as the leaves rustled above her now, glinting in the dawn, she realized with a pang of shame that Kenny had been trying to bury the body of his little dog that his Uncle John had shot. She patted the poplar's trunk. "Well, I guess you could afford a few branches, couldn't you, old friend? And you're still here. You'll be here when my kids have kids. Sometimes, when they're passing through, I hope they'll turn off the highway and come to see you."

She sketched the tree from many angles, trying to catch the thresh and sway of its mighty branches bending in the wind and, as sunrise approached, she circled, snapping picture after picture to catch nuances of shadows playing over the leaves in the strengthening light.

When she headed back to her parents' home, their little old farmhouse, dragged into the village and patched up after they had retired, a battered Chevy truck overtook her; Sam Bach was at the wheel. Sam, who had been two grades ahead of her in school, had bought old Granny Krebs's quarter after Granny "cashed in her chips." Now he was a two-bit sheep farmer. Father and he were great cronies in the Masonic Order. Father was always telling Sarah how Sam had replaced a pane of glass for him, or spaded his garden. Or hauled his garbage to the dump.

The truck stopped and Sam peered at her. "Sarah MacKenzie!"

"Cross."

"Oh, yeah. Cross." He squinted at the sun, which was still but little above the horizon. "Didn't figure city slickers like you got up much before noon."

She gestured with her camera. "Shadows are most interesting at first light and just before sunset. I got some good pictures, I think."

"Of what?"

"The poplar, of course."

"Oh, that damned thing." He smirked. "So what are you really doing, wandering around by yourself at this time in the morning? You get into a fight with your old man?"

She forced a grin. "My 'old man' is in Edmonton. Couldn't take time off from his job."

So I lied. I'm not about to tell Sam Bach that Clarence's job at *The Edmonton Journal* didn't last a year or that his Speedy Deliver venture folded on him three months ago.

"So, you took off on him! Musta been some fight, eh?"

She couldn't resist. "Man, you should have been there! First I hit him over the head with the fry pan, then he chopped my toe off with the axe, then I tried to strangle him with my bathrobe cord, but when he went for his trusty old .38 –"

His smirk turned a little sick. "Awright, awright. Look, I'd offer you a ride, except, well –" He gestured to a couple of coyote hounds lying on the seat beside him.

"No problem. I can walk."

She strode along, eating Sam's dust and castigating herself. Do I always have to give Rattlesnake Park something to yap about? I can just hear Sam in the beer parlour. "Stuck-up bitch! Why, we all remember her when –" Do they think I don't remember me "when"?

Mother, who was cooking pancakes, looked at Sarah in surprise when she entered the house. "Oh, have you been out already this morning, dear?"

"I'm not the only early bird, Mother. I saw Aunt Jane on her way to post a letter. She'll spot my car. And there might be others before I can load my gear and get away. God, do they smell me when I show up in Rattlesnake Park, or what?"

"Well, you know what small towns are like," Mother said in her "hush-now-let's-forget-it" tone. "And I'm sure you'll find time to paint. Something….pretty, maybe?" Her eyes flicked to the picture propped against the back of the couch – sage-brush, impressionistic almost to the point of abstraction. Shades of umber and grey, austere and peaceful as a prairie winter. Sarah had wanted to give Mother and Father something really good.

The gate creaked, and in a moment Aunt Jane's bulk filled the doorway. She looked Sarah up and down. "Well, you finally made it, huh?" She lumbered across and glanced into the spare bedroom. "Where's the boys?"

"I'm not here visiting, Aunt Jane, I'm here to work. I left the kids in Edmonton. Maria ought to be taking them for their swimming lesson about now."

"Maria?"

"My au pair. She's very –"

"Au pair! Oh, lah-de-dah! When I had my kid, I stayed home and looked after him."

Mother hopped in like a killdeer drawing a coyote away from its chick. "Just look at the painting Sarah did for us, Jane. "I think it's...it's quite...unusual."

Aunt Jane frowned, stared at the painting, removed

her glasses, stared at it again. "Do people buy stuff like that?"

"Can't account for some peoples' taste, can you, Aunt Jane? Damn fools from Imperial Oil even bought a couple from my show."

"You're kidding." She gestured with her thumb. Her voice was sly. "Couldn't sell that one, huh?"

"As a matter of fact, I turned down a thousand for it."

And God knows, I could have used the money.

Mother started visibly. "A thousand dollars?"

Aunt Jane blinked. "Well, you said it. 'A fool and his money....'"

Sarah swallowed rage and ducked into the bathroom. When she came out, Aunt Jane was saying, "Seems like after he got out of the coop he started working for the phone company. Been there five years. Person's got to take their hats off to a kid like Kenny when he finally pulls his socks up."

"Indeed you do," Mother agreed, "Wouldn't Granny Krebs have been pleased?"

Sarah hunched her shoulders defensively and let her breath go with a snort.

"Well, now, don't you go turning up your nose at Kenny, Miss. They tell me he's a real nice fella now. Gonna be foreman on the crew that's running a phone line out to the farms to the north of town."

Sarah shrugged, sat down at the table, and lifted two pancakes onto her plate.

So, the snot-nosed-wonder got his act together. Oh, I know I shouldn't despise him after all this time. God knows, I was odd man out too, but....

She ate quickly and gulped the last of her coffee,

"Well, excuse me, ladies, I'm off to work."

"Couldn't you just take time to show Aunt Jane those sketches, dear? Some of them are lovely."

"Sorry, no time for the wicked or the working woman."

Mother cast an apologetic glance towards Aunt Jane and fluttered about, loading a basket with sandwiches, apples, cupcakes, and thermoses of coffee.

"There's enough food here to do me for a week," Sarah said as she took the basket from Mother's hand. "Don't wait supper for me, okay?"

"You're not wandering around out on the prairie alone again tonight, are you?"

"Why not? I've done it all my –"

"But what is there to see?"

"Sunset, Mother. Far, far distances. Stars. Stars I never see in the –"

"But Sarah, people say –"

"I don't care what people say. How's a person supposed to paint prairie without seeing prairie?"

The wind had really started to blow. It was picking up bits of grit from the road and flinging them into her face as she loaded the car. She knew it would be impossible to set up an easel in the open field where the poplar stood. Instead, she spent a frustrating day in the shelter of the river bank, trying to catch impressions of wind-driven water dancing in reflections against the cliff on the far side.

At sunset, the wind died; the air was filled with the scent of dusty sage. On the way home, she parked the car at the side of the road, hiked up a knoll, and sat, staring at stars until the night grew chilly and wet with dew. Faintly sinister northern lights were gathering when she finally headed for home.

As she pushed open the gate into her parents' yard, a truck pulled up in front of Dorcas and Jimmy O'Conner's tumble-down shack across the street. Sarah could just make out that it was loaded with heavy spools of what must be telephone wire. When the driver rolled down the window, she heard the faint clink of beer bottles.

"Hey, Sarah, baby –"

Kenny Krebs!

"Wanna go for a little ride? We could have a coupla beers, then maybe –" He giggled. "The little man's just a-hopping and a-jumping. Know what I mean?"

Sarah dived into the house, shot both bolts, and leaned against the door, her heart racing, but the only sound was the gentle burble of Father's snoring.

At least that rotten bastard of a Kenny isn't going to try to follow me, she thought, flexing her back against a sudden spasm of pain.

At dawn the chinook picked up again.

Damned wind. And in three days I have to go back to the city.

She loaded a lunch and her painting gear into her car and headed down into the coulee south of the CPR tracks, where she could find shelter from the wind. She was working well; her sketches captured the quality of sage-tough, desiccated land, of flying clouds and the endless roll of tawny hills back and back into distance.

"But I've *got* to get the poplar before I leave. To catch the spirit. Done right, it would do for prairie art what that old spar tree that stands stark against the sky did for Carr's on the West Coast." Unexpectedly, she shivered. "Geese walking on my grave?"

Oh, Sarah, knock it off.

When she returned to the house, late in the afternoon, Father and Sam Bach were departing for their monthly Masonic evening. She imagined Sam telling Father, "That Sarah, she used to be a pretty nice kid, Jamie. She sure has changed, though. You know that?"

Sure, he'll say that. And he was as busy as the rest of them, making fun of my clothes or my pigtails.

Shame stabbed her again, as hurtful as it had been when she was ten. The storekeeper's wife had given Mother some of her daughter's dresses for Mother to cobble into something fit for Sarah to wear. Mongoloid Milly, the storekeeper's daughter, sat about the store all day, farting, breathing through her mouth, and muttering to herself. Sam Bach had been the first to notice that Sarah MacKenzie was wearing Milly Thomas's cast-off dresses.

When Sarah entered the house, Mother was bustling about setting a fresh pot of tea and scones, warm from the oven, onto the table. Just as they settled down, the yard gate creaked and slammed. In a moment, Dorcas O'Conner walked into the house. When Sarah had started school, Dorcas had been a "big kid" in Grade Five.

"Well! How's the professor?" she asked, banter cloaking venom.

Sarah forced a laugh. "Ho! A lowly sessional instructor yet. Not a professor, Dorcas."

"Lowly? Huh! You guys – working seven months of the year. Talk about having it soft.... You don't even look after your own kids."

"Somebody does, though, and some of us teach more than seven months a year, as well as –"

"Ah, poor diddums!"

Shut up, Sarah. Zip your lip, Kid. Button it. If anything happens to Mother or Father, it's Dorcas O'Conner and Sam Bach you'll have to call on until you get down here. Well, if you can down get here. And you've already made Sam mad.

"Never could figure out how come you got so high up in the world," Dorcas pursued. "You were never that swift at your multiplication tables."

"Still have a little trouble with seven times eight, Dorcas."

Mother chirped, "I've just made a nice pot of tea, Dorcas. Won't you join us?"

"Don't mind if I do. I got the spuds on boiling for supper, the kids are watching TV, and Jimmy won't be home for half an hour." She flopped into a chair. "Know what?" She paused for dramatic effect. "I heard that Luke Raisbone caught Marjorie in bed with the hired man. Beat the shit outta the guy, and blacked Marjorie's eye."

"Marjorie?"

"You remember, dear. I sent you an account of Luke and Marjorie's wedding out of *The Taber Times*."

"Oh, Marjorie Strider! Whoopee-ding! I wish Luke had blackened her other eye for me."

"Sarah!" Mother exclaimed. "If I thought for one minute that you mean the awful things you say –"

Whatever makes you think I don't, Mother dear?

"I suppose you're going to tell us you didn't even know that Johnny Wasdon died?" Dorcas's tone was censorious.

"Yeah, I heard about the demise of the greatest principal Rattlesnake Park School ever had. Almost wept a river! I can picture him and little old Miss McCrostie now, toddling home for their nice warm little dinners, and leaving me to fend for myself with that raunchy pack of farm boys."

"Ah, c'mon, you know you enjoyed it."

Sarah carefully buttered a scone. "So, what are you up to these days, Dorcas?"

"Kids and didies."

"Didies? I thought your kids were teenagers?"

"I thought so too. And then along comes Mummy's little mistake." She sighed. "No big-city glamour for us poor suckers."

"Big-city glamour! Classes, and my studio – that's 'glamour'?"

"But Aunt Beth says you had an...exhibition? Or whatever?"

"Sold a few canvasses too, so maybe I'm getting the hang of this painting business."

Dorcas stared at her, puzzlement and spite on her beefy face. "You mean you're just getting the hang of it? How come you're teaching at a university then?"

Mark one on the wall, Dorcas. There's a dig that'll improve with the telling! "Oh, there's quare things in the world and it's truth I'm saying." Sarah said, laying on a mock Irish accent.

Dammit! Did I have to give her the impression that I'm hot stuff? That I'm really something? If anybody from Rattlesnake Park came barging in and saw our shabby house....

Dorcas was examining Sarah's sagebrush painting. "A thousand bucks for that thing?"

"Who told you that?"

"It's all over town. Jeez! I can't even tell what it is for sure." She took three slurps of tea. Mother nipped a bit of cake. Her dentures clacked as she chewed.

And Father's sound even worse. *How am I going to stand it when they can't look after themselves and I have to listen to it at every meal? If it wasn't for Dorcas helping with the housework and doing the shopping for them while Sam does chores around here, I'd probably have them with me now.*

She dragged her attention back to Dorcas, who was saying, "I never knew him when he come to the door."

"Knew who?"

"You know bloody well who. He said you scuttled into the house like a gopher with a hawk on it's tail when he —"

"Oh, Kenny Krebs." She pulled her shoulders in defensively.

"Done all right for himself, I guess. Foreman on that telephone crew and all, but he's such a slob. Drank his beer, cleaned ours out, and was looking for more. Blabbered on about the kids he'd gone to school with until Jimmy practically threw him out." She laughed and examined Sarah with goat-yellow eyes. "Couldn't get it through his head that you are a university professor. No love lost between you two, huh?"

"All I remember about Kenny is that he always had a cold and he snored while he was wide awake."

"Sarah!" Mother sounded indignant. "It wasn't the child's fault. Granny couldn't afford to have his adenoids attended to. I remember when she brought him home. Poor little scrap. His mother abandoned him, you know. It's beyond me how any mother could treat a baby like that."

"Not beyond me," Sarah said with savage glee. "If he'd been mine, I'd have fed him to the pigs."

"Sarah!"

Dorcas stared at her, open-mouthed.

Oh, Christ, now I've done it.

"The child had a very hard life, Sarah," Mother lectured. "Granny had nothing but those five scrawny cows and her bits of cream cheques. I used to give her my flour sacks and sugar bags when I could spare them. She'd bleach them and cobble them into shirts and sheets."

But she never cobbled a snot rag for Kenny.

Sarah pushed away from the table and tried to stretch the spot of tension from between her shoulder blades. "I don't know about you two, but I find it hot in here." She moved to the open door and sat on the floor with her back against the doorjamb.

"The moment Kenny got home from school Granny used to make him turn right around and drive those cows in to water at the town's artesian well," Mother went on. "Barefoot too, unless there was snow on the ground."

"And the darling little soul had to pack such a big stick to beat the poor old cows," Sarah cackled.

Shocked silence.

When she glanced over her shoulder, the inside of the kitchen was already shadowy, but she could read their discomfort. "Sorry, I'm not into this 'local-boy-makes-good' crap where Kenny Krebs is concerned."

A green Ford pickup pulled up beside the ragged

picket fence across the street. Jimmy O'Conner, who worked on a road grader for the municipality, climbed out of the cab and disappeared into the shack. In a moment he yanked the door open, stuck his head out and roared, "Sarah, if Dorcas is over there, tell her to get to hell home here. The kid's shit himself and the spuds is boiled dry."

Sarah ducked aside as Dorcas flew past her and out the gate.

Mother began gathering the tea things. "I do wish you'd be a bit more careful what you say in front of people, Sarah," she fretted, treasuring the delicate cups in her thin old hands. "It doesn't give a very good impression. Why have you got such a scunner on Kenny Krebs?"

Before Sarah had to manufacture a lie, Mother was distracted by the phone. Realizing that it was some member of the Women's Auxiliary who would talk for an hour, Sarah reloaded her camera and mouthed, "I won't be long, Mother. I just want to get some more pictures of the poplar."

As she passed Dorcas and Jimmy's shack, a pot spilling blackened lumps of burned potatoes sailed through the window and landed on top of the garbage heap under the kitchen window. Inside the shack Jimmy and Dorcas were yelling at each other and the baby was howling.

The dark was coming down and the familiar road seemed cold and lonely as Sarah headed north. She could feel the gravel, even through her hiking boots.

WHY HAVE I GOT A SCUNNER on Kenny Krebs? She snorted. Oh, Mother, if I told you, you'd have seventeen fits and thirteen conniptions even now.

During that February, a month before her eleventh birthday, when half the class was absent with mumps, Sarah discovered, to her horror, that she and Kenny Krebs would be alone in the school one day at noon.

Kenny, a skinny, underfed little runt, was putting in time until the law allowed him to quit. So were several other great lumps of farm boys whose attention was on their balls, not on the dates of the kings of England. Sarah knew they eyed her covertly; she overheard lewd half-secret conversations.

"Double dare you."

"No. You."

"Drop dead. My old man would skin me."

"Shut up, dummy. Want her to go blabbing?"

But Sarah never did go blabbing. To blab, when the boys hadn't touched her, was to put herself completely beyond the pale. She sensed that so long as there were half a dozen together, they could brag and posture as much as they liked, but they weren't likely to touch her. But let one of them get her alone? Especially Kenny Krebs, who was always trying to weasel his way into the gang? She felt sick.

Sicker when she heard that mischief-making little bastard of a Ronnie Beans pause on his way out the door as he headed home for lunch. "Now's your chance, Kenny. You've got her alone. Don't take any guff."

Kenny looked flustered. He wiped his nose on his sleeve, gave Ronnie a sickly grin, and nodded.

Sarah dived into the cloakroom, yanked on coat and boots, threw the old canvas school bag containing her lunch over her shoulder, and raced for the barn. She scrambled up the boards of the stall, mounted

Skeezix, backed her out, and faced her towards the open door.

If Kenny takes one step into this barn, so help me, I'll run him down, she vowed as she unwrapped her sandwiches. Boiled eggs mashed in vinegar, again. Today her stomach revolted at the smell.

The skinny, fox-like little dog that had followed Kenny everywhere since some farmer had dumped it in town, was waiting patiently for him in a sunny spot on the south side of the school. At the smell of Sarah's sandwiches, it came to the door of the barn, staring at her with starving eyes. At the last Women's Institute meeting, Sarah had overheard Granny Krebs telling somebody that she couldn't afford to feed a dog. Sarah tossed the little beast her sandwiches; it gulped them down, choking in its eagerness.

Fifteen minutes went by. Skeezix moved restively and jerked against the reins. Sarah's empty belly rumbled and she needed to pee. Snow melting from the roof of the school trickled from the eaves and froze into thick icicles. Then Sarah spotted Kenny peeking around the corner of the school. When the little dog ran to him, he tossed it most of a lard sandwich, the only thing he ever brought for lunch, then took a few steps towards Sarah. "Going someplace?"

"Nope."

"Why're you on your old nag?"

She shrugged.

"C'mere, I got something to show you." His voice cracked. "Uncle John gave me a bunch of steelies. Wanna see 'em?"

"Nope."

"I'll give you a couple. Stand you to a few dubs too.

Then we could have a little game of –"

"Drop dead. I heard you and Ronnie Beans."

A dirty tide of red blood flooded his face. They stared at each other across forty feet of distance. "All right, sister," Kenny snuffled, "you asked for it." He stalked across the yard to a place where the snow was still deep, scooped up handsful and formed them into iceballs with the heat of his hands. The sun had melted a patch of bare ground; he saw a way of improving on his invention. He began building the rest of his iceballs around chunks of gravel.

Gonna blast me out of the barn when he's got enough ammunition!

She was about to make a run for it when, to her immense relief, Ronnie Beans appeared. He stopped at the corner of the school and took in the scene.

"Well, Kenny, did you?"

"How's a guy supposed to fuck her?"

"You mean, you couldn't?"

"She won't get off that goddamned horse."

Ronnie flopped against the school, pointed at Kenny and howled, all but strangling on his own laughter.

"Shut your stupid face!" Kenny screamed, firing an iceball that caught Ronnie in the middle of the forehead. A geyser of blood erupted, scarlet against the snow. More kids arrived, girls squalled, Marjorie Strider vomited, somebody ran to fetch Wasdon, and Ronnie bled.

"What happened here?" Wasdon roared to a cowed and frightened schoolroom once he had succeeded in stanching the blood flow.

Nobody said a word.

Snorting with frustration, Wasdon gritted, "If Miss McCrostie and I can't trust you people to behave yourselves while we go home for a decent lunch, I don't know. I just don't know." His eyes flamed over the class and landed on Kenny. "Come up here, Mr. Krebs. You'll take your punishment in front of the whole school."

Kenny didn't bawl. Nobody made Kenny bawl. Not even Granny when she laid it on him with a caragana stick as thick as her thumb.

Just before 3:30, Sarah's nose started to bleed. Looking disgusted, Wasdon dismissed the class, made her lay her head back against the seat and hold her finger hard on her upper lip. By the time the bleeding stopped, Sarah needed to pee something awful. Wasdon's thunderous countenance, that afternoon, had forbidden any such frivolous requests as trips to the biffy, no matter how urgent.

Certain that all the kids had gone, and being in imminent danger of wetting her pants, Sarah decided to pee in the barn. She was squatting, bare-bummed and helpless, when Kenny Krebs sprang from behind a stall, grabbed her, and threw her onto her back. Before he landed on top of her, she saw his "thing" sticking out of the fly of his pants. It horrified her. So did the snotty face coming down onto her own. Then she remembered Marjorie Strider saying, "Mummy says if any guy gets fresh with you, all you gotta do is give them old nuts of his a good hard handshake."

Sarah heaved with her whole sinewy body, threw Kenny onto his side and grabbed. She didn't think she'd given "them old nuts of Kenny's" a very hard handshake; she was amazed when he started rolling in the horse manure, doubled up and letting forth grunting roars of agony. His little dog, thinking it was some kind of a game, hopped about, barking with excitement.

Sarah scrambled to her feet, yanked her pants up, and stared at Kenny.

Oh, God! He's gonna die. Oh, God! I've murdered him. Oh God! What's Mother gonna say? If he dies, she's gonna.... Oh, God!

"Kenny," she quavered, "are you all right?"

"You lousy bitch! You goddamned lousy bitch, I'm gonna –"

Something told Sarah that she'd better scram. She untied Skeezix, led her outside, grabbed a hank of mane in her left hand, swung herself up, hooked her right heel and her right elbow over Skeezix's backbone and squirmed aboard. As she pounded away, Kenny slammed her so hard between the shoulder blades with an iceball that he almost knocked her off the horse.

Her nose started to bleed, streams of it this time. She tore for home, wiping fruitlessly at blood. Her hands were scarlet, her coat sleeves soaked, that spot between her shoulder blades burned like fire, and she was scared to death that she'd killed Kenny Krebs.

Supposing he dies? He sounded like he was gonna. When Mother finds out she'll blame me. I was dumb enough to pee in the school barn. Then she realized, Kenny's not gonna die. He can't be. People that throw iceballs that hard aren't gonna die. She nodded her head with sudden understanding. And he's never gonna tell anybody about what happened this afternoon, neither.

She slowed Skeezix to a walk.

Straighten out your goddamned face, MacKenzie. You go home bawling, and Mother's gonna to start asking questions.

At the road allowance, where she went west to her parents' quarter while Kenny went east towards his Granny's, Sarah met Kenny's Uncle John. He was leaning against the old poplar, carrying a rifle and a length of dirty rope. He scowled at her. "You'd better get along home and get that nosebleed fixed up." As she rode away, he yelled, "You seen Kenny? Little bugger's late, and I wanna shoot that goddamned dog and get it over with."

She pretended she had not heard.

For the next two weeks, Kenny was absent from school. Somebody said he had come down with mumps. When he returned, he was very pale and lethargic. Ronnie Beans asked him what happened to his little dog. Kenny split Ron's lip with one punch. He didn't bawl when Wasdon strapped him that time either.

SARAH HAD BEEN SO DEEP in memory that, at first, she didn't notice that the new poles of the telephone line marched down the east side of the road allowance.

"But *surely* he would have taken the line across the road," she gasped as she broke into a trot. "Not even Kenny Krebs would...."

But when she reached the top of the hill, she saw a straight line of telephone poles receding into the distance. Where the poplar had stood was a pile of broken branches and dying leaves.

❧

SARAH TOUCHES THE PICTURE LOVINGLY. A thrill of pleasure passes through her. She can almost hear the rustle of its leaves and see the thresh and bend of the mighty branches moving in the wind. She remembers an art critic saying that *The Poplar* was like the best of poetry, capturing essence in powerful understatement.

She dashes away tears and straightens Miss Hindman's little nude.

Imagine, Mother hanging onto that nude through thick and thin all through those hard years on the old farm, and it was worth ten or twelve thousand, even then. She grins sardonically. Listen to yourself, Sarah. If you sold it now, you could be living in "The Pink Palace." Maid service, a fancy stereo, a TV, and meals fit for a queen.

While she struggles to finish dressing, Tommy, in the next room, starts kicking his door and howling, "I want to go home! I want to go home! I want to go home!"

At least, I'll never do that. At least, I don't think I ever will. Besides, there's no home to go to.

That always gives her a pang, her house being rented, but it is the rent and her pension that pays her bill at the lodge.

She unfolds the goddamned walker ("Six legs to stand on and all of them useless"), leans heavily on the contraption, and shuffles into the corridor.

Mrs. Mayberry has her door open again.

And there she sits on her commode, as amiable and brainless as the golliwog my grandmother sent me for my birthday when I was four.

Sarah's eyes flinch away, but Mrs. Mayberry isn't

bothered. "Good morning, Mrs. Cross. Ain't that sun a treat?"

"Shall I close your door?"

"Oh, mercy! What does it matter, dear?"

Plenty of brass still, that one. I'll bet she was good at selling real estate.

Sarah heads for the crowd waiting for the elevator to go down to the dining room for breakfast.

Herd of goddamned scarecrows.

Then it hits her, suddenly and painfully, that she is one of those scarecrows.

With breakfast over, the day stretches interminably before her. Oh, she could go to exercise classes in the lounge. Probably will, if for no other reason than to alleviate the boredom. It hardly seems worthwhile trying to make the one draggy leg obey, but she can still fling her arms about, and does so. Then it's back to her room until lunchtime.

I could nap, or…. I could start the painting. The light is wonderful in here this morning, but…. If only I could remember….

She has turned the radio on to the CBC station that broadcasts classical music and is stretching out in her recliner, looking forward to some Mozart, when there is a rap on the door. Before she can tell whoever it is to go away, the door opens and in comes that god-damned whey-faced Bible-thumper. "Ah, Sarah, and how are we today?"

"*We* were a hell of a lot better before you came barging in."

He laughs indulgently. "Now, now, it's just that we are concerned about your spiritual well-being. Is there any-thing we need to discuss before we join the others for mid-week service this morning?" he asks as he plants his rump on her bed. "It is never too late to come to the Lord, Sarah. His mercy and his forgiveness are infinite, and let us never forget that he died in agony on the cross that we poor sinners might have eternal life."

"You know perfectly well I've never 'joined the others' before and I sure as hell ain't about to start today." She eyes his pained expression with satisfaction, leans forward, taps him on the knee confidentially, and says, "There's something I need to discuss with you, though."

"Yes, Sarah, anything."

She lifts a conspiratorial finger. "There's times I have one hell of a time in the can. Like shitting bricks, y'know? Now, from the looks of you, I'd say you have a little tendency in that direction yourself. Isn't that right?"

His face has turned a gorgeous shade of magenta.

"I was wondering, what say we go halvers on twenty pounds of prunes? You could cook 'em up and fetch me a jar every time...."

That does it.

He springs to his feet. "Old age is no excuse for utter crudity."

"Young age is no excuse for utter stupidity, either. Now, get to hell out of here. And turn the radio up a little before you go."

He doesn't, but he goes. Sarah relaxes to the strains of *The Magic Flute* and the sure knowledge that the Bible-thumper will give her a wide berth from now on.

Then there is the trek to the dining room for lunch. Hot dogs today – none too hot, and there is no mustard.

As she passes the lounge when she heads back to her room, she sees Marcie and What's-Her Name setting up the bingo game.

At least they've quit pestering me to go to *that*.

She tries to read a little, but her eyes blur and water. Before she lies down, she turns her radio on again, then opens her window to kind air and the salt tang of the sea. When she wakens, an hour later, the room is chilly and the town, stretching below the lodge, is shrouded in fog. She has been dreaming about Father and Mother.

❧

FATHER AND MOTHER were of the hard-bitten generation of Alberta farm folk who denied themselves everything beyond the bare necessities. When Sarah was growing up, there was seldom so much as an aspirin in the house; the only doctor she ever saw was one who came to bind Father's ribs and set his shoulder after the bull had almost killed him. The years had not changed the habits of a lifetime. Long-distance phone calls were for emergencies only; therefore, when Father phoned that Christmas Eve, Sarah knew something was seriously wrong.

"That you, Kid?"

"Yes, Father. What – ?"

"Your Ma's on the sick list. I was wondering, there some way you could come down?"

Alan, who was ten, took the angel that was to grace the top of the Christmas tree and headed for the ladder, one eye on the top spike.

Josh hit him amidships. "No, Alan! Gimme that angel. Mom said I could."

"No way. You'd fall down and break your –"

"Boys! Sh-h! This is long distance. Grandpa's on the –"

"But Mom, you *said* –"

"Just a minute, Father, I can't…. Alan, give me that angel. Now, there's chocolate cake in the…. Just a *minute*, Father. You can both have a piece, but don't…." The kitchen door slammed behind them and Sarah took a deep breath. "Now, tell me, what's the matter with Mother?"

"Damned if I know." She could hear him gulp. "She don't take no interest in nothing. Don't eat, and she's got one hell of a cough."

"How long has she been like this?"

"Coupla weeks. I asked Jimmy O'Conner if he'd run her up to the doctor in Bow Island, but she don't wanna go."

Doctor? This is serious. I've got to get down there. Oh, God! Three hundred and fifty miles on those roads – and this *would* be the year Clarence isn't free. Boxing Day sale coming up. "My day to unload half of McRobb's 'Best-in-the-West Clunkers.'"

She was breathing shallowly, the nails of the hand clutching the receiver biting into her palm.

Well, there goes my Christmas plans. I thought I could invite a few friends in over the holidays and at least take the kids skating, but –

"Sarah?"

"Don't worry, Father. I'll *be* there, quick as I can."

The boys, who had helped themselves to generous slices of cake and returned to the living room, stopped chewing and stared at her.

"We're going to Grandma and Grandpa's, after all? You said we were gonna stay home this year."

"Oh, Jeez, Mom, it's *boring* down there and there isn't even beds for us guys. Just sleeping bags on the floor."

"And it's cold."

"Yeah, and I saw a mouse in Grandma's cupboards."

"Mice won't eat Santa Claus, so quit complaining. And think of your father. He'll be here alone on Christmas Day."

Alan's eyes grew round. "You mean, you're gonna drive?"

THE ROAD WAS A TREACHEROUS ribbon of ice under a moon scudding through storm clouds. The kids had been asleep in the back seat for hours. Sarah's hands were numb from gripping the wheel. She passed cars abandoned in the ditch and accidents with ambulances and the hysterically flashing lights of RCMP cruisers. She took a curve too fast and fought the temptation to feather the brakes. A trucker roared past, slapping her with the wind of his passage and blasting the air horns.

"Bastard! You son of a bitch, you!"

"Mom?" Alan quavered, "Are you all right?"

"Yes, sure, Alan. Fine."

"When are we gonna stop for supper?"

"We'll be in MacLeod in half an hour."

"And how long after that?"

"Maybe an hour. Don't whine, Alan."

"Jeez, you're grouchy."

Kid, you're just lucky I don't bite.

THE IMMEDIATE CRISIS had been dealt with – tranquilizers and antibiotics. Father was beating the pants off the kids at checkers out in the living room. ("Little buggers can just as well learn that when I play, I play for keeps.")

Sarah, sitting on the foot of Mother's bed, lit her third cigarette. Mother frowned. Sarah took one deep drag and stubbed it out. "So, what *are* you going to do, Mother? You can't stay here any longer with no doctor in town and having to depend on neighbours for transportation."

"That's what I keep telling Daddy."

Sarah winced. They had always been Beth and James to each other; now they had become Daddy and Mommy.

"What would you like to do?"

Mother studied the backs of her wrinkled hands. "I don't know, Sarah. I don't know."

Oh, yes, you do. You want me to ask you to come and live with us. And the worst of it is, there's room in our house, but, oh, God, it's bad enough now. I shudder to think of them overhearing the rows that break out between Clarence and me. Then there's the false teeth and Father's dirty old pipes and his cigarette lighters.

She laced her fingers and avoided Mother's eyes. "Maybe...maybe I could look around for an apartment close to our place. What do you think?"

Hurt flicked across the anxious old face. She sighed. "Well, our pension cheques would take care of the rent, and leave a little over for groceries, I suppose, but...."

Sarah glanced into the living room where she could see Miss Hindman's exquisite little nude.

Stewing about money, and her with a small fortune

hanging on her wall. Well, the nude *is* hers. She's hung onto it thorough thick and thin all these years, and I don't feel like getting into a hassle about it now.

"Maybe it would be best to move to Edmonton," Mother sighed, "but how would we get Daddy away from Rattlesnake Park? He plays checkers with old Pete O'Donnel most afternoons. Then there's the Masonic Lodge on the first Thursday of every month. What with Daddy being past master and all...."

"I know some Masons that'll take him under their wing; you'll have the Church and the kids to keep your cookie jar empty."

"If you could find an apartment close to the Church, maybe...." Her voice wandered off, vague, faint.

"Shouldn't be hard. Let's talk to Father."

The old man looked up, faded eyes blinking behind his thick glasses. "Some goddamned boarding house? Not on your life."

"Boarding house? Who said anything about a – ´ ?"

"I stayed in one of them christly places back in '21, the winter I was feeding cattle for Burns in Lethbridge. Bloody woman kept them floors so shined it was like trying to walk on glare ice, and her spuds never was cooked enough."

"I'm not talking about a boarding house, Father. I'm talking about an apartment."

He eyed her suspiciously. "What's the difference?"

"What's the difference!" Alan hooted, pounding Josh on the shoulder.

"All right, you two, outside." Sarah made a mental note to speak to Alan when she could get him alone.

When the door closed behind the kids, she sat

down to face Father and relit her cigarette. "You've never been in an apartment, Father. They're – well, kind of like a bunch of little houses all under one big roof. Everybody has his own door. Locked. Nobody comes in unless you invite them. You'll have your own kitchen. Bedroom. Furniture. Everything."

He dragged his jackknife from his overalls pocket with a trembling hand. The blade was narrow and frail from years of whetting. He started reaming his pipe; the smell was sickening and he got more dottle on the carpet than he got into the ashtray. "I don't wanna live in no goddamned apartment. I wanna stay right here."

"But what if one of you gets sick in the middle of the night and needs a doctor?"

"What if we do? We're eighty years old. Whadda you think some christly doctor's gonna do for us?"

"Different story three nights ago." The bite came into her voice in spite of good intentions. "I recall some old guy worrying about his wife. And I have some vague memory of driving more than three hundred miles over skating rinks to get down here."

He shut the knife and returned it to his pocket. Tears leaked out of his eyes and coursed down the channels of his face. He made no attempt to wipe them away. It was as though he didn't know they were there. "Well, I guess it's what Mommy wants, ain't it?"

BY THE FIRST OF APRIL, Father and Mother were ensconced in an apartment two blocks from Sarah's place. Whenever she came to visit, she found them sitting like uneasy travellers waiting for a train.

"Relax. You're *home*. Why don't you go out for a

little walk? It's a beautiful day."

"We're fine, dear. Just fine."

"Sure a treat to lean your eyes against a tree once in a while, Kid."

"And it's lovely to have the boys come in every night after school."

But three weeks went by, and they still looked as though they were waiting for a train.

Sunday was Sarah's day off – no marking, no prep, and she and the family always went out for dinner at a good restaurant. Mother and Father were invited to go with them.

Mother had a hearing problem. In a noisy place, she was confused. She read the menu aloud and exclaimed in horrified tones at the prices. Waiters were embarrassed, other diners amused. Both oldsters had problems with their dentures. Mother's clacked; Father's downright didn't fit; if something got under them, he was not above taking them out of his mouth and scraping them off right at the table.

"God, Sarah," Clarence complained after the third disastrous dinner, "I know they're only an old farm couple, but –"

"Salt of the earth doesn't count, eh, Clarence?"

"Oh, for Christ sake, don't get sore."

"Don't worry, sweetie, you won't be embarrassed by eating out with them after this. I'm cooking for them at home, and if you don't like their manners, you can go eat on the porch."

Clarence didn't speak to her for three days; she lay in bed at night, not knowing whether she was madder at him or madder at Mother and Father.

It's so bloody stupid, them going on like this.

Mother could have a hearing aid. Two if she wanted. They could both have dentures that fit, decent clothes, and a maid to clean house for them. But would Mother sell that nude? Not on your.... God, they get to me, they really do. Well, if I could arrange for them to meet some people and get them off my back, maybe –

She spoke to Duncan, her next-door neighbour, who was well up in the Masonic Order. Could he possibly take Father to Lodge with him? He did so. Once.

Mother, however, found another lady in the apartment who belonged to the Church. Mrs. Bains and Mother trotted off twice a Sunday and every Tuesday afternoon to Auxiliary meetings. Father sat at home staring out of the window.

"What am I going to do with him?" Sarah groaned one night as she and Clarence were getting ready for bed.

"I don't mind playing checkers with the old guy once in a while, but Jeez, I've got friends of my own. Guys that give me leads. If it hadn't been for good old Darrel telling me about that guy that was looking for a T-bird –"

"You sold it?"

"Finally, but I'm telling you, the guy that bought it can squeeze a buck until it hollers."

"So, what did you make?"

"A hundred and fifty."

For three day's work? My God!

"What're you thinking?" His tone was edgy, suspicious.

"I was thinking about Father."

"Why don't you try getting the old boy a pet?"

"The apartment doesn't allow dogs or cats."

"They wouldn't have to know about a coupla gerbils."

"Gerbils? Father'd say they were nothing but mice."

"Why not a budgie? They're kind of fun."

Why not? If I got a real baby, it would ride around on Father's shoulder, and maybe even learn to talk –

On Saturday afternoon she set out on her quest. Just before supper, she struggled into the apartment, loaded down with stand, bird, cage, and supplies.

"His name is MacGillicuddy, Father", she said, transferring the stunned-looking little bird from her finger to his.

Father looked a little stunned himself as he stared at the budgie. "Be damned. Huh! Be damned."

"He'll be a lot of fun when he gets tame, you know?"

He glanced towards her then away. "Yeah. Yeah, I guess."

I should never have bought that bird without asking him first, she fretted as she headed home to mark a pile of exams. Well, if it doesn't work out, I'll have to take the little beast home for the kids.

But within a week MacGillicuddy ruled the roost in the apartment. When he was not riding on Father's shoulders he was ripping newspapers, tearing corners off calendars, or pestering Mother when she was working on her tapestry. There was birdshit on everything, and Mother and Father thought MacGillicuddy was the cutest thing they had ever laid eyes on.

"He doesn't have to be out of his cage *all* the time, Father. Half an hour's exercise is –"

"Hell with that noise. I ain't keeping him penned up."

MacGillicuddy landed on the frame of Miss Hindman's painting, and tested one corner with his beak.

"Mother! Are you going to let that destructive little stinker ruin – ?"

Mother sprang from her chair, "Oh, you naughty – Shoo! Shoo!" She removed the painting from the wall and pressed it to her heart. "I shall put it in with my lingerie," she said stiffly, her face colouring when she looked at Sarah. "It will be safe there, and I need only take it out when I want to look at it."

God almighty, after all these years…. Well, at least *she's* had a real love.

When Mother returned from the bedroom, Sarah took a deep breath. "If you're going to have MacGillicuddy flying loose all the time, I'd better see if my cleaning lady can fit the apartment into her schedule before this place gets too bad. She's quite reasonable. Ten bucks an hour."

"Ten bucks an hour for a woman to vacuum and dust a little? Christ! I worked all day, spike-pitching on a threshing outfit for a buck and a half. What's wrong with the bloody place? Looks all right to me."

Outside, Sarah sat in her car, pounding the steering wheel. Dammit all to *hell!* I can't let them live in a *sty.* I'll have to clean the place myself.

Within two months, the boys grew weary of taking turns visiting their grandparents after school.

"Grandpa's always trying to make me fix his stinking old lighters," Alan complained. "I don't know how a guy's supposed to put a wick in the fool things. Can't he afford a new one?"

"You have to realize Grandpa never had money to waste. If he thought something could be fixed, he struggled with it."

"Yeah, but *he's* not struggling."

Josh giggled. "He sure wastes money now. Sent me to the store three times last week to buy flints."

"No kidding?" Alan whooped. "I went a coupla times too."

Sarah was alarmed. Father had asked her to buy flints every time she had been over to the apartment in the past month too, but there was a development in the Art Department which distracted her. Joseph Chapel, the famous artist who was supposed to appear as a guest lecturer at summer session, had contracted some mysterious disease. Pressure was being brought to bear on Sarah to pinch-hit in his place; there were endless meetings, endless discussions. She saw her parents only for Sunday dinners and on Thursday nights when she tidied the apartment and took Mother grocery shopping.

One warm spring night, as she was driving home from work, she saw Father sitting on a bus bench beside a busy intersection. Alarmed, she circled the block and turned into the garage's parking lot behind him.

"Father?"

He continued to lean on his cane and stare at the street. "Five hundred and eighty-nine, five hundred and ninety."

"Father!"

He glanced at her, then gravely consulted his pocket watch. "You realize there's been five hundred and ninety two cars pass this spot in the last half hour, Kid?"

"Has there?" A chill passed over her.

"Eee-yup."

"Well, it's…it's a nice day to sit in the sun anyway, isn't it? Where's Mother?"

"Damned if I know. She went someplace."

"Someplace?"

He shrugged irritably. "Something about the Church. Listen, you gotta come over and help me get things straightened out at that bank. They got everything buggered up."

"Buggered up? What do you mean?"

"Just what I said, for chrisake. Can't you understand English?"

She stared at him. "Father, are you feeling all right?"

"A hundred and fifty today."

Percent or years? she wondered bleakly. "Look, hop in the car and we'll.... Well, why don't we go over to the pub there for a tall cold one before I run you home? I could use a beer myself after a day's work."

"A *pub*? You?"

"There's nothing wrong with a woman going into a –"

"Should be bloody well ashamed of yourself," he tossed over his shoulder as he hobbled away.

"Oh, look, Father, don't.... C'mon, I'll give you a lift."

"The hell you will." He didn't even glance back.

The moment she got home she phoned the apartment. At the tenth ring she heard Mother fumbling with the receiver. "Yes?"

"Mother? Father said you were –"

"You *saw* Daddy? I've been so worr –" Sarah winced as the receiver, forgotten, clattered against the wall. "James MacKenzie, *where* have you been?"

Realizing she had been forgotten, Sarah hung up the phone and pulled a deep, shaky breath just as

Alan and Josh burst through the door.

"Mom, you gotta *do* something about Grandpa. He came home and tossed *three* new packages of flints on the table."

"And then he tried to send me to Safeways to buy *more*," Josh sounded deeply aggrieved.

"And he's always bugging us to play checkers."

"Beats us every time. What's the fun in that?"

"I'm afraid Grandpa's slipping. The poor old guy hasn't got much to think about except checkers and flints."

"Well, it's not our fault, and we're sick of his checkers and his flints."

"Look, I'll make you a deal. Supposing you and Josh come home after school and prepare the veggies, tidy the kitchen after supper, and load the dishwasher, and I'll visit Grandpa and Grandma after work and run errands for them?"

Alan's face lightened with relief. "Mom, I'll peel spuds and carrots till the cows come home," he vowed, in an eerie imitation of his Grandfather's voice.

The kids shouldn't be tending grandparents or peeling spuds either; they should be out playing ball with their buddies, she thought. But I am so *tired*. Never a day off. I don't know when I last touched brush to canvas, and there's that damned summer session coming up. I know I'm going to get stuck with it, and that means boning up. It's years since I did studies of the human figure. She sighed. Well, God knows we could use the money. Clarence never sold enough cars last month to pay his own gas bill.

The following afternoon, when Sarah walked into the apartment, Mother was working tearfully at her tapestry while MacGillicuddy danced across it, shitting on the beautiful work and trying to snatch the needle from her fingers. Father was sitting in his old rocker, one elbow propped on the table and, as always when he was troubled, his fingers toying with the few silver hairs on top of his head.

Sarah looked from one to the other. "Is something wrong?"

Mother indicated a grubby letter lying on the table. "A letter from Mrs. O'Donnel. Old Pete's dead."

"Oh-h. Father, I'm so sorry."

"Sorry? Hell! Old bugger went out with his boots on. Him and that old truck of his lost an argument with a CPR freight and he never knew what hit him. How lucky can you get?" He sighed and picked up a smelly old bullet lighter. "Listen, Kid, I been wrestling with this sucker all day. How about seeing if you can't ram that wick into her for me?"

"Father, I can't 'ram that wick into her' and I'm not going to waste time trying."

"All right then, *don't*. But I want you to go get me some flints."

"I could ram his flints and his bloody lighters up his nose," she raged, as she headed for the drugstore. Then she was leaning against a utility pole gulping tears. "Poor old fella. His best friend gone. He couldn't even go to the funeral, and there's me, bitching at him about his lighters."

Half an hour later, she walked into the apartment and triumphantly handed him an expensive new lighter. "Present for you, Father. Butane. Especially designed for pipes. You'll never have to fuss with flints or wicks with that one, and I'll throw all those junky old lighters out for you."

"Throw 'em out? Good lighters? The hell you say." He turned the new lighter over and over in his hands. "Too fancy for every day. Fella's liable to lose her. I'll keep her for when I get decked out in my glad rags." He returned the lighter to its box, slipped it into a drawer and looked up at Sarah. "Well, where's them flints?"

She took a deep breath and handed over the flints that prudence had warned her to buy.

"Eee-yup." He bent to the window, squinted at one end of his old lighter so that he could see to insert a dime into the slot to remove the scarcely-used flint. He tossed it onto the rug and replaced it with a new one. "Old bugger died with his boots on.

"I ever tell you about the first time I seen Pete? We was both kids, new to the country, him and me. We got us a job on Margeson's haying crew, Pete mowing and me raking. Crazy bastard of a Margeson had me driving two stud horses. Worked pretty good for a couple of days, then one reaches over and lifts a little hide offa the other with his teeth, and all hell breaks loose. By the time they was done fighting, there wasn't enough hayrake or harness left to fix. Margeson come along, mad as hell. Gave us our time and run us offa the place. Eee-yup. Ten miles to town, and we hoofed it. That night was the first time Pete and me got tight."

For the next few weeks, Sarah was frantically busy putting the finishing touches on a number of canvasses she had been invited to include in a provincial exhibition and, at the same time, struggling to prepare for the summer session. Her visits to the apartment were hurry-up affairs consisting of changing beds, gathering up washing, taking out garbage, and throwing mouldy food out of the fridge. Whenever she gave the rug a hasty going over with the vacuum cleaner, she could hear it suck up dozens and dozens of flints, but, to her relief, she noticed that MacGillicuddy was being kept in his cage lately, and Father had stopped fussing about flints and lighters.

One night, as she was about to leave the apartment, MacGillicuddy was begging most appealingly to be turned loose. When she opened the cage door for him, Mother exclaimed, "Oh, my dear, I wish you hadn't done that. He's so hard to catch, and Tom doesn't like him. Silly really, for a grown man, but he's frightened to death of birds."

"Tom? Who's Tom?"

"Friend of mine," Father said gruffly.

"A friend? Where did you meet him?"

"Right out there in the hallway. Eee-yup. Smart fella, too. Studying for his Ph.D. up at the university, but I can still lick him at checkers."

"You mean, he lives in this apartment?"

"Eee-hup."

"But how old is he? I mean, what is he studying? I mean…. Look, you've got to be careful. This is the city. How do you know he's not a cr – ?"

A rap sounded on the door.

"Come on in, Tom. She's open."

"Oh, James," Mother gasped. "The budgie – !"

MacGillicuddy, who had been joyfully circling the room, made for the open door where the stranger was standing. The stranger squawked, ducked, and, as the budgie swooped past, grabbed MacGillicuddy by the tail. Tail and bird parted company. MacGillicuddy crash-landed in the hall. The stranger stood with a package of flints in one hand and MacGillicuddy's jewel-blue tail feathers in the other. "Oh – tundering Jasus! I.... Oh, Jamie, Mrs. MacKenzie, I'm terrible sorry. I didn't mean.... I wouldn't –" he fumbled as Sarah brushed past him to retrieved MacGillicuddy.

"Goddamn that Sarah, anyhow," MacGillicuddy said in exactly Father's voice when she picked him up.

Thankfully, the stranger had not heard. He was staring at the feathers in his fingers with an expression of extreme distaste. He went and handed them to Mother, then wiped his hand on his pant leg. "I suppose I should take him to a vet, wouldn't you think? I.... I don't know anything about birds."

"Forget it, Tom. Little bugger'll grow a tail, good as new. C'mon in. You fetch me them flints?"

Tom looked as though he had been reprieved from the gallows. "Sure did, Jamie. I think I've got it figured out how to put a new wick into that lighter for you too. I'll have a go at it once we've finished our game." He went to the drawer where the checkers and the board were kept, hauled them out, and packed them to the table.

Acts like he owns the place! Who is this guy? The accent sounds Irish, except it's not. And where does he get off, calling Father "Jamie?"

She was further amazed when the stranger said, "Well, you old rascal, I suppose you've been studying that checker book I loaned you, and you think you're going to clean up on me, don't you?"

"I'm sure as hell gonna try."

"All right, then. Set 'em up."

As Sarah returned MacGillicuddy to his cage, Mother said, "Tom, in all the excitement we forgot to introduce you to our daughter. This is Sarah."

Tom glanced up, jerking his head in acknowledgement. His expression was judgemental, almost hostile.

Thinks I'm neglecting Mother and Father. What right does he...? Who the hell does he think he is? How do I know *he's* not a con man?

Although she couldn't afford the time, she pulled a chair up to the table to watch the game. She used to play checkers with Father when she was a kid. Once in a while, she even beat him.

Just let me *catch* that bastard letting Father win, or –

But Father and Tom played with deadly concentration, matching each other, move for skillful move. When Sarah rose to leave, they scarcely grunted in her direction.

She tiptoed along the corridor, studying name plates on apartment doors. There it is. Thomas Harrison Ford. So he does live here, but I'm going to check him out as soon as I get home. Bastard thinks I'm neglecting Mother and Father. But maybe I am too, she admitted miserably as she got into her car. God, I don't even know who they're associating with these days. Poor old Father, begging strangers to buy his goddamned flints and fix his lighters. Why couldn't I have just done it cheerfully? Then there's that business at the bank. I've got to find time to take him over and see what he's fussing about or, the next thing I know, Tom will be cleaning out his account for him. Not that there's much to clean, but –

Then it hit her. Miss Hindman's nude! That's what he's after. But when would he have seen it? Unless he's been snooping through drawers? Unless Mother's shown him –

She raced home and fell over herself to get to the phone.

Her friend, Shirley, one of the powers-that-be in the School of Graduate Studies at the university, said, "Thomas Harrison Ford? Oh…. Tom! Where'd you meet our favorite Newfie?"

"In my parents' apartment."

"Your father must be the checker player Tom talks about. Old Jamie with all the lighters and the flints? And you thought Tom was up to no good?"

"It had occurred to me."

"Relax. The only person Tom is likely to con is himself."

Sarah went weak with relief and embarrassment.

THE SUMMER SESSION ENDED on a throbbingly hot August day. Sarah couldn't quite face the apartment after work. She planned to go over after supper. She changed into shorts and a loose tank top and was flopped out on a deck chair in the back yard, sipping a bottle of beer and watching the kids and Josh's little dog, Paddy, race through the lawn spray, when the phone rang.

"Alan, could you get that for me, please? It's probably for one of you kids anyway."

She was lying back, eyes closed, when she heard the living room window slide open behind her. "Mom, it's that Tom guy. Something's wrong with Grandpa."

She tore into the house and snatched the receiver from Alan's hand. "Tom?"

"You'd better come, Mrs. Cross. Your mother says Jamie went out for a little walk and a breath of fresh air and.... Well, I've called the ambulance."

Sarah beat the ambulance to the apartment. When she pushed through the crowd gathered on the stoop, dropped to her knees and looked into Father's face, she knew that he was dead.

It was midnight before the questions were answered, the hasty arrangements made, and Mother and MacGillicuddy ensconced in the house. The night was hot, breathless. Everybody had gone to bed. Sarah poured herself half a tumbler of scotch, topped it up with water, went out into the back yard, and stretched out in a lawn chair.

Her breath caught somewhere between a laugh and a sob when a memory popped into her mind from the time when she was a little kid. Father and Pete were headed for the beer parlour in Rattlesnake Park. Father promised Sarah a packet of Cracker Jack if she would keep Fanny, his collie bitch, from following them. Sarah tried. Trouble was, after she got Fanny dressed in baby clothes, she'd left the bitch unattended while she went to look for shoes to complete the ensemble. When she returned with the shoes, Fanny was gone.

All their lives Pete and Father had giggled about Fanny, decked out in baby clothes, parading through Rattlesnake Park looking for Father, with a dozen eager suitors trailing in her wake.

Her eyes blurred, she took a gulp of whiskey, and looked up into the stars.

FOG HAS SETTLED ON THE HARBOUR. Ships, inching through the murk, moan sullen warnings, but the lodge, on the top of the hill, is in brilliant sunlight.

"So, in the end of all, they both died with their boots on," Sarah mutters. "How lucky can you get?"

Four o'clock, and still no Beth. The goddamned day is so goddamned long. Could it be that she has forgotten?

She tires of the radio. This afternoon they have been playing such old artists as Sarah Vaughn and Tommy Dorsey. Sarah detests both. She switches the radio off and wanders irresolutely about the room. "Maybe I'll go down to the lounge. Find somebody to talk to."

The lounge has three people in it. An old guy who leans both hands on his cane and mutters to himself. Sarah has never discovered his name, never wanted to. The old bugger gets mad for no good reason and hits people. There is an old lady, reputed to be over a hundred, sound asleep in her wheelchair, mouth open and head flopped over as though her neck is broken. And there is the one-legged-demon, Josie, with her inevitable game of solitaire and the friends with whom she converses so pleasantly, although the friends aren't there. Josie, the "former prostitute," as one of the "quality" residents sniffed. Sarah never bothered asking her how *she* knew.

Sarah picks through a pile of newspapers on one of the scarred coffee tables, fishes out a real estate guide, and leafs through it until she comes upon a page advertising duplexes.

"One hundred and forty-nine thousand," she reads. "Why pay rent? You be the landlord and let your tenants pay your mortgage. Hurry. Offer won't last long."

"Cursed duplexes." She is swept again by a sense of betrayal and impotent rage.

❧

THE BUSINESS OF BUYING the duplex had started on Clarence's fiftieth birthday. Sarah woke at two in the morning to find his side of the bed empty. She rose, shrugged into a robe, and padded down the hall towards the light coming from under the dining room door. Clarence was seated at the table, a mug of cold coffee in front of him and all their business papers spread before him.

"What are you doing, Clarence? Is something wrong?"

"Do you realize that when I retire I'll only have my old age pension and about two hundred and thirty dollars a month Canada Pension?"

"Well, I'm not retiring for fifteen years. There'll be my Canada Pension plus a fairly decent pension from the university. We'll be all right."

"And have them say, 'Poor old Clarence Cross has gotta live off his wife's pensions because he never could hold down a decent job'?"

"It doesn't matter what 'they' say," she soothed. "It's not as if you haven't tried." Okay, so it's a lie. I should have dumped him years ago. But I didn't. And it's a little late now. So –

"Y'know, I could have taught music, even without these fingers?" he said, holding up his left hand and staring ruefully at the two stumps. "I could have been a damned good piano teacher, even if I couldn't play, but I couldn't stand the thought of listening to a bunch of brats murdering Brahms day after day." He gave a deprecating snort. "But that's what you do all the time, I guess, herd a bunch of characters that'll never learn to be artists while they muck around with paints and charcoal and stuff."

"Some of them learn."

"Yeah, and there'd have been the odd kid that might have learned to play too." He shook his head. "I was never cut out to be a businessman, that's for sure, and I never could work up much steam about selling insurance or used cars or whatever." He made a wry face and stabbed one finger at his chest. "Too soon old and too late smart, that's me."

She dumped his coffee mug, poured fresh for him and a mug for herself. "What were you looking for in the papers?"

"I've been thinking, there's a guy in the same fix as I am down at the hatchery. Denny Grogan. Wife's gone into real estate. They got it all figured out. They're selling their house, putting the money into a duplex, and renting out one half. Regular little gold mine with all these oil workers in town looking for accommodation. I don't see why we couldn't do the same thing."

"Sell our house? Nothing doing, not when we've finally got it in good shape and paid for."

"We don't need all this space now that your mother's gone. And a duplex doesn't have to be a dump."

"But it would be small and cramped and, with tenants needing a place to park, I couldn't expect to have the garage for a studio."

"The kids won't be with us much longer. You'd soon

have a spare bedroom for a studio."

"And listen to you complain about the smell of turpentine all the time? I don't know why we're even discussing a duplex. It's silly."

"Pretty soon this house is going to be too big for us. Alan's twenty. Been working for the city for two years. It's a wonder he hasn't pulled out already."

"What are you trying to do? Push the kid out?"

"No, but…. And then there's Josh. University this fall? He doesn't knows what he wants to study. Should get out and work a year or two."

Sarah struggled to maintain her composure. "What he *needs* is to take some courses to sort himself out. Art, Creative Writing. Whatever. This is the kid that picked up a recorder and taught himself to play when he was five, don't forget, and he's already getting the odd bit of poetry published. But he could decide to settle on art. He's always –"

"Alan never needed courses to sort himself out."

"Right from the time he was a little guy, Alan knew what he wanted. Give him a toy truck and a backhoe and he was happy."

"So, what are we gonna do about the duplex?"

Duplex? Are we back to that nonsense again? "Nothing, so far as I'm concerned. This is our home. I've painted every wall in it. Planted trees when they were nothing but buggy whips, and now some of them are thirty feet tall."

"My father's wedding present paid for half this place."

"And *my* salary paid the mortgage nine times out of ten!"

Why did I have to rub it in? she asked herself, as

she lay in what used to be Mother's room, staring up at the bare branches of the lilac which had grown up outside the window. Now he'll sulk. Sit up playing piano records until all hours and go to bed reeking of beer.

Two weeks went by. Sarah was still sleeping in Mother's room and Clarence was still sitting up half the night, drinking beer and playing piano records. Sarah and he barely spoke to each other.

Then Clarence made a big to-do about getting tickets to an Oiler's game for himself and the boys one Saturday night. "That's okay, just me and the guys, isn't it, Sarah? You never understood the game anyway."

"I'll be glad to have the evening to myself."

When the three of them returned, Alan and Clarence wore the air of bright-eyed conspirators while they discussed various plays in loud "guy" voices; Josh, who took no part, stomped off to bed without even saying good-night. The following morning at breakfast Sarah caught him watching her with a guilty, confused expression.

Clarence has said something to the kids, she realized. Something to do with me. Now what's he up to? Well, no doubt I'll find out soon enough.

That night she was working in her studio when Alan knocked on the door. She was a little surprised. He seldom came to her studio. Usually it was Josh who walked in and made himself at home. Sometimes he played patience while she worked and sometimes he amused her by reading *Mad* magazine aloud to her.

"Come in, Alan," she invited. "I'll only be a minute here."

He sat on the edge of the old couch, watching her,

his clasped hands caught between his knees.

She laid down the pastel she had been working with and removed her mask. "What's up?"

"Mom, couldn't you at least *talk* to Dad about his duplex idea? He feels awful with you being so mad at him all the time."

"Did he put you up to speaking to me? He had no right to drag you into this matter."

"Well, Mom, it's no fun for us guys, either – you two scrapping. It's got me and Josh scrapping, too. The thing is, Mom, I've got friends that live in duplexes. I don't think you realize how nice they can be. And with a good tenant in the other half and money coming in all the time, Dad might not feel so...." He trailed off, offering her a sick grin and a shrug before he sidled outside. In a moment she heard his old pickup clatter away.

She opened the studio door to the smell she loved, damp earth and early spring. She shut off the lights and sat in the doorway, smoking in the dark. The tip of a new moon was touching the bricks of the fireplace chimney, buds on the elm tree she'd planted twenty years ago were beginning to swell, and she could just see tulips in the bed beside the house nodding like stately ghosts.

Well, it's *my* house too, and there's no bloody way. Clarence can sulk till hell freezes over.

SHE HAD BEEN INVITED to be the guest speaker at an art teachers' convention in Calgary the following weekend. Between her classes and the preparation for her speech, she was working every waking moment; she became overtired and caught a cold.

Several times, when she had been driving in after work, she had noticed strange cars leaving the house, and several times, after she had gone to bed, she'd heard Clarence talking on the phone. She was too exhausted to pay much attention.

By the Friday morning, her cold was better, she had her speech prepared, and her bags packed. She was looking forward to a break in routine and a chance to talk to old friends, but when she was ready to leave, her car refused to start. The guy she called from the CAA said the starter was shot. The garage said they wouldn't be able to work on it until that afternoon. She toyed with the idea of taking the Air Bus but, along with the cold, she had had a slight ear infection; she knew it would flare up again if she flew.

Why not the old Greyhound? It's only a few hours, and it'll give me time to gather my wits.

Since she was to be met by the organizer of the convention and taken straight to luncheon when she arrived in Calgary, she had dressed in her best wool suit, a rich carmine red worn with a silk scarf of darker tones that brought out the colour in her dark eyes and in her hair, still black with only the odd thread of silver, and still worn in a flowing pony tail.

She bought her ticket in the bus depot, strolled outside and mounted the steps of the Calgary Express. When the driver looked up to take her ticket, she found herself staring into a pair of shining Celtic-blue eyes. Jock MacDonald.

"My god, Sarah!" he exclaimed, "It's you."

"Well, Jock MacDonald! So, you're still driving for Greyhound." She was striving for a polite distant tone.

His eyes hungrily searched her face. "I've read

about you. I've even snuck into your exhibitions when I had layovers in Edmonton but…you've never been around."

This is ridiculous. I've got to shut it down. "What do you think of my work?" Cool, professional.

"I'm no judge, but…." He paused and his voice was humble, "I guess it's real good stuff, isn't it? From what the paper said, anyway. So, what'll you be doing in Calgary?"

"A convention. I have to speak this afternoon."

An older man, obviously a Greyhound official, bustled out of the depot and stuck his head in the open door of the bus. "What's the holdup, Jock? You're late pulling out."

"Oh hell!" Embarrassment flared in his face as he put the bus into reverse and looked up at Sarah with a pleading expression. "There's an empty seat right behind me, if you wanna move my jacket."

She laughed. "Jock, Jock, are you still playing that game?"

"I wouldn't have been, not if I'd had brains enough to know a good thing when I saw it a long time ago."

"Oh, sure. Flattery will get you everywhere." There was a barb in the tease.

"It's not flattery." When she looked up into the mirror, his eyes met hers in an expression of pained humility. "I've never forgotten you."

"What a good line. How many girls have fallen for that one?"

"Sarah, don't make fun of me, please. I've…I've driven this route for years, hoping that maybe, someday –"

Her heart tripped painfully. You'll never know how often I've thought of you, either, if I have to be honest with myself. Maybe if I'd known you were so close –

"Could I pick you up somewhere tonight, Sarah? That is if you can get away? Please? I've got the house all to myself."

She was trembling. It was all she could do to keep from touching the rough serge of his uniform. She wrote the name of the hotel where she had a reservation and passed it to him.

THAT NIGHT, sated for the moment, they lay like young lovers, touching all the length of their bodies, trading puffs on the same cigarette. Sarah glanced about at the room which Jock's wife, who was visiting a sister in Regina, had decorated with crochet. Everything. Pillows, curtains, bedspread – even a flounce around the edge of the bed table.

"Give you the feeling you're caught in some kind of goddamned spider web?"

"It's that bad?"

"No. No, it's not. It's just that she could tell you the double whatever the hell in crochet, and I've lost count of the Arran sweaters piled up in those drawers that she's knitted for me. Works for her Granny. A little wool shop downtown. A good little business and she sure knows her way around it, but she couldn't tell you who the prime minister is, or whether the Black Hawks play hockey or football. What about yours?"

Careful, Sarah. Don't start something you're not prepared to finish.

She shrugged. "Oh, we rub along, but the kids are great."

"We never had any. Maybe if we had, Esther could

have figured out something to do besides that god-damned crochet and knitting stuff."

She kissed him lingeringly. "Well, my love, I have to go. Sorry to leave you, but I've got to get back to my hotel."

"I'll drive you."

"Call me a cab. I don't want anybody asking questions."

When she came out of the bathroom, he was seated on a chair waiting for her. He pulled her to him, entering her completely. They whimpered with pleasure and devoured each other with hungry open-mouthed kisses. "Well, babe, I guess we buggered it," he murmured against her hair. "At least, I buggered it. But anyhow, we've had tonight."

"And that's it? Tonight?"

"Christ, you mean it?"

"It can probably be arranged the odd time. If we're discreet. There's an old rancher in west of here. He lets me pull my camper onto his place for painting expeditions any time I've a mind to. He never comes near me, so –"

WHEN THE TAXI PULLED UP in front of her house in Edmonton, Sarah was surprised to find the place in darkness. She climbed the steps, unlocked the door and switched the lights on. The house was empty, echoing. Rugs, furniture, pictures – everything – gone. She was staring about with a sense of weird unreality and very real fear when Clarence and Alan's faces appeared over the banister. "Surprise!" Back in the shadows she saw Josh, his expression frightened, ashamed.

"Surprise!" Clarence and Alan chorused again.

"We just about broke our necks getting everything moved into the duplex for you, Mom," Alan burbled.

"Duplex?"

"Josh even got your studio all set up. It's got sky-lights and everything. You're gonna love it."

"Clarence, what in God's name... ?"

"Wait'll you see it," he interrupted, "An up-down duplex, brand new, and we've got a good tenant that's paying five hundred a month. And just wait till you hear the packet we made on this old dump."

"Sold? *Sold?* You had no *right!*"

"Sure as hell did. This place was in *my* name."

"Your name!" Josh's voice quivered with fury. "That counts for a lot. I never saw you doing too much painting or papering or gardening around here. I told you not to do it, Dad. I *told* you –"

"Keep your trap shut, young fella, or –"

"I wouldn't blame her if she walked out on you. Just walked to hell out on you right now."

Clarence swelled with insult. "I've a good mind to drill you one, you lippy young bugger."

Sarah stepped between them, her hand on Josh's arm. "No, Josh, this is between your father and me."

She turned on Clarence. "Haven't I ever told you about the time Father bought the Aldridge quarter without telling Mother?" Her voice was shaking. "Haven't I ever told you how much Mother *hated* it?"

"Oh, God, Sarah, don't start. I was just trying to do what's best for us."

"Just trying to do what's best for us? You know, that's what Father said too."

AFTER SARAH'S INITIAL SHOCK and outrage at Clarence's having sold the house without her consent, she had to admit that the duplex was very nice. New, convenient, bright. The builder, a good one, had razed an old house to make room for the new and had preserved some stately old trees in the back yard, as well as shrubs, a rock garden, and several beds of well-tended perennials. Although it was near a traffic artery, the duplex was situated in a respectable district of middle-class homes less than ten minutes from Sarah's work at the university. For five days she almost forgot that there was a tenant named Eric downstairs, although Clarence had shown her the man's references, impressive ones, from somewhere in New Brunswick.

Sarah was working in her new studio on that first Saturday morning. She was touched at how carefully all her things had been moved and set up for her. Josh had done a wonderful job. While she was admiring the flood of light streaming through the skylights, she was jolted by a blast of county and western music from the suite downstairs.

What kind of garbage is that Eric character playing? And so loud too. I'm not putting up with that, and I'd just as well tell him so right off the bat.

She whipped out the back door, down a flight of steps and down another to the basement suite's back door.

At the fifth ring the door opened. The music hit her like a blow, and Eric, a fat, bearded young man, so drunk he could scarcely stand, blinked at her. "Wal, hello, Mrs. Landlady. How's tricks?"

"Look, Eric, I must insist that you turn that record player down. It is disturbing me, and since we both live in the same house, we have to be considerate of each other."

"Don' like my hurtin' music, and you a good ol' western gal too? Wal, what the fuck. I think it's pretty nice."

"I'm not discussing the matter with you. Turn it down."

He shut the door in her face, and as she moved away, she heard him mutter, "Persnickety goddamned landladies. I hate 'em all."

The "hurtin' music" diminished so that she could scarcely hear it, but her morning's work was ruined; she couldn't concentrate, and any pleasure she might have taken in the duplex evaporated.

I knew this setup had to be too good to be true, she thought. We're going to give that guy his notice right away.

But when she told Clarence, he said, "Well, he *did* turn the music down, didn't he? We can't afford to be that picky. A coupla months with that suite not being rented, and where's the advantage of owning a duplex?"

"You said there were all kinds of people from the oil patch crying for accommodation."

"Yeah, and most of 'em drink."

THE DUPLEX WAS FILLED NOW with prickly unease. In spite of herself, Sarah listened for untoward sounds from downstairs and watched Eric's comings and goings with suspicion. Often, when he had been drinking, she could hear his "hurtin' music," not quite loud enough for her to protest, but just loud enough to scrape her nerves. Alan and Josh made fun of him, but she knew they too were uneasy. Josh, particularly, was sullen and unlike himself.

Several times, after she had gone to bed, she heard Clarence talking to the boys.

What's he trying to do? Reassure them, or justify himself for making such a stupid mistake as to sell our house? she wondered. But what's the use? What's done is done.

She punched the pillow savagely. Damn it all to *hell*, I feel as if I have to *be* here, keeping an eye on things, when the summer's passing and all I want is to be down in the foothills.

ON THE LAST DAY OF JULY, Sarah surprised Alan carrying a cardboard box of his belongings out to his pickup.

"What's going on?"

"Me and a couple of other guys from work are going in together on an apartment, Mom. We figured...well, we figured it was time."

"And you didn't even discuss it with us? You think you're making enough money? Living in an apartment is not quite as cheap as living at home, you know."

"Cheap? Not with the old man doubling my board, it's not. But, like he says, I'm a big boy now. I can't expect a free ride forever."

"Did you think I wouldn't have something to say about this?"

"Forget it, Mom. It's all arranged. I'm going."

Sarah watched him drive away with a sick sense of loss. I can't believe he'd leave, just like that. And he'll never be home again. Clarence, doubling the kid's board without even discussing the matter with me! Has he been after Josh too, and the kid hardly out of high school? Surely he wouldn't.

When she questioned Josh, he denied it, but the day after school closed he burst into her studio, cocky and confrontational. "Got a job with a trucking company, Mom."

"A job? With a *trucking* company? But what about university? I thought you were going up there today to see about registration."

He shrugged, his expression evasive.

"What kind of a trucking company, Josh?"

"They do industrial cleanups and stuff like that. They're starting me on a sucker truck." Then, reluctantly, "Some of the guys move drilling rigs too."

"But you're surely not going to be moving drilling rigs?"

"Not likely."

"Josh, you really should be thinking about university."

"Aw, Mom, maybe Dad's right. I don't know what I want to study, and while I'm trying to figure it out, I'd just as well be paying you a little board."

"Dad has been letting on that we're going to end up in the poorhouse in our old age, hasn't he?"

Josh coloured and picked at a loose thread on his shirt. "Well, you can't be too flush when Dad would let our old house go for this place."

Sarah jammed her brush into a jar of turpentine and wiped her trembling hands on a rag. "Josh, we don't need to worry that much about money. Dad's just...." She stopped herself with a deep, unsteady breath.

Just shut up, Sarah. You've never criticized Clarence to the boys, nor to Mother and Father either. Not even when he drove you crazy hopping from job to job and you were ready to divorce him.

Would have too, she realized, except for Mother. Her daughter a divorcée? How would she explain *that* to the good Father and the ladies of the Auxiliary? I haven't been near that bloody Church since I was thirteen, but I *still* dance to its tunes.

That night, when she was sure the house was empty, except for herself and Clarence, she pitched into him. They had the worst fight of their marriage. Each hurled accusations and insults at the other which would never be forgotten or forgiven.

The next morning, Sarah packed her camper and headed for the foothills. For three weeks she worked, rejoicing in the clear, bright air, the spice of pine, juniper, and sage, in dawns, sunsets and the magical hour of the gloaming. The duplex she cast out of her mind, absorbing herself instead in the earth and the creatures of the foothills, cattle chewing cud and puffing in the summer sun, in glimpses of mule deer, of a fox vixen and her cubs, and red-tailed hawks sailing above the hills. She produced a number of canvasses with a sureness of technique that moved closer and closer to some mystic abstraction of prairie.

Several times Jock appeared. Sarah and he feasted on food he'd brought and, when the sun had set and the Rockies were purple against the gloaming, he dragged the mattress outside where they made urgent love. Sated finally, they lay, half asleep, sipping whiskey and staring up into the great wheel of stars while tiny brown bats fluttered above them and deer mice skipped across their blankets. By tacit consent, they did not discuss their real lives; they were content to rejoice in the now, in the intense pleasure each took from the body of the other and brought to the body of other. Tomorrow? There was none.

But, as the days went on, shortening considerably towards the end of August, Sarah knew that she must face her job and the duplex again. She drove back through a day of dreary rain with the odd snowflake riding on the wind.

She and Clarence greeted each other with frigid civility.

FIVE DAYS LATER, the city was sweltering under summer's last heat wave. It was a Saturday night. Josh had not returned from work. Sarah lay awake listening for his truck. Alberta was "oil-patch drunk," overflowing with money, with strangers. Saturday nights were crazy with drunken parties, with accidents. Ambulances passed, banshee screams ululating and the faint reflections of their warning lights pulsing on the bedroom walls.

Trust Clarence to be manoeuvred into buying a duplex half a block away from a main traffic artery leading to the University Hospital. She was fuming when she heard drunken voices. Eric and one of his "cousins" stumbled down the steps to his suite. She could hear Eric fumbling to fit his key into his door.

She was drifting towards sleep when she heard the "hurtin' music."

Clarence wakened with a start and hopped out of bed. "That son of a bitch. I've been fighting with him for three weeks. I'm going down there and tell him –"

"He's drunk. Why don't you wait till morning?"

He opened the screen and stuck his head out. "He's got a girl down there! He's not turning my place into a whorehouse."

Sarah could feel the muscles in her shoulders bunch.

That afternoon a sober and respectful Eric had introduced a couple of girls, cousins from down east, he'd said. Would it be all right if they stayed for a few days? Sarah sized the girls up as a pair of tough looking little tarts, but since the request was polite and reasonable, she could not very well refuse. She had not told Clarence.

"You've read the book on landlord-tenant relationships, Clarence. They make it plain enough. 'Morals of the tenant are not the landlord's concern.' Anyway, he told me those girls are his cousins."

"Girls?"

"Two of them. Rap on the floor with the broom. He'll get the message."

To her relief, Clarence did so, and the "hurtin' music" diminished to a murmur.

"Now, let's get some sleep," she sighed. "Tomorrow I've got to sort out all the stuff from the old house that's piled in the garage and get it ready for a yard sale."

A high-pitched woman's scream, a truck door slamming, and a shriek of laughter jolted her awake.

Clarence bounded out of bed, raced down the corridor and out the back door. Sarah could hear his bare feet pattering down the outside steps to the first landing. "What's going on here?" he yelled.

Another truck door slammed. The suite door slammed. Somebody was kicking the house. "Gimme back my shoe, you fucking bitch, or I'll kick the fucking door down."

"Fuck off. I told you the kinda crap you want was gonna cost –"

"Gimme back my shoe, you two-bit whore."

Scuffles, grunts, crashes. Clarence yelled, "Stop this ungodly row! Give him his shoe, you little fool. Now, fella, get the hell off my place."

A pickup roared away and Clarence yelled, "What kind of a girl are you, dragging riffraff like that onto my property?"

The girl's voice was as strident as a trumpet. "Don't try following me into Eric's place, you old asshole, or I'll boot your balls for you."

A slap. A startled squawk, then, "You old son of a bitch! No guy slaps *me*."

Grunts. Doors slammed. Feet, stumbling up the stairs, quivered the house. "Sarah! For God's sake –" Clarence cried, as he tore past the bedroom with the two girls and Eric on his heels.

When Sarah reached the living room, she found Clarence dodging karate kicks that one of the girls was aiming at his head. Eric and his other "cousin" made ineffectual grabs at her. "Hey, Linda, take it easy, okay?"

"You got the old bugger on the run, you don't need to –"

"No asshole slaps me. I'll kick his fuckin' head in."

Sarah fell into an armchair and stared helplessly at the scene which played before her like some bizarre comedy. She couldn't take it seriously. She had to suppress an urge to giggle. Paddy, Josh's little dog, paraded up and down, grumbling to himself like an impotent old man.

Clarence grabbed the girl's foot. She snatched his hand and twisted his thumb. He yelped and yanked away from her.

Eric grabbed her. "Hey, that's enough, Linda." She tore away and went at Clarence again. When he warded her off with his good hand, he reminded

Sarah of a frightened old woman.

Suddenly, she was scared. She stumbled to the phone. "Please, can you send the police?" she quavered. "A girl is beating up on my…my husband." She pressed her fingers to her lips and squeezed her eyes shut. My God! A *girl* is beating up on my husband.

When she dropped the phone back into its cradle, Linda was standing over her, arms akimbo. "Cops, huh? Well, don't you get any idea of laying charges, lady, or I'll be laying charges of my own. The old bastard slapped *me*, y'know." She turned to her buddies. "C'mon, guys, let's split." When they filed through the back door, Sarah rushed after them, slammed the door, and shot the deadbolt.

Clarence stood in the hallway, goosily examining his thumb. "Crazy bitch – I think it's broken."

Without a word, Sarah brushed past him, went to the fridge, took out a package of frozen peas and shoved it at him.

When the police rang the doorbell, shriek after shriek of laughter rose from the suite downstairs.

"Disturbance here, ma'am?"

"Well – I think it was just a misunderstanding, officer. The girls have…have gone now."

Eric's "hurtin' music," up full volume, penetrated the floor as though it was cardboard. One of the cops gestured with his billy club. "I recognize that music. There's been trouble with that character before. Want us to go and shut the racket down?"

Sarah couldn't look him in the eye. "I think he'll settle down in a minute or two."

The other cop noticed Clarence's thumb. "War wounds? Sure you don't want to lay charges?"

Clarence hesitated, then shook his head.

Let us be thankful for all mercies, Sarah thought. All we need is for some hooker charging *him* with assault.

The cops had gone and Sarah, too keyed up to think of sleeping, was heating the kettle for cocoa when she heard the rasp of a key in the back door. Paddy, whimpering with anticipation, rushed down the hall. When Josh walked in, six feet of tough, young, work-dirty brawn, and scooped the little dog up in his arms, it was all Sarah could do to keep from bursting into tears.

"What's going on, Mom?" He broke off, hearing the music. "Holy...! He's at it again." He picked up the broom and rapped authoritatively on the floor. A shriek of mocking laughter and the music reluctantly diminished. Josh looked at Clarence. "So, how are you enjoying being a landlord, Dad?"

Before Clarence had to answer Sarah forced a laugh. "There's seldom a dull moment. I'll say that for it. Would you like some cocoa?"

Hiding his thumb, Clarence sidled toward the bedroom. "Josh can have my share. I'm going to bed."

Josh watched him out of sight, then whispered, "What's wrong with his hand, Mom?"

"I think he caught his thumb in the car door."

"Don't you think we should take him to the —"

"He's a big boy. He knows the way to the hospital." She changed the subject abruptly. "You're getting home awfully late."

"And leaving early. We're heading for Edson to move a rig tomorrow morning."

"A drilling rig? Oh, Josh —"

"They pay double overtime for Sundays."

"But you said you were driving –"

"They put another guy on the sucker truck. From now on I'm swamping for Mickey Sawyer." He laughed, his expression defiant. "I'll make more money next month than you and Dad combined."

"God, Josh, don't you know they're bribing you with danger pay?"

"As long as a guy knows it's dangerous…. I'm quick and I'm careful, Mom, and I'll be able to salt away enough money to put myself clean through university. No student loans and no sponging off you guys."

"That's not…. Josh, please, find something else. Anything."

"And be a quitter like Dad? No way." His face was very young and very frightened when he saluted her and marched off down the corridor.

Sarah was still awake when she heard his alarm go off at 4:30. She saw his shadow as he slipped down the hall and she stole out of bed to stand at the window to see his pickup pull away into a brightening dawn through a city now filled with sleep.

After breakfast, Clarence took his injured thumb to the emergency ward at the hospital while Sarah started sorting and organizing the stuff in the garage. At almost noon, she looked up to see Eric and his two "cousins" slinking through the yard on their way to Danny's Doughnut Dive on the corner. They offered her sickly, apologetic smiles as they passed. She watched them out of sight, found a clean page in the notebook where she had been tabulating items for the garage sale, and, with a firm hand, wrote a termination of rental agreement and slipped it under Eric's door.

SHE WAS TOO TIRED to shower before supper. She was saving that luxury until after the dishes were done. She was mashing a potato with her fork and watching a pat of butter melt into it when the doorbell rang. She was reluctant to answer, but Clarence made no move to do so. She plodded down the two steps into the living room and through the hallway.

A heavy man of perhaps forty or forty-five stood in the doorway. He was dressed in clothes twenty years too young for him – tight jeans with a wide belt and a huge silver buckle, a pale green shirt with the sleeves folded back in a certain dandyish manner and polished cowboy boots. Straight out of the oil patch. Alberta was full of his kind, but it was his face that arrested Sarah. Rather a handsome face, except for the nervous, shifting eyes and an oddly congested, almost purplish complexion. "Clarence Cross live here?"

"Yes. Will you step in?"

"You're Mrs. Cross?"

"Yes."

"And you got a kid named Josh?"

She was headed to the kitchen to summon Clarence. Now she swung around to face the stranger. For the space of two breaths they stared at each other.

He dropped his gaze. "You're not gonna like this, Ma'am. Josh was...." He suddenly began to weep. Great tears splashed onto his hands and onto his shirt front, sprinkling it with spots of darker green. "Josh was...killed on a rig they were moving up at Edson this afternoon."

She felt nothing. At first. For a moment, she clung to a wild hope. Not true. Not true. It is the RCMP that bring that kind of....

But when she looked at the man's face, she knew that it was true. Her knees went rubbery. She backed against the wall to steady herself. "Who are you?"

"Tex Gordon, Ma'am. General manager of Cal-Tex Trucking."

Clarence strolled out of the kitchen, still chewing a mouthful of steak. "What's going on, Sarah?"

"Josh was…Josh is dead," she blurted, as though by telling him she could somehow make it not so.

Clarence stared at her, blinked, threw back his head and wailed.

Sarah stood trembling between the two men, the one weeping silently, shoulders heaving, the other sobbing in squall after anguished squall.

Sarah felt nothing. Yet. None of the pain, not a glimmer of the rage that would be her constant companion for years to come.

She sat on the edge of the couch and picked a coarse yellow thread off her jeans. Unbidden, a memory of Josh when he was eight popped into her mind.

One summer evening he and his buddies were playing around a house under construction. Somehow Josh fell, snagged his arm on a nail sticking out of the cement forms and opened up the inside of his upper arm. Sick with fear, Sarah had rushed him to the University Hospital, assuring him all the while that the stitching would hurt no more than having a tooth filled. When this proved to be true, Josh told the young doctor that he wanted at least fifteen stitches, one more than any other kid had had in the whole neighborhood.

"Fifteen it is, buddy, even if we have to put one in

the end of your nose."

And they had both laughed.

Her hands quivered as she rolled the thread into a dirty little rope in one direction, unrolled it and rolled it into a dirty little rope in the other.

"What happened to Josh?"

Tex fumbled through something about a gin pole and a suspended piece of the rig swinging and crushing Josh when a truck moved. "Nobody's fault. Coulda happened to anybody. Just in the wrong place at the wrong –"

"And you were paying him so handsomely, weren't you?"

He winced, turned away and wiped his nose on his sleeve. "Ma'am, I'm awful sorry. I'm just so goddamned sorry. If there's anything I can do...if there's anything at all –"

"Do? Now?" Hysterical laughter bubbled just below the stirrings of rage. "What do you *suggest?*"

His adam's apple crawled up his throat and down again and the purple congestion drained out of his face, leaving it pasty, sick. He sidled towards the door. Before he ducked outside, he glanced back at her with an expression compounded of fear and shame.

Anything you can do, anything at all, eh, buddy? Well, how about standing him up and making him walk?

She turned to look at Clarence who was perched like a sick chicken on the edge of his chair, his injured hand held before him like an offering. From time to time, he gagged and swallowed as though he was fighting nausea.

Blames himself. How's he going to live with that?

How are the two of us going to stand the sight of each other? Well, I've got to pull myself together. Clarence never will. Somehow, we've got to get through these next few days. And then? I don't know. I just don't know.

Old Paddy waddled over to her and laid his head on her thigh, looking up at her with puzzled, pleading eyes. As she ran her hand over his bony head she heard Eric's "hurtin' music" rise very softly from the suite below.

❧

SARAH TOSSES THE REAL ESTATE SECTION back on the table and picks up the TV guide.

Thursday. The Seth Thomas clock says quarter after four. Damn! Where is Beth? She promised…. Oh, it's an hour till suppertime, and I'm sure she'll…. Well, why not watch a little TV? If I can get past Josie without a war.

Josie has taken upon herself the guardianship of the lounge TV. It is almost necessary to ask her permission to turn it on, let alone change channels. Josie's taste clashes with Sarah's; therefore Sarah is seldom in the lounge to watch TV.

I really should get Beth to bring up my set, she thinks. Surely she could afford one of her own now. But TV's not much use without the cable, and I can't afford…. Oh, nonsense. All I'd have to do is give up the hairdresser and the chocolate bars.

Channel 9. Something about the Faroes. The Faroes? Ah, yes, islands in the Atlantic off the north of Scotland. Very much like Newfoundland, I think.

She goes eagerly to turn the set on. No channel changer here. Josie is instantly at her elbow. How the hell can she move so fast with only one leg and a walker?

"What were you wanting, dear?"

"Channel 9, Josie. It's all right, I've got it. It's a documentary on –"

"There's reruns of that cowboy show on 13."

"I don't want a cowboy show."

Josie glowers, her toothless face as mobile as a rubber mask. "There's them that do."

"Oh? Then why didn't *they* have the TV on?"

Josie scowls and returns to her game while Sarah settles into a comfortable chair.

And suddenly, so real that she can almost feel the air on her skin, there is a sea coast, and the cold, cold clear light of summer dawn a long, long way north. It might indeed be Newfoundland.

"That's what I've been dreaming!" she mutters, "Newfoundland."

She strains forward, gooseflesh rising as the camera pans great flocks of gulls, kittiwakes, puffins, and murres, screaming and circling above wind-punished cliffs that shear off into the sea. Offshore is an iceberg, towers, spires and minarets of turquoise, sapphire, and blinding white, riding on a navy sea.

Sarah is completely caught up in the scene; the room around her ceases to exist. She is leaning forward, jaw sagging, trying to store shape and colour and form within her, when Josie flounces up to the TV and switches to the cowboy show. For a moment, Sarah does not realize what has happened. Then, "Josie! Goddamn you, don't you dare –"

"Stuff it, you old bitch. You're not the boss."

Sarah heaves to her feet, rage empowering her, and shoves with both hands. Josie totters, loses balance and crashes, her one leg tangling with the legs of her walker. The rubber mask of her face twists like the face of a bawling baby.

Ignoring her, Sarah switches channels again, but the documentary is finished. Nothing now but credits scrolling on the screen. She stares at them, feeling cheated, feeling lost.

Josie moans like a wounded seal.

The hundred-year-old has wakened. She is gesticulating with both hands towards Josie sprawled on the rug.

"Can I help it if the silly bitch falls over because of a little shove? She had it coming, butting into my affairs."

She glances at the clock. Twenty-five to five. Damn, *where* is Beth? She wouldn't have forgotten my birthday, surely?

The lounge is bustling with the charge nurse, Marcie, and two other attendants, all down beside Josie, patting her, fussing over her.

Disgusting. Sarah untangles her walker and shuffles toward the door. As she heads for her room the old bugger with the cane swipes at her.

Josie's scream freezes her in the doorway.

The charge nurse is saying, "Now, now, Josie dear, just lie still. I don't think you're hurt." She turns to the attendant whose name Sarah can never remember. "Call Dr. Dean. I'm sure there's no fracture, but just to be on the safe side –"

"Fracture? Because of one little shove?" Sarah is

startled at how quavery and weak her voice sounds.

Marcie comes to her. "Let's get you to your room, Sarah, dear. Maybe you can have a little rest before supper."

"I don't want a little rest before supper. What's wrong with that silly cow?"

"There's something nice for you in your room. Wait till you see."

"Beth?" So eagerly that she forgets Josie, forgets to resent being distracted like a naughty child. She lurches along as fast as the walker will allow, shoves her door open, and stops on the threshold. On the table beside the radio is a box of toffee and a cut glass vase filled with red roses. Propped against the vase is a plain white envelope.

"Aren't you a lucky girl to have roses and toffee for your birthday?" Marcie says. "Your granddaughter is having your TV sent up too, and she's paid for a whole year of cable for –"

"But where is *she?*"

"I think the note will explain."

Sarah goes cold. She knows what the note will say. An offer too good to refuse…. Please forgive…. I will always love….

"She's left me here!"

Marcie can't hold back the tears, but Sarah is savage with herself. Straighten out your goddamned face, Sarah MacKenzie Cross. You will *not* bawl.

"Sarah, I'm so –"

"No, Marcie. Just…go away. Please."

As Marcie moves towards the door, Sarah calls, "Do you think you could round up a little tea and toast and bring it here to my room in the morning? I want to start working while the light is good."

"Working?"

"I saw icebergs on TV this afternoon. Castles in the sea. The light was fabulous. I'm going to sketch in the composition after supper." She hesitates, then forces herself to ask, "Do you think Josie's leg is…is broken?"

Marcie laughs. "I know it's not, but trust our Josie to make the most of any occasion."

Sarah grins. "How'd you like to take her those roses? You can tell her they're from me, but you're not to tell her that I'm sorry."

ACKNOWLEDGEMENTS

I GREATLY APPRECIATE the assistance of my instructors in the Creative Writing Program at Malaspina University College: Keith Harrison, Stephen Guppy, and especially Kevin Roberts, who read the manuscript-in-progress several times. I would also like to thank the many friends who have read this book and offered insightful comments, as well as Dorothy Causton for her help with proofreading. In addition, I would like to thank Art Charbonneau and Dale Weir for their help with setting up the manuscript.